Crime Time: Mystery and Suspense Stories

Crime Time: Mystery and Suspense Stories

John Jakes

Five Star • Waterville, Maine

Five Star First Edition Mystery Series.

Published in 2001 in conjunction with Tekno-Books and
Ed Gorman.

Set in 11 pt. Plantin by Al Chase.

Printed in the United States on permanent paper.

Library of Congress Cataloging-in-Publication Data

Jakes, John, 1932–
   Crime time : mystery and suspense stories / John Jakes.
     p. cm. —(Five Star first edition mystery series)
   Contents: Dagger—Celebrity and justice for all—The
opener of the crypt—Cloak and digger—Unc probes
pickle plot—Unc foils show foe—Girl in the golden cage
—Tex—Little man—its been a busy day—The man
who wanted to be in the movies—Dr. Sweetkill—The
siren and the shill.
   ISBN 0-7862-3157-2 (hc : alk. paper)
   1. Detective and mystery stories, American. I. Title.
II. Series.
PS3560.A37 C75 2001
 813'.54—dc21   2001033054

Table of Contents

Preface

Some authors have more problems than a math test. One of mine, and a major one, when I started writing and selling fiction more than fifty years ago, was this:

I read too many genres enthusiastically. Westerns, crime, science fiction, historical—I wanted to write them all. Thus for nearly 25 years, until I focused on the historical novels that became my career for the next 25, I was a scatter-shot author, bouncing around from genre to genre. It's my belief that this is one reason I didn't excel in any of them. Not that I didn't enjoy the work. I loved writing crime stories and kept at it intermittently for two decades. I've even done a few since, always with pleasure.

Writers often start out by attempting to imitate a favorite author. In the crime field, I tried to imitate more than one.

John Dickson Carr a.k.a. Carter Dickson was the first. I think I own his entire body of work, in various yellowed and dog-eared editions. What I call his atmospherics—weather, the moody play of light and shadow—enthralled me. His influence infuses the books I write today.

Carr's convoluted puzzles enthralled me too, though I was never able to imitate them with any success. A very early novel, consigned to the trash because it was non-salable, involved an American clone of Gideon Fell. Detection of the villain hinged on—I cringe to admit this—punctuation in a super-obscure English poem. Blame it on the fact that I was a graduate student in literature at Ohio State at the time. I don't have a copy of this awful effort any more. Strike one.

John Ross Macdonald, who later dropped the first name in deference to another Macdonald, was at the top of my list of private eye novelists. I ventured into that field too, both in long and short lengths. Somewhere I have a single copy of a cheesy little paperback that started out, with high hopes, as a novel featuring a pair of interesting investigators named Johnny Hood and Romo Spain. My then agent, Scott Meredith, couldn't sell it to a major publisher, and it wound up at some fly-by-night house whose moguls decorated the cover with a breasty babe falling out of her dress, under the title *The Defiled Sister*. I don't recall any defilement of anyone's sister in the story but what the hey, this was paperback merchandising back then. Strike two.

Johnny and Romo did survive briefly, to appear in "The Girl in the Golden Cage," which is included in this collection.

My idol of idols in the 1950's was the other Macdonald, the great John D., whom I still consider one of the most egregiously underrated authors of the last half of the nineteenth century. Mainstream critics and publications belatedly came to this realization only after he moved from paperback originals to hard covers, but even then they never did him full justice.

John D. wrote terrific crime novels for Gold Medal, the Fawcett imprint for paperback originals. My lifelong colleague and friend, Evan Hunter—(the first real live author I met, in 1952, in the Scott Meredith office at 580 Fifth Avenue)—had cracked Gold Medal too. I gnashed my teeth in juvenile envy and attempted to do likewise.

My failed effort was a work called *Gonzaga's Woman*, which in my conceit I believed was fully the match of any book by John D. It had to do with a crime lord, Gonzaga—(I suppose I got that from the name of Bing Crosby's university), his girlfriend, and some poor schlepp who got mixed up with them. Gold Medal of course rejected it, but Scott Meredith placed it with Universal Books, a second- or third-tier house that lasted a few hours longer than the publisher of *The Defiled Sister*. Strike three.[1]

That fairly well sums up my none-too-glorious novelistic career in crime. I had considerably better luck with shorter pieces, and you will find some of them in this book. All are old friends; here are comments about a few.

"Celebrity and Justice for All" is the newest story, written in the wake of the O. J. Simpson trial, when my gorge rose unmanageably because the posturing by attorneys on both sides seemed to be more important than the crime or the criminal.

"The Opener of the Crypt," a sequel to "The Cask of Amontillado," originally appeared in a fantasy magazine. The editor asked me to rewrite the manuscript so that the language becomes increasingly florid—"Poe-esque"—toward the end.

"Cloak and Digger" was part of a cycle of short-shorts probably inspired by my addiction to "The Man From U.N.C.L.E." There were twelve stories initially, each with a number in the title ("The One of Nails," "The Two Dead Dodos" etc.). The secret agent who foiled the villains was called Roger. Whether that was his first name, last name, or both, I never decided.

At one point toward the end of the cycle, Hans Santessen, who had bought most of the stories for *The Saint* magazine, asked to borrow my file of carbons. Foolishly I gave it to him.

---

[1] When I finished writing this preface, I searched several used-book databases and discovered to my astonishment that copies of *Gonzaga's Woman* are still available, $15 and up. Thanks, but I'll pass.

He died not long after, and the file disappeared. I have copies of published versions of only a few of Roger's adventures, and no information about the rest, which I call The Lost Roger Stories.

The Uncle Pinkerton mysteries appeared in *Ellery Queen's Mystery Magazine*. They sprang from my addictive reading of the show business trade paper *Variety*. The stories were challenging, both because of the puzzles and the "Variety-ese" which I imitated as best I could (nothing can beat the most famous *Variety* headline—STIX CRIX NIX PIX). I spent some early years in Indiana, where both my parents were born, so the background came naturally.

Fred Dannay published the first story with great enthusiasm, hoping it would be a series. I wrote only three adventures of Unc and his nephew before abandoning them. As for casting film versions in my head, Unc could only be played by Jonathan Winters, Woody by—who else?—Woody Allen.

"Little Man—It's Been A Busy Day" features my 5'1" private eye Johnny Havoc, who perambulated through four novels as "the champion of short people everywhere." I liked Havoc because he was always being punched out by the big bullies of the world, and had to work himself out of fixes with his brains, not brawn. In each Havoc novel I included what I called a Keystone Kops chase.

Other stories represent endeavors with private eyes, spies, and a miscellany of violence. I hope there's something in all of them that will entertain you after all these years.

John Jakes
Hilton Head Island, South Carolina
October 2000

Introduction

I was twenty-six when I first learned there was a place called Indiana. I made this amazing discovery through a young writer named John Jakes. This was back in 1952. Jakes is still here. So am I. I'm not sure about Indiana.

I was working at the time for a literary agency—the same one, incidentally, for which Don Westlake and Larry Block later worked. My exalted title was Executive Editor. This meant I was earning forty bucks a week. My job was to read the stories our professional clients sent in, comment on them (if they needed revision) or (if they were salable) pass them on to my boss with marketing suggestions. Most of our clients were pulp writers earning from half-a-cent a word to five cents a word, depending on the quality of the magazine buying the story. We also represented a handful of "true" confession writers, who earned top dollar for baring their breasts, so to speak. The confessions, of course, were as fictitious as anything we submitted to the pulps.

By 1952, when I first began working at the agency, the pulps were fast disappearing. But out there in the vast American wilderness, far from the big bad city, our clients kept writing, and we kept peddling their wares to the surviving handful of magazines still publishing science-fiction, western, romance, sports, action-adventure, and—thank God—detective fiction. One of those clients was a young writer name John Jakes.

Jakes had sold his first story in 1950, when he was just eighteen. By the time he came to the agency, he had an im-

11

pressive track record of sales, even though he was still in college at the time. His stories and novelettes arrived with amazing regularity. I kept wondering when this guy found any time to study. Each time a manila envelope with his return address came into the office, I knew I was in for a treat. I'd pop it open and inside would be a neatly typed manuscript sandwiched between two pieces of gray shirt cardboard, crossed side to side and top to bottom with white tape. I'd tear the tape and yank out the story like a kid opening a Christmas present. The green index card I later clipped to the story would invariably begin with the words "Another top-notch Jakes yarn," and then go on to summarize it and offer marketing suggestions. We usually sold each of his stories within ten days after the agency received it. He was that good.

Frankly, I found this a bit intimidating.

Here was this genius kid out in Drowsy Cows, Indiana, probably racking up A's in all his courses, probably quarterbacking the football team, probably dating all the prettiest girls on campus, and in his spare time knocking out these "top-notch" yarns that sold in a minute flat. Meanwhile, I myself was struggling to learn how to write. For despite the big-shot "Executive Editor" title, I had just begun writing in earnest when I first encountered Jakes's work. I was learning from magazine editors, and I was also learning from the man who ran the agency, but most of all I was learning from the professionals we represented. It did not take me long to recognize that there was a whole *lot* to learn from this kid in Indiana who was six years my junior and a hundred light years ahead of me.

Well, just take a look at what's in this collection.

What you must remember is that Jakes was writing mostly science fiction when he began. Detective stories were something he tossed off when he wasn't hot-rodding around campus with all those gorgeous blondes. Considering this, the range of the work is amazing. In the seeming wink of an eye, Jakes moves casually from Private Eye to Man on the Run to Sci-Fi Legal Thriller to Spy Story to Spy Story Spoof to Murder Anticipated, to a gaggle of dazzling Private Eye Variations, mixing assorted characters, styles, moods, backgrounds and venues with all the sure-handed skill of a river boat gambler shuffling a full deck of marked cards in plain view. The versatility *alone* is startling. But from story to story, as we travel with Jakes on the road from his college-boy apprenticeship to his best-selling maturity, we witness as well an incredible transformation. We are watching a wonderful writer finding his voice. What starts out as merely damn good only gets better and better until at last it is best.

Let me share with you now the sense of joyous anticipation I felt whenever a Jakes story landed on my desk. I can still remember that taped shirt cardboard. I once wondered how come a college kid sent his shirts off to the laundry instead of washing and ironing them himself. In retrospect, I'm glad he spent the time writing. But come. Join me. Tear off the tape. Reach between those gray cardboard layers. Yank out the story. Ah, good! Another top-notch Jakes yarn.

Ed McBain
Weston, Connecticut

Dagger

They had been three inseparable comrades, drawn together by their work—Jimmy Ridgely, the trumpeter; Len Hunt, the piano player; and Laurie. Lovely Laurie, who sang, and lifted them from a low-class outfit to a small group with something of a style. They had drunk many beers together, told many jokes together, sipped many cups of coffee together in the cold early morning hours when the rest of the people in town were asleep. And now their world had been torn apart, and only two of them were left.

Lieutenant Stagg sat behind the desk, a thick-jawed man who needed a shave. His hands juggled the Nazi SS dagger. Behind him, rain slanted down the glass, the chilling rain of the predawn hours.

"This is your knife, isn't it?" Stagg said to Len Hunt.

Hunt was seated on the other side of the desk, a slender, slightly stoop-shouldered man with unruly straw-colored hair. His eyes were bleary. They had dragged him out of bed and down here to police headquarters to tell him that Jimmy Ridgely had been murdered and that he was the boy tagged with doing the job.

Hunt's voice was raw-edged. "I told you," he said, "that it was mine. I got it in Berlin, during the war. I keep it in my dressing room. It's kind of a good luck charm. Everybody knew I had it." His voice grew heavy with the repetition of the words.

Inside, his stomach churned. He glanced quickly at Laurie, sitting on a bench along the wall. She was bundled

14

into a woolly green coat, and her hair was tangled, and she wore no makeup. Her blue-gray eyes were rimmed with red, but she was lovely. Still lovely. He looked quickly away.

Stagg threw down the dagger. "You people make me tired. Hunt, we know damned well how you felt about Miss Connors here. We talked to your manager."

Wolf? Sure, Len thought, Ted Wolf would know. Aging gray-haired Ted. He knew. So did everybody else. But that didn't make him guilty, just feeling the way he did.

One of the detectives leaning against the wall scraped a match loudly and lit a cigarette. Stagg sighed heavily. "Hunt, were you in love with Miss Connors?"

Len wound his fingers together and stared at them. Why didn't it work out, like a piece on the piano? Clearly, logically, the chords in proper sequence. No, it was jumbled, tangled in a mass of feelings and half-thoughts.

"I want the truth," Stagg rumbled. "Were you in love with Miss Connors?"

"Yes," Len said quietly. He did not look at Laurie. "I still am."

Stagg picked up the dagger again and leaned back. "That's what I thought." He turned toward Laurie. "Miss Connors, you're a very attractive girl. I've learned from Mr. Wolf that most every man that came into the club . . . well . . . fell for you. But you and Hunt here were the closest people to Jimmy Ridgely. That's why we tagged Hunt."

Len glanced at Laurie again. Her head was bowed. He got angry then, and jerked to his feet, facing the big detective. "You haven't got a bit of evidence."

"I've got a motive," Stagg said. "Jealousy. Ridgely and Miss Connors were to be married Saturday. You were jealous. It was evident to everybody at the club, Hunt. To everybody, get me? The way you mooned around. All right, you

15

got sore. After the last show, you and Ridgely and some of the others shot craps with Ted Wolf until almost four. And then you got Ridgely to come to your dressing room. That's where we found him. With the SS dagger . . . yours . . . stuck in his chest. The scrub-woman put in the call." The words carried a note of finality.

"Damn it," Len shouted, "I went right home after the crap game. I didn't see Jimmy. He walked off. He was acting funny, so I let him go."

Stagg picked up a pencil. "Did he lose much in the crap game?"

"He won three bucks."

"Oh." The detective's face sagged and he put the pencil down. "Just checking."

"Damn it . . ." Len said loudly again.

"Easy, buddy," the detective against the wall said. "Don't talk like that around here."

Len let the breath rip in and out of his chest. He heard Laurie sobbing quietly. Sure, it broke him up when Jimmy announced their wedding. So what? He loved her too much to try and mess things up for her. And now this cop. . . .

Suddenly, his breathing quieted. A loose grin appeared on his face. He was waking up now, throwing off some of the warm daze of sleepiness. He was beginning to pick up the loose ends, with which they wanted to hang him so methodically.

"You got anything more to say?" Stagg asked.

"Yes, I have," Len said. "I went back to my hotel right after the crap game with Wolf. I got my key from the night clerk."

He jabbed a finger at Stagg. "Check him. I hit the sack and your boys woke me up, just about a quarter of six. Check it, and find out how right you are."

16

Stagg shook his head. "The clerk probably wouldn't remember exactly when it was. You could have killed Ridgely and grabbed a cab back to the hotel. Besides, Wolf told us he saw you leaving with Jimmy Ridgely. You walked out of the bar together, when the crap game broke up. There was time."

"Wolf's a liar," Len said sharply.

"We'll decide that. He's coming in to sign a statement this morning. We've already contacted him by phone."

"He had too much to drink," Len said. "He was drinking a lot."

"Look," Stagg said harshly, "quit playing games with us."

Len breathed deeply. Far, far down in his stomach was a core of cold, terrible fear. Here was the deadly question. He felt sweat bead his palms as he stared at Stagg. Laurie's rhythmic sobs counterpointed with the lonely tap of the rain on the window. Outside, the sky was growing gray.

"Tell me something," Len said quietly. "Whose prints were on the knife. Mine?"

Stagg looked quickly at the cold gray blade of the dagger lying on the desk blotter. "There weren't any prints." Len felt a quick surge of inward triumph. "But you could have used gloves."

Len started to button up his topcoat. The detective against the wall straightened up and stuck one hand in his pocket, his eyes gleaming warily.

"I'm getting out of here," Len said, staring straight at Stagg. "I'm taking Miss Connors with me. And until you get some kind of evidence that sticks, don't try to tag me with killing Jimmy."

Stagg juggled the knife, and slammed it down on the desk abruptly. "All right. But I'm warning you, Hunt. Don't make a move out of this town. Around here, when somebody dies, we look for motives. You're it this time. So we'll keep

17

working on it until we find some evidence like you want. And then we will make it stick."

His words were threatening, but Len saw the slump of his shoulders beneath the faded blue suit. He was a tired man, tired as Len himself, and in almost the same position, except for the fact that he had already established Len as the killer in his own mind. Both of them were looking for the hand that had pushed the knife into Ridgely's chest. But Stagg would try to make Len's hand fit the dagger.

Len walked quickly over to Laurie and touched her shoulder. She nodded without glancing up. The detective who had leaned against the wall followed them without making any pretense of hiding. They walked out of the station and Len turned up his collar against the chill rain.

Across the street was an all-night restaurant. They went in, ordered coffee, and sank down in a corner booth. The detective yawned as he relaxed on a stool near the jukebox.

Laurie's spoon rattled against the cup. "Len . . ." she said quietly. It was the first word she had uttered since Len had walked into the police station nearly an hour before.

Len reached out hesitantly and put his hand over hers. "No, honey, it wasn't me."

"I . . . I . . . didn't realize . . . until that policeman asked you . . . how you felt . . ." She took a quick drink of the coffee, still not looking at him.

"Let's not talk about that now." His voice went lower. "Jimmy's dead, and somebody killed him."

Her eyes came up slowly, round blue-gray pits of loneliness. "Who?"

Len shook his head. "I don't know. But I know I don't want to get stuck with it. And right now, I'm scared. Scared they'll make it stick somehow. Stagg looks like a one-track man. He can't be thrown off, unless we turn up the real guy."

She smiled, briefly and bitterly, and stirred her coffee again in an aimless way. Her eyes wandered to the rain-spattered window. "Out there, someplace. But who is he?"

The detective shoved a nickel in the jukebox, and in a moment the music poured out of the speaker. The detective hunched over his coffee and grinned sourly at them. Len listened, his insides knotted up. Laurie was listening, too, and she started to cry once more.

It was one of their few records. Laurie sang, and Jimmy's trumpet came out high and shrill and sweet, ripping up and up, translating the words that Laurie sang into emotions of brass, making them live. *With a Song In My Heart.* That was all that was left, Len thought hatefully. A few grooves in a couple of dozen records, and some memories in the minds of a handful of people. Oh, he wasn't a great horn man. Others had been better, others would be a lot better after him. But they had been three, Len and Laurie and Jimmy, and somebody pushed the SS dagger into Jimmy's chest and stopped the sound of that horn.

It meant something when you knew the guy.

"I've got an idea," Len said hesitantly, as if he wasn't sure.

Laurie took a handkerchief from her purse and wiped at her face. "What . . . what is it?"

"Wolf." Len pronounced the word softly. "His name cropped up quite a lot in what Lieutenant Stagg said. "Wolf told them I was in love with you. Wolf said Jimmy and I left the crap game together. He's too damned eager to volunteer information."

"Why would he want to kill Jimmy, Len? He managed the band, and it would hurt him to lose him. Jimmy had his own reputation, at least around here."

Len shook his head. Nothing was straight in his mind. Only a suspicion. "No reasons, honey. Just wild ideas, right now.

19

But if Stagg works on his wild idea, I damned well better work on mine. And fast." He patted her arm. "You need sleep."

She nodded. "I'm kind of dead all over, Len. I can't feel anything."

"It'll take a while for the shock to wear off. Come on. I'll take you home."

He paid the bill and hailed a cab out on the street. Traffic was beginning to move, and although the rain still slashed down, the sky had grown considerably lighter. Len stifled a yawn as he climbed in after Laurie. He was tired, but he knew he wouldn't get any sleep for a long time yet. He couldn't afford it.

A squad car pulled away from the front of police head-quarters and started out after them. Len turned around with a disgusted sigh. Laurie leaned against the side of the cab and closed her eyes.

Len sat staring out into the rain, watching the ribbons of water obscure the buildings. *Wolf.* He kept hearing that name. *Wolf.* He kept seeing the face, fiftyish, balding, bag-cheeked, somehow worried and pressed all the time. *Wolf.* Managing the outfit. *Wolf.* Rolling the dice in the after-hour sessions, rolling them like his life depended on it, rolling them like a fanatic pleading to a strange god.

He was the only other person that even approached the edges of the picture. Barring, of course, somebody around the club that nobody ever noticed. If that was it, then Len knew he didn't have a chance. The cell would be waiting for him; Stagg would see to that.

But if Wolf fitted in somewhere . . . but damn it, where? Nervously, Len lit a cigarette. They were nearing Laurie's apartment, one of a series of brownstone walkups. Quickly, Len thought the thing over. He had to follow it up, while the idea was fresh.

What motive would Wolf have? Did he love Laurie, too, as Len did? Had it become twisted in him, making him take the dagger from Len's dressing table? No. Len stared hard at the glowing orange end of the cigarette. It didn't fit. Ted Wolf was a businessman. He had no personal connections with anyone in the outfit. Strictly percentage. Irritatingly, Len knew he was right, but he couldn't remember why. Something didn't click into place.

The feeling of certainty vanished before the lack of evidence. Maybe Wolf *did* have some emotional connection with them. Maybe it was hidden down deep in his brain, festering, swelling, with none of them knowing about it. Maybe . . . maybe . . . Len ground the cigarette out on the floor. Too damned much depended on *maybe*.

The cab pulled to a stop before one of the brownstones. "Here you are, mister," the cabby said.

Len told him to wait and walked up to the door of Laurie's apartment on the second floor. Her eyes still held their dazed, unbelieving look. Len took the key from her trembling hand and opened the door.

"Promise me you'll get some sleep," he said quietly. She nodded. "I'll let you know if anything breaks." He glanced away. Even now, he couldn't help seeing how beautiful she was. And somehow, he hated himself for it. He patted her shoulder again and stalked off down the hall. He heard the door shut behind him as he headed down the stairs.

The cabby took him back to his apartment. The police car stayed right behind them, and parked across the street from the hotel. Len mixed himself a drink and went to the window, staring down at the car. The symbol, he thought. They're after me, and they'll get me, just by dogging me, unless I do something.

He swallowed the drink hastily and felt it jolt into his

stomach. He looked at his watch. Quarter after seven. Well, he couldn't see Wolf for a while yet.

As he stood under the shower, letting the icy points of water dig into his skin and restore it to life, he kept thinking back over the whole thing. What was it he wanted to remember? What part of the thing made him so sure Wolf could not have killed out of jealousy? Somehow, this unseen factor ruled out the one alternative and brought in another. But it was one of those things heard once that sinks to the bottom of the mind and lies there, growing sluggish from disuse. If only he would remember.

He sighed loudly and stepped out of the shower. The thick towel felt good on his back. He decided to give himself a couple of hours. It would come to him. Things like that always did. Names he couldn't remember at the moment, no matter how he tried, always came, in time.

Another drink made him warmer, but he stopped at two. He had to keep his mind clear and alert. He dressed in a better suit and walked two blocks to a diner, where he had bacon, eggs and toast. His body had thrown off its tiredness. He knew that he would be exhausted tomorrow, but now he felt normally awake and perceptive.

The detective got back into his squad car when Len found a cab and started out to see Ted Wolf. The squad car stayed behind the cab all the way.

Ted Wolf lived in a not-quite-exclusive apartment hotel near the river. The detective posted himself at the curb as Len stepped into the vestibule and pressed the buzzer. A moment later, he heard a voice over the speaking tube.

"Who is it, please?"

His breath cut off short. That was it. The voice belonged to a woman. Ted Wolf's wife.

"It's Len Hunt, about Jimmy Ridgely."

There was a gasp. "Oh." The door clicked abruptly and Len jerked it open. The elevator rose to the fifth floor with horrible slowness. Down the hall, a door stood open, and beyond the door sat Mrs. Wolf in her wheelchair.

Len walked in and closed the door. Mrs. Wolf started to speak, but instead she pressed a white handkerchief to her mouth and doubled over, coughing. The handkerchief showed faint reddish stains that had not come out in laundering. Only one kind of person coughed like that. Len felt his stomach quiver. Somewhere, a connection.

"I'm sorry, Mr. Hunt," Mrs. Wolf said, wheeling herself into the living room. She was a thin gray-haired woman whose skin had somehow taken on that same dead grayish color. Len stood awkwardly until she asked him to sit down. He did not want to look at her, because he could see that she had once been a beautiful woman, until paralysis and tuberculosis had torn the beauty away.

"I'm sorry," she said again. "We heard about the death last night. The police called. Ted left about half an hour ago. He was going to police headquarters, and then to pick up our tickets."

Tickets . . . the word stung Len's mind. Now he remembered part of it. It was a subject seldom mentioned by anyone, least of all by Wolf himself. He had heard it at the club, how Wolf was devoted to this pale trembling frame of a woman. How she was slowly dying, how he cared for her, tried to prolong her life, took her to doctors, spent money . . . devotion . . . fanatical devotion. And tickets . . .

"Were you leaving town, Mrs. Wolf?" Len asked carefully.

If only she was innocent of everything, if there was really something there.

"We are going to Arizona next week." She smiled wanly.

23

"The doctor said it was imperative that we stay there for six months. But I'm afraid we couldn't get the money together, Mr. Hunt. So we're only going for one month. This climate is bad for me . . . I . . . She stammered and bent her shoulders again, the cough wracking her. Flecks of red stained the handkerchief, and her hands fluttered wildly to conceal them. "Is there anything I could help you with?"

"No, I'll have to see Ted. Would . . . would it be all right if I waited for him?"

"Certainly. He promised to be back by nine-thirty, if you don't mind waiting that long."

"No," Len said, trying to keep the terrible eagerness out of his voice, "I don't mind."

"You can wait in Ted's study if you like. I . . . ." She touched her hair self-consciously. "I'm going to see what I can do about making myself look a little nicer. It's awfully early in the morning, you know."

"Thank you," Len said. He walked toward the study.

"Well . . ." Mrs. Wolf said awkwardly, "I hope you'll be comfortable. Make yourself at home." She wheeled herself off down the hall.

Len stepped quickly into the study, his head whipping from side to side, taking in everything. Money. *Money. Not enough money.* Of course not. The club was small, the band smaller.

Not big time. Not the big money. Not enough for so many medical expenses. Where was it to come from, the money that Ted Wolf had needed so desperately and then failed to get? Wolf wanted to keep his wife alive for a few more months. *Money* . . . it tied up somewhere . . .

Tensely, Len listened. The rain hit the windows of the study, and far down the hall, Len heard a radio being switched on. He crossed quickly to the desk and began sliding

24

the drawers open noiselessly. In the bottom drawer was a cheap gray tin box, locked.

His hands trembling, his stomach cold with anticipation, Len dragged out his apartment key and started to jimmy the box. Such a flimsy box, really. But how much deception would there be between a man and his invalid wife? She probably would never suspect him of anything, probably never ask or meddle into any of his affairs.

Len cursed quietly and twisted the key. The tin rasped as the lock snapped and broke. Len's breath came heavily. He made himself put the key back in his pocket before he opened the box lid. What would be in it? Something? Or nothing?

He sat back in the chair, took another deep breath, and listened. The radio still played. Water gurgled in a bathroom. Len reached out and opened the box and looked inside. His breath cut off as he let the three pieces of paper flutter to the desk. He looked at the first piece of paper. *IOU to Ted Wolf, $3,500.* He licked his lips and looked at the next slip. *IOU to Ted Wolf, $2,800.* The third IOU was for $4,100. All three were signed in a scrawl that Len knew all too well. *Jimmy Ridgely.*

Calmly now, Len put the IOU's into his coat pocket, closed the box, and replaced it in the drawer. He walked to the window and lit a cigarette, staring down at the rain-swept street five stories below. Now all he had to do was wait. Ted would be home by nine-thirty.

The manager of the band closed the door at eleven minutes after nine. Len rose from his chair. Wolf saw him through the open study door and started to speak, but Len motioned for him to be quiet. Wolf walked into the study. Len saw that the face of the man was gray, almost like his wife's, and that the flesh sagged even more than usual.

25

"Len . . ." Wolf said. "What's all the secrecy?"

"Were you down at police headquarters just now?" Len said.

"Why . . . why, yes." Wolf laughed sheepishly and fumbled for a cigarette.

"Giving them a statement to make them surer than ever that I killed Jimmy?"

"Len, what's gotten into you?"

Len took the IOU's from his pocket and held them up. "This."

Wolf drew the unlighted cigarette from his lips. His eyes, circled with puffy pads of flesh, grew smaller. "What are you trying to say, Len? Spill it, before I get sore."

"I'm saying that maybe you killed Jimmy Ridgely. I'm saying that I'm almost certain you did."

"You're insane . . ." Wolf began.

Len shook his head. Beyond Wolf, Mrs. Wolf had wheeled herself into the doorway. The words of greeting froze on her lips when she heard Len speak, and she sat there, a loose vacant expression of horror on her face as she listened. Wolf himself did not see her behind him.

"It's a wild hunch," Len said. "It's been a wild hunch all along, but I stuck to it, because otherwise they'll get *me* for it. See my reason?"

Wolf stuck the cigarette back in his mouth and lit it. His eyes shone brightly, a little wildly, in the glow of the match. "Let's hear what you've got to say."

"You got your crap game going at the club after hours, only this wasn't one of the regular ones. This one was private. You were looking for a sucker and Jimmy was it. You needed money, money to take your wife to Arizona and keep her alive. Jimmy lost to you; he lost a lot. These IOU's show that. But I figure you picked a wrong guy in Jimmy, because he couldn't pay off. Last night, you collared him after the game . . ." Len grinned sourly. "After he won three bucks."

"Go on," Wolf said, his voice deadly soft.

"I'm not saying you planned it. Maybe you had too much to drink and you and Jimmy were in my dressing room. Afterward, you saw a good chance to implicate me. You wiped the prints off the knife. Or, maybe you took the knife ahead of time. Anyway, you told Jimmy to pay off and he told you no dice. You lost your head, Wolf, and pushed my knife into his heart. Right into his heart, Wolf." Len's voice rose. He stepped quickly forward and grabbed the man's coat. His voice grew savage.

"Isn't that right?"

Snarling, Wolf jerked away. His hand flashed toward the desk, closing on a dull-edged letter opener.

"You got it right, Len," Wolf whispered. "I got sore and he went into your dressing room. He left his coat there. I got sore and the knife was on the table . . . but you can see why I did it. I needed the money . . . he wouldn't pay me . . . he couldn't . . . you see. . . ."

Len reached for the phone. "Tell the police."

"No!" With an agonized shriek, Wolf rushed forward and jabbed the letter opener at Len. Len dodged, striking out with his fists. They whirled around and Len felt the opener tear the flesh of his cheek. He pushed at Wolf and the man stumbled backward, his arms swinging wildly, off balance.

Len tried to grab him, then. But he hurled on, striking the window. He shrieked and flapped his arms and rolled slowly backward over the sill amid a tinkling of breaking glass. The rain whipped in through the window. Len choked and looked away. It was five stories down.

Then he remembered Mrs. Wolf. She sat in her wheelchair, her head cocked ridiculously to one side, a pitiful smile on her lips. She was sick now, sicker than she had ever been before.

"I loved him so," she murmured. "I loved him so . . ."

Len put his arms around her. In a couple of minutes, she began to cry, slow agonized sobs that mingled with her coughing. She slumped over in the wheelchair. Len walked wearily to the desk. He picked the IOU's up from the floor, stuck them in his pocket, and picked up the telephone.

"Police headquarters," he said.

Lieutenant Stagg was not happy about it. But the testimony of Mrs. Wolf established with certainty that Ted Wolf had admitted to the murder of Jimmy Ridgely. When Len walked out of police headquarters at five that evening, he was cleared. The detective followed him to the door. Len looked back. The man lit a cigarette and did not move off the steps.

He walked all the way back to his apartment. The club would be closed for a few days, thank God.

Laurie answered the phone when he called.

"I found the right one," he said.

"Who was it, Len?"

"Ted Wolf."

"Wolf? Why . . . ?"

He shook his head, not thinking that she could not see him.

"I'm tired. I'm going to bed. I can tell you at dinner tomorrow night, if that's all right."

"I'll be here," she said.

Len put down the phone. His eyelids felt heavy and his body ached from nervous strain. It was all over. Laurie, lovely Laurie. And Jimmy, dead. No marriage for them. Death. Sorrow. But there was time, he thought. Time ahead. Plenty of time for them, now that she knew, now that Jimmy's killer was dead.

Len walked over to his phonograph. From the rack, he pulled out three records. Their discs. *With A Song In My Heart.* One by one, he broke them and threw the pieces into the wastebasket. And then he went to bed.

Celebrity
and Justice for All

There was this dream. His mother, whom he couldn't stand because all her life she transmitted silent signals: she didn't like him. As he was coming up through law school, or taking crap with two hundred fifty other hungry associates in Wasserman & Sheinberg, he'd try to tell her about some accomplishment, some shining nugget of logic in a brief he'd contributed to, and the old lady would smile her phony smile and study his earlobe while he talked, and when he was through she'd say, "All right, Mickey, but remember what's important. Publicity. Did anyone take notice? Was your name in the paper?"

She was gone now, thank Christ; she'd hung on till she was ninety-seven, driving him nuts; she was *still* hanging on in the dream which he suffered through many times each year.

He woke up in a sweat with his heart pounding. His first thought was, *Got to win. Today's the day. Got to win.*

He couldn't precisely remember it, but he felt he'd had the dream again last night. He hated his mother most because of one thing. The old bag was *right.*

His chauffeur was waiting outside the mansion half an hour later. Because of the day's foul fog, yellow and slimy, he could barely see the man, let alone the deep-green Jaguar super-stretch with the special solid gold justice-and-scales upright on the hood. "Arm the defenses," he said as he jumped in; day like this, greaseballs from the underclass might dart out of the fog at an intersection and try to cut away the hood ornament with a pocket torch.

The chauffeur, a big ugly Peruvian Indian recently arrived

30

on an illegal immigrant sub, knew enough Spanglish to grunt and throw the switches. Soon they were rolling, out the armored gates, away from the forty-room mansion where he lived in his lonely splendor. He'd just gone through a fifth divorce. He couldn't keep a wife, or maintain a family. His hours were too long, he was too dedicated to the law.

By eight, he was in his office on the hundred and seventeenth floor of Heston City North, a complex of guaranteed earthquake-proof cylindrical towers named in honor of the old-time actor who'd starred in some picture about "the big one." Heston City was opened two years ago; so far, so good.

The office of Miguelito Chang, Esq., occupied half a floor, a whole one-hundred-eighty-degree arc of the building. Beyond the armor glass, you absolutely couldn't see a sign of life, let alone any other illumination, because of the yellow shit that passed for the LAX atmosphere. Never mind, he knew the important building was out there; the building on which his dreams were centered this day of all days, this day when he might, oh God yes, just might achieve the acme of professional recognition because of the case whose verdict he and the entire worldwide media community were certain would come in before five o'clock.

To confirm that, he voice-activated the sixteen monitors spread on the inner wall in rows of four. "Up six." The volume of six slowly escalated, bringing in the modulated tones of the silver-haired, pseudo-humanistic king of morning talk, Philo Downey. What a phony. Okay, but he was seen in one hundred and four countries, last count.

". . . guest this morning is Billy Esperanza, parking lot superintendent at Criminal Courts out in LAX. Señor Esperanza has seen and heard it all during these seventy-six weeks of the trial of the half-century, right, Señor? Seventy-six weeks in which an all-star team led by one of the country's top defense lawyers, Mickey Chang, has been fighting to keep the Trailer Court Terrorist, Sheela Marie Kooperman, from getting the big-needle verdict."

The parking lot superintendent, for Christ's sake. Stupid. Really reaching.

On the other hand, who was left after nearly three and a half years since Sheela Marie's arrest? Everybody had been interviewed, you couldn't blame Philo. "Remember what's important . . ."

He slipped his thousand-dollar no-lapel cutaway into the wardrobe and patted down his pleated shirt. Had to stop sweating so much. Had to stop the fast lubbing of his heart. He'd gone through so much fucking stress during pretrial hearings, case preparation, then the actual trial: witness coaching, opening statements, direct and redirect, closing arguments, facing the glare of media lights outside Criminal Courts every day, dozens of mikes shoved in his face by dipshit recent graduates who thought Blackstone was some old timer who did tricks with floating light bulbs, it was a wonder he wasn't dead of stroke or myfarc. But this, by stupid coincidence, was finally *it;* the big day; make or break . . .

"Now tell us in one word, Señor Esperanza, will the twenty-six good citizens and true bring in their verdict this afternoon as we've heard for days? In one word, now . . ."

"Absolutely definitely," said the Señor, flashing a big mess of gold front teeth.

Mickey went, "Hah," and clapped his hands. He took a shot of Caff from the bottle in his desk and rang for Miss Prynne.

Miss Prynne came in sinuously with her hidden petticoats swishing under her tight charc-gray pseudo-Vic outfit that was supposed to minimize her build, but you couldn't mini-

32

mize tits and ass like Miss Prynne's with a block of cement. Miss Prynne was up for her third centerfold in the *Legal Review*, but Mickey hadn't heard from the rag's lawyer in two days; made a quick note to jab him.

"Good morning, sir," Miss Prynne said demurely, as though he hadn't been sampling those goodies intimately for five months.

"Hiya, hon. Want to give me the layout?"

"Slim Gross at ten. He's to have his rough outline and sample chapter—"

"Slim, I remember. Fucking hack." But the ghost writer knew how to turn out a celeb best-seller. He was doing *My Plea to You*, the third authorized memoir of Mickey's client, Sheela Marie Kooperman, a sixteen-year-old blonde beauty who'd been knocked around and abused by two step-fathers in Sandy Lakes Modular Estates, a two-bit Florida trailer park, and had been so traumatized that she'd per-suaded a boyfriend to steal a weapon for her, a rapid-fire NRA Special, with which she'd invaded a private golf com-munity in Boca Raton and gone from house to house, putting a lead period after the lives of thirty-eight householders. Mickey had led the defense team, winning a coastal change of venue and a seventy-five-percent cut of all major and subsid-iary rights; he'd been on the telly almost every day with his all-star team of colleagues from seven countries, and he'd run a hell of a defense, if he did say so. *Ladies and gentlemen of the jury, you heard my client weeping as she told you of her deranged state. She lost control. She was not responsible. Firstly, she was a victim of abuse, parental and societal. Secondly, she was a victim of impossible expectations inflamed by constant media merchan-dising overkill. A consumer with no wherewithal to consume the electronic banquet pitilessly shoved at her by four hundred chan-nels of sell-sell-SELL. But she saw a lot of fat cats who did gorge at the banquet, and she snapped. "They all got so much more than me, I been deprived, that's why I did it"—there, ladies and gentlemen, there is the plaintive cry of a hurt, wounded victim who has been physically and spiritually raped again and again, by lust-crazed white Euromales, and by a society that rewards and favors our rich brethren while it throws our starving underclass on the ash heap.*

Mickey counted seven jurors openly crying at the end of that little number—three of them men, for Christ's sake. He'd won, and today would validate it—the proof, the payoff, began at half after five . . .

He visualized the Jaguar super-stretch pulling up, himself in white tails and modest black boutonniere, pressing through thousands of fans, law buffs, fans who'd been hanging behind the barricades since before daylight.

There'd be cameras, scores of paparazzi—and Miguelito "Mickey" Chang would walk away with the big one. He'd hired a chippy from the swank Puss-to-Go agency, some bim who'd be appropriately clingy when the camera panned around just seconds before the announcement. He had to hire someone, he didn't know any girls who'd go out with him after his five divorces and his reputation for ferocious pursuit of excellence in his profession. Miss Prynne screwed on the QT, in-house only, for bonuses and perks. But the tension—God, it was terrible. Mickey hated to sweat, it was undignified and, sometimes, had a repulsive smell. But he just couldn't help it, today was make-or-break.

Remember what's important. . . .

"Three o'clock, here in the office, you have a wash, trim, and touch-up from Mr. Phyllis."

"Right. Noted. Did we get the jury report from our mole?"

"Yes, chief, confirming what everyone's been hearing for the past three days." Miss Prynne seated herself and crossed her legs provocatively so that the outline of a garter showed beneath her skirt. "He says that unless the sky falls, the jury will come in between four and five this afternoon."

"Philo Downey said so, too. I set up the schedule based on that. Rotten coincidence, the ceremony at practically the same time. But the ceremony was calendared a year ago. So okay. Randy's ready for the defense?"

"Mr. Greenstone is calendared, yes, sir."

"Tell him to come in sometime before lunch. I want personal confirmation."

"Of course, sir," Miss Prynne said, rising and leaning over his desk so he could smell her passionfruit perfume.

She gave him her hand. "I want to wish you all the luck in the world." They shook, and Miss Prynne lightly tickled his palm with her index finger.

"Be there whenever I can get there," he promised. "I'll show you my prize."

"I'm counting on it, sir."

She wiggled out of the sanctum; but even the sight of her marvelous ass, which he would enjoy again that evening sans pseudo-Victorian getup, didn't, couldn't occupy his mind for long. Today was *the* day. Biggest day of his life . . .

Mickey spent the morning on various phases of client merchandising. He yelled and screamed for a half-hour with the business affairs veep at Dreampix, who wanted rights for a second MOW on Sheela Marie. Finally, Mickey lost his temper. "Seven and a half percent adjusted gross or nothing, you fucking putz!" He was so exercised, he tore the speak box out of the desktop jack and flung it. Two minutes later, Miss Prynne entered with a new box, jacked it in, and whispered, "Mr. Spielman calling back."

The business affairs veep rolled over and said yes. Mickey called him a visionary Christian gentleman and promised to do brunchy-lunchy soon.

Slim Gross was fifteen minutes late. He was one of those sorry writer types, of which there were a zillion out here. Slim belonged to the subgenus *erzatz hick,* alternately bragged about his West Texas upbringing and yapped about his Yale lit degree. He had a studied sappy country-boy smile on his pale bearded face, a carefully sprayed forelock hanging over his forehead, antique stonewashed jeans, and Texas boots complemented by a collarless shirt with rhinestone studs and a formal jacket.

"I've got a new angle for the lead chapter I'd like to pitch, Mickey," the writer began, proffering his document which Mickey could see was prepped on the cheapest of computer paper; this guy was strictly Grub Street West. But he could be brow beaten, which made him a bargain.

"Leave it," Mickey said with an imperious wave; his eyes were elsewhere.

Slim picked at his forelock. "I was hoping—wondering— could we discuss it today? Maybe get an okay or—" Slim gulped. "Possibly an advance on the advance? My life's companion just vamoosed, and she's suing me for everything. I'd even be willing to cut the royalty to five and a quarter in exchange for a little consultation with the fir—"

Mickey laughed. "*This* firm? Forget it, kid. You couldn't afford the associate toilet cleaner in this firm. I'll read this and get back to you next week."

"Mickey, I'm really desper—"

Mickey jumped up in majestic wrath. "Do you know what day this is? Do you know what's happening this afternoon?"

Shamed, Slim hung his head. "Yes, sir. The verdict in the trial of the half century."

"Asshole. The awards. The *awards.* Get out. And take this shit with you. I already know I don't like it."

He threw the copy at Slim, who caught it like a drunken wide receiver; fortunately, Slim wasn't so cheap that he couldn't afford brass brads; at least the pages didn't fly all over.

Slim slunk out. Mickey sat down, mopping his face.

"That was tacky," he said. "Jesus, that was so tacky." He excused himself: he was excited. He laid his hand over his thumping heart to feel just how excited. From another drawer, he rooted out a 400 mg. pop of Tranx to take the edge off the Caff.

Everything seemed to calm down then, proceed less stressfully for the next hour. At half past twelve, Miss Prynne announced his colleague, Randy, over the box.

Mickey's brows quirked up. Odd, her using the box instead of announcing another member of the firm personally.

"Randy," he said, racing from behind the desk to shake his colleague's hand. "Great suit." Randy Greenstone was wearing a handsome deep purple number that could have come from nowhere but the atelier of Mr. Rodeo, "Suiter to the Stars."

"Just great, you'll look super this afternoon—eyes of the whole world on you, all that shit. Sit down, pal."

Something was drastically wrong, Mickey could see that in his colleague's demeanor. Randy Greenstone, a wholesome blond South African ten years Mickey's junior, was a sharp defense attorney but less oriented to the limelight than Mickey. Randy had had but one wife, with whom he shared six children. He did fool around some, but not so flagrantly anyone would make print or pix about it. With one exception.

"Mickey," Randy said, "you know my daughter Bunny—"

"Yeah, swell girl, lot of pluck, that girl."

"Well, she's the star of her team, and—Mickey, I don't know how to say this."

Mickey felt a chill. Decidedly less friendly, he said, "Just spit it out."

"There was a last-minute schedule change for the Wheelchair Soccer League. It's the state championship, you know."

"I don't know from shit about kids doing headers in wheelchairs," Mickey said with outright menace. His heart was doing a real speed number again, but not for the right and proper reason. "Quit jerking me around. What—?"

"Bunny's match was scheduled under the lights at eight o'clock, but they shifted it back to four, don't ask me why. I told Felicity and Bunny I'd be there, promised . . ."

"At four, you will be at Criminal Courts. You will be at Criminal Courts because I can't be there to front the team, I will be home getting ready for the big one, do you understand me?"

Mickey was practically screaming, while Randy seemed to be practically weeping as he said, "I can't do it, Mick, I can't disappoint my daughter."

"You think I'm going to miss the ceremony because of that, is that what you think, you putz?"

"Maybe we can hire an attorney from ABA Central. I know one, fairly imposing, older guy, done a lot of whiskey adverts. His practice has dried up, and he's starved for cash. He looks a little like me, he could front—"

"Bring in a ringer just for image, are you out of your fucking mind? They'd be on to us yesterday. You are the second lead of the team, and you are going to be there to hear our client get the big n.g. from the jury."

Randy agonized, hung his head, but ultimately said: "I can't. I can't disappoint Felicity and Bunny."

The floor was sinking. The room was reeling. His arteries were closing off. He was going insane. This putz was ruining *everything* . . .

But Mickey was nothing if not a masterful performer. He threw his head back and uttered a jolly "Hah-hah!"—admittedly insincere-sounding—and then he got in the groove, waving as he reached for the phone.

"Oh, well, okay, that's how you feel, family first, sure. You go to your fucking soccer game for cripples while I make a little phone call to Lew Monarch." Lew Monarch was the king of night talk, a brassy-voiced interrogator who could be nice as cappuccino yogurt if he liked you, dangerous as a cobra if you had a secret and he wanted it.

Finger poised over the fifty-button auto dial, Mickey said softly, "Maybe I'll just tell him I know a certain criminal practice attorney who prepped the Tupper twins—you remember the Tupper twins, don't you? *We Had to Do It* was on the *Times* list for nineteen weeks, the MOW had a thirty-six share—and maybe I'll suggest to my pal Lew that you not only prepped them both as witnesses, you prepped one of them in a different way by peeling off her clothes, in a hotbed motel, what was she, sixteen? Make it fourteen."

Randy whispered, "You dirty headline-chasing son of a bitch."

"Yeah? Sorry. That's the game, kid. This is the big day. You aren't going to blow it for me." His fingertip hovered ever closer to the Lew Monarch button. "You enjoy your soccer game, and then Felicity and Bunny can enjoy hearing about the Tupper twins on Lew Monarch next week."

A mantle of defeat dropped over Randy. "I'll be in court at four."

Mickey lifted his hand, grinned. " 'Course you will. Your family'll understand. Now go wash your face and prepare to be a celebrity big-time, counselor. Sheela Marie's going to get off. N.g.—no needle. Your family wouldn't want you to miss that moment of triumph for our team."

Randy about-faced and left.

Mickey's moment came later, just before the closing of the three-hour awards program. The femcee stepped to the glass podium and said with stentorian seriousness: "Ladies and gentlemen of the bar, we've come to the big one. The award for the best performance by an attorney in defense of a client accused of a capital crime."

A busty accountant showing a lot of cleavage minced out on stiletto heels and handed over the envelope. Mickey was half-blind with sweat and excitement. His hired date squeezed his arm, whispering, "Oh, wow, oh, wow, Mickey," but she could have been an orangutan for all he cared. Two hundred and seventy million pairs of eyes were watching the worldwide cast of this star-studded event. Ever since the epochal O.J. days, trial lawyers had been superstars.

The pounding of blood in his ears was so loud, he hardly heard the recitation of nominees, cases, and verdicts, presented together with flashing audiovisual displays on the huge stage of the Music Pavilion. He was fixed, focused, attuned only to the fateful amplified sound of the envelope ripping . . .

The femcee, Supreme Court Justice Clara Thomas-Hill, peeped into the envelope. Smiled . . .

Come on, come on, for Christ's sake!

"And the winner of this year's Clarence Darrow award is—the man who led his dream team to this afternoon's stunning exoneration of his client—the winner is *Miguelito 'Mickey' Chang!*"

"Oh, WOW!" his companion screamed orgasmically as he rocketed from his aisle seat and raced forward amid the glaring, flaring follow spots that hit him, lit him up, while the ninety-piece symphony orchestra in the pit played the love theme from Sheela Marie's first MOW.

And then he was onstage, at the podium, the femcee handing him the beautiful statuette, the pot-bellied Great Defender grittily rendered in bronze, shirt sleeves, suspenders, and all. "Oh, gosh, it's heavy," he gasped in his best little-boy voice, nearly bringing down the house with laughter.

The Supreme Court justice kissed him on the mouth and whispered congratulations. Mickey was dizzy with visions of what the moment would mean. Book deals, film deals, merchandise deals; limitless possibilities . . .

He was so overwhelmed, he forgot to reach inside his jacket for the acceptance remarks he'd worked on for a week. All he could do was improvise, standing there in the lights, the music, the glory—*Jesus Christ, they're on their feet in the orchestra! Also the balcony! A couple thousand of the best and brightest of the profession—a standing ovation!*

Finally, they settled down, but he was still so overwhelmed, he wasn't quite coherent. He raised the glittering Clarence over his head and wiped his eyes with his other hand.

"What a system. It's a great system, our system of justice. The greatest."

He was crying.

"I didn't win this by myself. I have so many people to thank."

He was crying, bawling; couldn't stop.

"First of all, there's my mother . . ."

The Opener
of the Crypt

I first read the story when I was young. Even then it seemed real in a way none of the other stories I read were real. As I grew up I tried to tell myself that it was nothing but a boy's imagination which gave me that sense of reality. But then I would read the story again and it wouldn't be a story any longer. It would become a real and vital truth, distorted somehow, but still real. A voice at the back of my mind always spoke to me then, whispering with a hollow solemn softness.

This is truth, the voice would say. *This is fact. This is not imagination or legend.* And I believed it. It filled every part of me, and as a grown man I was more aware of the truth than I had been as a child. And so I worked at my job on the *Gazette* and led my life along the streets of Paris. But I read the story again and again, until it was a part of me, until I knew that somewhere, sometime, it had existed.

Of course, I wanted to prove it to myself, to justify that quiet voice in my mind, but for years I never had the chance. And then one summer evening when the sky over the city was filled with a pale twilight, I had dinner with Dr. Armand, a good friend of mine and an historian of high standing. I remember how it was as we sat smoking our cigars and sipping our brandy. How I came one step closer to the realization of the truth that lived in my mind.

Dr. Armand reached over to a small table beside his chair and picked up a letter. He nodded his white head at me. "This ought to interest you, Paul."

"What's that you have?" I asked.

He glanced at the finely written script. "A letter from a friend of mine in Rome. It seems he was touring the seacoast last month and he ran across a highly interesting house in a small village."

I took a puff on the cigar. I tried to be calm, but something stirred inside of me. "What's so interesting about this house?"

"Well," said Dr. Armand, his gaze going out the window to the peaceful evening sky, "it's quite an old house, and almost fallen to the ground, but one of the innkeepers said it once belonged to a family named Montresor."

I sat there stupefied.

Dr. Armand waved the letter again. "Coincidence, of course, but I thought it might pique your curiosity." He chuckled quietly and continued his talk on various topics. But I didn't hear. The voice was in my mind again, speaking softly to me. *He does not believe. But you know the truth.*

"Yes!" My voice was intense.

"What did you say?" Dr. Armand looked at me, puzzled.

I made up a hasty excuse and left him, after I had pressed him for all the details. When I got back to my flat, I couldn't go to sleep. There it was—something to prove what I believed. This bit of news made me want more proof. When morning came I went to the editor of the *Gazette* and quit my job. I took my savings out of the bank, bought a small motor car and started south.

I drove rapidly. A desire filled me and pulled me toward Italy, toward that small village, toward proof that the legend was a living truth. It was more than a desire, because I felt vaguely that a force outside myself was pulling me there. I slept at the roadside slumped over in the seat of the car, and ate only when the growling in my stomach became painful. The countryside raced by and I was in Italy, roaring across the plains, through the river valleys, disturbing the sleeping plazas and throwing up dust behind me. I had to know!

I got tired, of course. Very tired. By the time I had gotten lost twice, found my way again and at last reached the coast, I was sore all over. My face felt dirty and I knew my beard had grown out. But it was worth it. With each kilometer I drove, I knew I was getting closer to the truth.

It was early evening when I finally reached the town. I had been driving along the coast for two hours with the sea spread out to my left in a glistening sheet. I pulled over the top of a small hill and stopped the car. The town lay before me at the foot of the hill. Music and shouting drifted up from below. The streets were brightly lit. My hands gripped the steering wheel. A skyrocket shot up into the air over the town and exploded in a shower of red stars, and I knew it was carnival season.

I drove down the hill. The streets were jammed with people dressed in costume, singing and dancing and running in every direction. I pushed my way through those streets on foot, paying hardly any attention to the people, watching the houses for the name of the inn mentioned in the letter.

At last I found it. I think I was a little crazy then, feeling so close to my goal, because I shoved my way roughly through the crowd and a couple of young men turned to look at me, their eyes glaring through slits in their masks. I went through the door of the inn, ignoring them.

The landlord's name was Giacomo. He looked me up and down, his ancient tanned forehead wrinkling into a frown. I was a foreigner and I was not in costume. He certainly must have felt that something was wrong. And from the way I must have looked, bearded and dirty, my clothes rumpled, I suppose I couldn't blame him.

"What does the signor wish?" the old man asked me. He poured himself a glass of wine and downed it quickly.

I could hardly say the words. Excitement had made me tense, nervous. "I . . . I am looking for an old house."

He laughed loudly. I could tell he thought I was mad, and it made me angry. I wanted to lean across the table and choke the words out of him.

"We have many old houses, signor. This town is full of old houses."

"This is a particular house. It belonged to a particular family. The family's name was Montresor."

He thought a minute, staring into the wine dregs. Then he nodded. "Yes, the Montresor house is in this town. It is a ruin, signor, tumbling to the ground. No one goes there any more. Why do you wish to find that particular house?"

"Never mind. Where is it?"

He gave me directions to the southern edge of the village. I tossed some coins on the table and hurried out. This time I shoved people brutally out of my way, pushing against the sticky tide of humanity roistering through the streets. The rockets blazed above me, the noise dinned in my ears, but I pushed on, driven by my desire. People hurled angry curses at me but I did not heed them. At last I broke free of the crowd and found myself in a deserted street, quite dark, with immense patches of purple shadow hiding the walls of the houses in inky impenetrability.

I hurried along the street, which suddenly became a dead end. My heart fell. I stopped at what seemed to be an iron gate and took out a match. I lit it and held it up. The reddish light flickered in an eerie manner. My heart pounded within my chest.

For there, blazoned on the stone, was a coat of arms that I knew only too well. The large human foot grinding down

45

upon a snake as the snake sank its fangs into the heel of that same foot. Above the symbol was the motto, and I had only to glance at the first word. *Nemo* . . . My match was suddenly extinguished by a gust of stale wind. With trembling hands I lit another. *Nemo me impune lacessit.* And below the coat . . . I felt a force seize me and transform me into a wildly quivering creature of fear and anguish. The name, carved in capitals that were heavy and ponderous: *Montresor!*

The second match flickered out into darkness. My heart thudding wildly, I pushed at the gate. There was a horrendous screeching noise, and I stepped quickly backward as the gate came free of its hinges and fell with a mighty clang onto the stone of the courtyard. This was the very house, and I was close to the heart of my secret! I raced across the courtyard, conscious within myself that soon I would know the reason for which I had been drawn over the years to this dark and malignantly brooding place. I would know what strange and demonically real impulse made me believe the legend as truth and made me seek proof.

An oppressive air of obsolescence and decay filled my nostrils as I stepped through the front portal into the first of the dark rooms. I knew the way . . . oh, God! I knew the way and could not turn aside! For here was the place to which I had been destined to come. Why I had been so destined, only the spirits that brooded here could explain.

I reached up to the wall and found a torch resting in its socket. With violently trembling hands I applied a match and soon had a flickering reddish light to guide me. My feet clattered hollowly on the cold and hoary stone. I paced quickly through the various suites of ancient rooms, each with its own particular odor of rot and desolation. The entrance to the staircase loomed before me and I hurried on, plunging downward at a rapid rate, watching as the shadows unfolded in the guttering torch glare, watching as I saw the reality of my brain becoming the reality of matter itself. Then the air became suddenly colder and I stood on damp ground. Around me stretched endless rows of wine racks, long empty of their casks, deserted and left to the scurrying rodents and the webs of dust and age that spread like grotesque mantles over the empty tiers.

The voice called to me now, surging through my brain, whirling me on and on and I could not resist its mighty power. *Come, come, make haste, make haste, the task must be performed.* What task I knew not, but I raced on nonetheless. I was will-less now, a creature drugged by the commands of an unknown preternatural force. The nitre depended from the vaulted ceiling in strangely deformed shapes, and the torchlight danced and whirled on the primeval stone of the walls. I felt the chill of the air pierce to the very marrow of my bones.

Again the vaults descended and my light fell upon the hollow black sockets of ancient skulls, scattered askew on mounds of human remains; new terror thrilled through me as my mind signaled that I was descending beneath the river. Droplets of moisture trickled over the yellowed skulls, and rodents scratched and chittered among the piled bones. The voice spoke again, its volume increased now, its tone imperious and sonorous. *Come; make haste to perform the task!*

I passed through the low arches, descended once more, pursued my way through another lengthy passage, stepping over piles of those grisly remains, and once again hurled myself down an include, until at last I realized with a start of overwhelming terror that I was in the deepest crypt, far in the bowels of the dark earth. My torch was seized with a gust of fetid air that made it dim and lose its intensity so that an unearthly light of a bluish color pervaded the crypt. Here the bleached relics of human life had been mounded up to the very roof. And directly before me was a wall of masonry, and lying before it upon the ground was an ancient tool with which the masons plied their trade.

I stood in wonder and awe, realizing that here at last I had found the utter actuality of that which I had once merely sensed. The speaker thundered his monstrous tones into the remotest crevices of my brain and I realized that he was lodged behind the wall of masonry, imprisoned, yet powerful in all his fiendish strength.

Break the masonry!

The command echoed and re-echoed in my confused brain. I reeled dizzily and nearly dropped my light. I staggered forward, no longer a mortal, but an agent of some weird and terrible force from the great dark gulfs of supernatural power that lie far beyond the ken of mere human knowledge. I knelt and placed my torch in a heap of grisly bones, propping it up as best I could. And then I took the mason's tool into my hand and gazed at it wonderingly, my brow hot and feverish. I leaped forward, and with a fury that approached madness I attacked the masonry.

I have no conception of how long I labored. The torch dwindled slowly and I battered at the ancient stonework, chipping it away fragment by fragment, until the blood streamed off my injured hands and stained the stone with its red color. I worked feverishly, emitting whimpering sounds, howling insane curses to unknown gods, exciting myself to a pitch of brutal mindless automatism. At the end of this period of madness, I had created an opening in the masonry scarcely a foot square. I took my torch with faltering hand and thrust it before me into the aperture. And my demented eyes saw the speaker who had sought me.

There in the flickering illumination I beheld the figure floating, as in a mist, above the floor of the smaller crypt. I grew cognizant of the garb of motley, of the delicate tinkle of bells on the peaked cap, of the almost overpowering reek of wine. From out that spectral face two orbs burned, intense as the innermost fires of the underworld. The voice that spoke to me issued from that unearthly apparition.

"You have fulfilled the obligation placed upon your family by your ignoble ancestor. You have released me from my prison and set my spirit free to roam the outer spheres. The debt is paid."

"Who is speaking?" I shrieked in a frenzy. "Who addresses me thus?"

"Fortunato," was the reply. "My tormented spirit has survived my flesh."

"Fortunato!" I cried. "But why have I been chosen? Why has it been my task and mine alone to free you? Who am I to be called here thus? In God's name, speak!"

"You are Montresor," came the shade's reply.

"Montresor!" This I shrieked in a voice completely and utterly saturated with a wild madness.

"The last of the Montresor line. I have kept alive within you the spirit of that first Montresor, that infamous spirit which fed upon its own evil deed and transformed itself into the spirit of a man inflamed with guilt. I have placed a compulsion upon you to free me, and you have answered."

And then I was aware of what I had only sensed before, that the immaterial substance of that first hateful Montresor who walled up the insufferable Fortunato had been transferred to me, until I was in spirit and in actuality two separate and individual beings united into a single creature!

My torch wavered once more. I reeled unsteadily on my feet, my eyes filming with the mists of madness. I swooned, but in the instant before complete unconsciousness threw its healing cloak over me, I felt a presence whisper past me from out that small crypt, rushing by as with a great wind, flinging the tiny musical tinkle of bells behind it in supreme triumph as it ascended upward toward the earth and the starred heavens, liberated and unfettered after age upon age in the depths of the planet. I swooned completely.

And only at this moment have I awakened. My torch is extinguished. I am faint from my labor at the masonry, and am lying upon the chill earth of the crypt with its stillness surrounding me. I have not the will or the strength to stir. In the darkness there are the remotest of scurrying sounds. The rodents are awaiting my demise. I shall rest until the infernal shade descends, for my debt has been fully rendered.

Cloak
and Digger

Roger guessed that the opposite side had got on to his mission when a black Citroen roared into the street and three men armed with Sten guns leaped out and began shooting at him simultaneously.

Bullets lacerated the stones of the café wall. Roger's head had been in front of this spot a moment before. As the slugs whined murderously in the twilight air, Roger crawled on hands and knees between the hems of the checked tablecloths.

He heard a great crashing above his own panicky breath. French curses, liquid and rapid, punctuated the bursts of gunfire. The shooting stopped twenty seconds after it had begun.

But by that time Roger had already crawled into the shadows of the café, bowled over the mustached proprietor and raced up rickety stairs to the second floor. He went out through a trapdoor to the slate roof.

Clinging dizzily to a chimney pot, he looked down. A flock of geese that had been strolling through the cobbled main street of the tiny village of St. Vign flew every which way, honking at the Citroen which nearly ran over them as it gathered speed and rolled away. Then, with a tight-lipped gasp of relief, Roger located the source of the crash that had saved him—an overturned vintner's cart. He vaguely remembered the cart being unloaded before the shooting started, as he sat sipping Coca-Cola, reading the pamphlet in his pocket, *A New Glossary of Interesting Americanisms,* and trying to look like a tame philologist in horn-rimmed spectacles.

He had failed miserably, he thought. In the disguise, that is. But then, the opposite side always had first-rate intelligence. Lucky the vintner's cart had gotten in the line of fire. The poor vintner was drawing a crowd of people as he sobbed over his dribbling and bullet-riddled casks and cursed off would-be drinkers. The whine of the Citroen had died altogether.

It was chilly, hanging on the chimney pot in the wind. Below in the street a nun in the crowd pointed up at Roger. Quickly he scrambled down the slates. He leaped to the adjoining roof in the amber dusk.

As he went skulking across the rooftops, one thought came up paramount in his mind after his shock and surprise had passed: his still-urgent need to get aboard *The Silver Mistral Express* which was scheduled to go through St. Vign on its way to Paris in—Roger consulted his shockproof watch while resting on the roof of a laundry—exactly forty-eight minutes.

His first task was to reach the railway station, hoping the assassins would be frightened off making another attempt on him because of the attention their first failure drew. Sliding, Roger dropped into an alley and began to run through the grape-fragrant French twilight.

As he ran he heard a number of whistles and saw several gendarmes pedaling frantically on bicycles. Good, he thought, puffing. Wonderful. If they keep the Citroen holed up in some garage for—again the watch—thirty-two minutes, I'll make it.

Reaching the depot without incident, he paced restlessly along the platform, trying to read his pamphlet. At last, up the track, a light shone and an air horn cried out stridently.

When the crack train from the south of France pulled to a hissing halt in response to the ticket seller's signal lantern,

Roger leaped aboard with the pamphlet of Americanisms still clutched in one hand. The conductor badgered him in French for disturbing the schedule as the express began to roll. Roger ignored him. He held up the pamphlet in the vestibule light. On the inside front cover a car and compartment number had been noted in ballpoint. Roger turned to the right, stepped through a velvet-padded door, then hastily backed out again. He had gone the wrong way. The private saloon car was filled with men and women in formal clothes, opera capes and evening gowns.

"What's that?" Roger asked the trainman sourly. "A masked ball?"

"An opera troupe, *Anglais*. Returning from a triumphant engagement in the South," replied the trainman, kissing his fingertips. Then he scowled. "Let me see your ticket, please."

Roger handed it over.

"How far is compartment seven, car eleven-twelve?"

"Four cars to the rear," said the trainman without interest, turning his back on Roger and beginning to whistle an operatic aria. Roger kicked open the door on his left. He hurried, walking as fast as he dared. The cars were dimly lit; most of the doors closed. The wheels of the train clicked eerily in the shadows. Roger shivered. He felt for his automatic under his coat.

Finally he found the right car. Putting his pamphlet in his pocket, Roger knocked at compartment seven.

"Dozier? Open up."

Mouth close to the wood, Roger whispered it again: "Dozier! For God's sake, man, open—"

With a start Roger realized the sliding door was unlocked.

He stepped quickly into the darkened carriage, blinked, and uttered a sigh of disgust. He might have known.

Wasn't this precisely why he had been sent to board the

train in such haste? Because the agent—some agent, Roger thought, staring at the compartment's lone occupant—was one of the worst bunglers in the trade. An IBM machine had slipped a cog or something, dispensing the wrong punch card when the escort was being selected for the vital mission of accompanying Sir Stafford Runes from Cairo to Paris. At the last moment, higher-ups had caught the error and dispatched Roger by 707 to catch the train at St. Vign and see that no fatal damage had been done.

The agent in question, actually a coder from London who doubled in ladies' ready-to-wear, and who had no business at all in the field, was a fat, pot-bellied bald man with the first name Herschel. At the moment he was snoring contentedly with his hands twined over his Harris-tweeded paunch. Roger shook him.

"Dozier, wake up. Do you hear me? What's the matter with you, Dozier?"

Sniffing, Roger realized dismally that brandy had aided Herschel Dozier's slumber. With each valuable minute spent attempting to wake the slumbering cow-like fellow, Sir Stafford Runes sat alone, undoubtedly in the next compartment. Disgusted, Roger slid back into the corridor.

Which compartment, right or left?

He tried the one on the right, tapping softly. A feminine giggle came back, together with some sounds which indicated that if an archaeologist was inside, he was a young, lively archaeologist, not the red-haired, vain, aging Runes.

Moving back along the carpeted corridor to the other door, Roger hesitated, his knuckles an inch from the panel.

The compartment door stood open perhaps a thirty-second of an inch, allowing a hairline of light to fall across Roger's loafers.

Sweat came cold on his palm. He drew his automatic.

Was someone from the opposite side in there?

Runes, on an underground exploration in the vicinity of Nisapur, had unearthed what headquarters described only as a "vital plan" belonging to the opposite side. The plan, apparently, was so important that higher-ups had ordered Runes to discontinue his valuable role as a double agent at once and return to home base as fast as he could while still avoiding danger. Now Roger smelled danger like burning insulation on a wire.

Drawing a tight breath, he cursed the faulty IBM machine, gripped the door handle, and yanked.

The first thing he saw was the corpse of Sir Stafford Runes.

It sprawled doll-fashion on the seat, an ivory knife-hilt poking from the waistcoat. Against the talcumed whiteness of the dead man's puffy old features, the carrot brightness of his thick red hair looked gruesome.

Then Roger's eyes moved to the tall man who stood calmly in the center of the compartment, eyeing him with a stainless-steel gaze from under the rim of a shining top hat. From the man's lean shoulders fell the shimmering folds of an opera cape, which showed a flashing hint of blood-red satin lining as he raised one white-gloved hand in a vicious little salute. Roger slammed the door shut as the man said:

"Is it really you, Roger?" His voice was clipped, educated. "I'd thought they took care of you in St. Vign."

"No such luck."

Covering the gaunt man with his automatic, Roger nodded down at the dead body. The express train's horn howled in the night.

"So you did this, you rotten bastard. Just the way you ran over Jerry Pitts with the road grader in Liberia and fed Mag Busby that lye soup in Soho." A vein in Roger's temple began to hammer. "You rotten bastard," he repeated. "Someone should have squashed you a long time ago. But what are you doing in that get-up, Victor? Traveling with that opera company?"

"Of course, dear boy," the other puffed. "I'm representing them on this tour. I schedule performances wherever duty calls. Such as in Paris. Most convenient." A white glove indicated the speeding motion of the train, but for all the man's casualness there was glacial chill in his calculating eyes. "It appears that this time, however, with you as relief man, I've landed in a spot of trouble. I'd thought all I had to worry about was that fool asleep next door."

"This time, Foxe-Craft," Roger said quietly, "you've got a bullet to worry about."

"A bullet?" The urbane man's eyebrow lifted. "Oh, now, really, old chap, so *brutal?*"

"Did you think about brutality when you fed Mag the lye soup? Listen, mister, for ten years we've wanted you. You and your fancy gloves and your code name." A line of derision twisted Roger's mouth. "*Elevenfingers.* Proud of that name, aren't you? One up on the rest of us, and all that. Well, tonight, I think I'll take those fingers off. One at a time."

With a stab of satisfaction Roger saw a dollop of sweat break out on Foxe-Craft's upper lip. Roger made a sharp gesture with the automatic.

"All right, Elevenfingers—"

"Don't make it sound cheap," Foxe-Craft said, dangerously soft. "Not theatrical, I warn you."

"Where's the folio Runes was carrying?"

Hastily Roger searched the archaeologist's corpse. He performed the same action on the person of his enemy, a shred of doubt beginning to worry him as he completed the task, unsuccessfully. Apart from the usual innocuous card cases,

56

visas, antipersonnel fountain pen bombs and other personal effects, neither dead researcher nor live agent possessed a single item remotely resembling the flat, eight-and-a-half by eleven series of sheets, blank to the eye but inked invisibly, which Runes was carrying back from Nisapur. Roger raised the automatic again.

"Take a long look down the muzzle, friend. See the message? I can put some bullets in places that'll hurt like hell. And I don't care if I wake the whole damned train doing it. But you're going to tell me where the folio is. You're going to give it to me, or I'll blow you into an assortment of pieces no doctor on the Continent can put together." Desperate, angry, Roger added: "In five seconds."

Foxe-Craft shrugged.

"Very well."

As Foxe-Craft consulted a timetable card riveted to the compartment wall his eyes glinted maliciously for a moment. Then the toe of his dancing pump scraped a worn place in the carpeting. Looking at his wristwatch, the man who liked to call himself Elevenfingers said: "You're an American. Look under the rug."

"I'll just do that."

Carefully Roger knelt, keeping the automatic in a position to fire at the slightest sign of movement in the corner of his eye. Roger probed at the frayed edges of the hole in the carpeting. And at that precise instant, the game turned against him. *The Silver Mistral Express* whipped around a curve and into a tunnel.

There was a scream of horn, a sudden roar of wheels rocketing off walls. Roger swayed, off balance.

A tasseled pump caught him in the jaw, exploding roman candles behind his eyes a moment after he caught a fragmentary glimpse of traces of ash beneath the carpet.

Foxe-Craft *couldn't* have burned the folio, Roger thought wildly as he fell backward, flailing. I didn't smell anything—and that means *Runes* burned it because he knew they were on to us, but why did he burn the only copy in existence—?

No answer came except the roar of wheels and another brutal smash of a pump instep on his jaw, smacking Roger's head against the side of the compartment, sending him to oblivion.

Through his pain he had dim recollections of the next hour—hands lifting him, a fall through space, a jolt, the *clacka-clacka-clacka* of wheels gathering speed, then the chirruping of night insects. And silence.

Bruised, disappointed, briar-scratched and burr-decorated, Roger woke sometime before dawn, lying in a ditch a few hundred yards south of another railway depot, this one bearing a signboard naming the town as St. Yar.

Roger picked himself up and tried to wipe the humiliation of failure from his mind. In another two hours Foxe-Craft—and the train—would be in Paris, doubtless with the vital material in his hands.

Roger felt, somehow, that it still existed—that Elevenfingers had tricked him. But how? Starting off, Roger noticed his ubiquitous pamphlet in the weeds. He stared at it dully, finally putting it back in his pocket as he passed a sign pointing the way to a French military aerodrome two kilometers away.

Trudging into the village, Roger located an inn and ordered a glass of wine. The proprietor treated him with the respect given by all Frenchmen to those who look like confirmed alcoholics—torn clothes and hangdog expression. Dispiritedly Roger sat at a street-side table as the sun rose. Bells chimed in the cathedral. A French jet lanced the sky overhead.

To kill the futility of it all, Roger bought a paper at a kiosk and sat by a fountain reading. At a town quite a distance south, the wet-inked lead story ran, an unidentified bald man had been found in a ditch by railway inspectors.

Poor Herschel Dozier, Roger thought, it would be just like Elevenfingers to finish the sleeping agent, just for amusement. Another knife in the guts for nothing . . .

When he had finished the paper, he dragged out the pamphlet to try to dull his mind.

"What the hell do I care about interesting Americanisms?" he said, blinking in the sun. And then, as pigeons cooed around his feet and a postcard seller passed by hawking indecent views, the depth of his blunder made itself known.

Foxe-Craft's remark flashed like a bomb. With a whoop, Roger leaped up and ran to the café.

"Where can I get a taxi to the military aerodrome? I have to get a helicopter to Paris right away!"

The baffled proprietor gave him directions. Roger's identification papers, concealed in his heels, served him well. Within an hour he stood on the noisy platform as *The Silver Mistral Express* chugged in along the arrival track.

Roger felt for the automatic in his pocket, grinning tensely. Of *course* Runes had burned the folio. Too obvious. But if Roger was right, there was another copy—*had* to be!

Down the platform trouped the formally dressed opera company, Foxe-Craft in their midst. When he saw Roger he turned and tried to walk in the opposite direction. Roger raced after him. He gouged the automatic in the agent's ribs.

"*Really,* old fellow—" Foxe-Craft began.

"Shut up," Roger said. "You egotistical bastard. Think you're so damn clever. One up. Well, you shouldn't have opened your precise mouth, Elevenfingers, because now you're going to be tagged with a killing. I thought it was

Dozier in the ditch. But it wasn't. It was Runes. Bald, vain Runes."

Roger dug into the enemy agent's pocket, came up with his prize, carrot-red.

"First we'll go wake up Dozier. Probably he's still asleep."

Roger turned his find over, noted minute markings which looked like ink on the inner, rather burlap-like surface.

"Then," Roger added, gagging his captive, "we'll have the lab blow up the stuff that's written here. Inside old Sir Stafford's—"

A crowd began to gather. The divas and tenors of Elevenfinger's now-defunct opera troupe clucked curiously. Roger held up the carrot-colored wig and finished:

"—inside, or under—as we Americans say—his rug."

Unc Probes
Pickle Plot

Showbiz vagaries oft topsyturvy the travel skeds of scribes for *GALORE, The Newspaper of Amusement.* Viz., I wound up a road stanza covering a distrib conclave in Indpls. on a Tues., was then reshuffled via the Bell to catch a runer tryout in Chi. on Thurs. In between, I decided on a quickie junket to Weevers, Ind., which is down in the hills and also home base for my only relatives, who raised me after my folks passed on.

Annual summer vacation in Weevers is usually sufficient to re-acquaint me with my stix youth, but as my Aunt's birthday is in late Aug., timing was perfect to deliver giftie in the flesh.

As I motored in early Wed., a banner over the state route flacked MAMMOTH WEEVERS COUNTY FAIR. Subline noted that same had opened day before. Traveling with top down, I received the o.o. from locals who doubtless failed to recognize me in plaid sports coat and shades. I zipped out Elm Street to the big, old white house. Nobody home.

Next stop, Main Street. I located a slot in front of Floyd's Fountainette just as my Uncle Pinkerton hustled out the door of his hardware emporium opposite.

"Hey, Unc!" I waved, tickled to see him.

Unc ankled toward his old straight-stick Chev coupe. "Can't talk to any salesman right now. There's an emergency—"

I dodged truck freighting a load of bossies, doffing my shades the while. "Unc, it's me."

He signified beaucoup surprise. "Woodrow! What in tarnation are you doing here out of the blue?"

"Figured I'd make a p.a. at Aunt Ellen's birthday bash." I gave a quick summary of my layover between engagements.

Unc shielded his eyes from the sun, which was lofty in the temp. department even for Aug. "Well, it's surely a treat to see you. But your Aunt Ellen just phoned me from the Fairgrounds. Something mystifying's happened and she's all upset. I'm on my way out there."

"Let's take the leased soft-top. She really perks."

"Soft-top? Is that your entertainment-paper term for a convertible? All right, if it'll make things any snappier."

We jumped in and I laid down a strip getting off. I was about to inquire anent the current brouhaha, in which Unc was a natch participant as he has an egghead rep in Weevers, when I spied a deejay sitting with a mike turntable inside the window of the five-and-dimer.

"Is Radio Station WEEV running a promo, Unc?"

"Yes, Woodrow, that young fellow is new with WEEV. Jerry James is his name. He moved from Pennsylvania to join the station this spring. He's put on a whole raft of stunts like that. Mighty ambitious lad. He and his wife Betty are working hard to become part of Weevers society, such as it is. Matter of fact, it's his wife's pickles causing this puzzle that has your Aunt so worried."

"Anything with a deejay slant would make nifty *GALORE* copy, Unc. But what's the pickle angle?"

"It seems a jar of sweet gherkins has mysteriously turned into something looking like a jar of beets."

By now we had joined a caravan of rube wheels all influxing in direction of Ferris wheel, merry-go-round, grandstand, Exhibition Hall and other apparati comprising rural fest at the outskirts. Unc narrated the scenario thus far.

Because of her position as local culinary topliner, Aunt E.

had been inked to femcee pickle contest at annual Weevers county gig. Prelims were held afternoon of day before, with three winners named by Aunt E. for final judging today.

On arriving at Fair locale this ayem, Aunt E. plus chrmn. of committee for judging all goody events (viz., choc. pie, stewed rutabagas, and other hix concoctions too numerous to mention) discovered one of trio of the top jars had been flummoxed overnight.

"Late last evening, Woodrow, your Aunt Ellen confided in me that there wasn't a shred of doubt in her mind as to whose sweet gherkins she'd pick for the Blue Ribbon today. What's upset her is, she got so enthusiastic yesterday that she accidentally let on. Best sweet gherkins she'd ever tasted. Now she's afraid she kind of showed the two other finalists they weren't going to win, and thereby caused someone to take a malicious step."

"Whose gherkins got the nod?"

"Those of the so-called upstart wife of that radio-station boy. Apparently Betty James is a mighty good pickler."

"Say, watch that, Clyde," I cried to a rustic whose boat nearly dented my metal on the approach to the dusty parking field.

"Now, Woodrow," Unc said, "try not to insult the local population with your terminology. You know your Aunt thinks you're headed for hell in a hand basket as it is." But he grinned.

As we ankled, Unc backgrounded further aspects. Duo of other finalists was composed of lifelong Weevers residents, one having copped gherkins Blue Ribbon nine skeins running. Neither was likely to feel hotsy once Aunt E. let feline out of the container.

"There's LeRoy Tate waiting for us, Woodrow. He's the head of the Judges Committee I mentioned."

Same person hurried out of big corrugated tin joint marqueed Exhibition Hall. Tate was a thin type, had a WELCOME TO FAIR VISITORS badge hanging on his seersucker, and displayed mucho gloom in the eyeball region.

"Pinky, am I glad to see you. You're the only man in Weevers who can untangle this mess." His lamps hit me. I mentally itemed Tate as Assist. Principal from my days at Weevers H.S., but reaction was sans mutuality. "Say, who's this, Pinky?"

"LeRoy, you should remember Woodrow Ennis, my sister Nella's boy."

Lotsa goggling. "Not little Woodrow Ennis who used to write those poems about frogs and pussy willows for the high school paper?"

"The same, Pops." But as I had forgotten "Pops" was not a sobriquet to be casually employed in stix, I added as a save, "I'm still scrivening, though."

"Mostly in a foreign language," Unc smiled. "Woodrow reviews moving pictures and shows and things for a theatrical newspaper, LeRoy. He works in New York City. Behind the Hudson River Curtain, you might say."

"I sometimes wonder what today's youth is coming to," Tate muttered, leading way into premises. Exhibition Hall featured tractors, chicken feed troughs, bleating shoats, and other rural paraphernalia. The air was steam bathish, so spectators rubbernecking various exhibs were on the sparse side. From one wall booth with soft drink dispensers, a gray-haired gent gave Unc a glower.

Unc waved cheerfully nonetheless: "Hello there, Floyd." Then, softer. "Small wonder he's hardly speaking. He showed up at the lodge last evening late, around 10:30. Had trouble putting up his booth in time, I gather. He came for the regular Tuesday night pinochle game, but he wasn't too friendly even then. Marvella must have told him her pickles weren't going to win. Marvella is the wife of Floyd Bemis, Woodrow, remember?"

"Dig. Floyd's Fountainette."

"Marvella," said Tate, "is the nine-time gherkins champion. But I got to give her credit for being real calm this time. It's Lulu Clark who's kicking up a fuss."

Extent of my info about food prepping is that invisible folks do it somewhere behind the walls of eateries. However, there was no mistaking something amiss re the pickle presentation. Three large glass jars tagged *Finalist* decorated an aisle table. Bottles on left and right contained appetizing-looking gherkins. Bottle in center contained hideous beet-colored liquid so dark that pickles effectively did a hideout bit.

Three femmes stood several feet apart like starlets with a billing beef.

Unc said, "Hello, Marvella. Hello, Lulu. Howdydo, Mrs. James. Mighty fine-looking display here."

Unc bent to study the jars, hands in pockets of his wash pants. "No doubt that the contents of this one have been adulterated. No doubt at all."

"And I'll bet someone who's standing not very far away did it!"

Speaker was the youngest femme, a trim blondie in polka dot threads. One adjacent biddy glared. Other jane raised her eyes heavenward while putting on virtuous expression. The blondie buttonholed the chrmn.

"Mr. Tate, I slaved and slaved to prepare my gherkins. A special recipe. Can't I enter another jar?"

Tate's collar line displayed red. "Now, Mrs. James, I certainly sympathize with you in this real unusual situation. But one entry and one only is the rule. No offense meant, but we have to stick to the regulations because somebody who wanted the Blue Ribbon could accidentally bust their jar, for instance, then bring in one from a better batch at the last minute. I'm real sorry."

Blondie steamed. "I suppose you're trying to imply that my pickles spoiled and I'm just accusing somebody else as an excuse. Well, I *am* accusing somebody, Mr. Tate. I've learned how some narrow-minded people in this town welcome newcomers."

"Too bad," whispered Unc, "she's right."

One of the older femmes, an owl-nosed gray-haired character type with floral handbag and geranium-pot headgear, declaimed, "Well, Miz James, since you're so snippy about it, it's no secret that ever since you and your husband moved to Weevers it's been push, push, push."

"Ladies!" exclaimed Tate. "Unless we get to the bottom of this, the pickle contest will be ruined. Pinky, what do you think?"

"Well, this may not be a crime for Sheriff Gus Gumley. On the other hand, it certainly may be a crime. And I go along with never having seen sweet gherkins spoil so they turn that weird color. Maybe someone did doctor them. Let's investigate."

"Investigate to your heart's content, Pinkerton," said Lulu Clark. "I didn't do it. But why do we have to have shoddy carnival people from the midway eavesdropping?"

"Lulu," said Unc, "this is my nephew Woodrow Ennis."

"My stars!"

"I used to take piano lessons from your husband at the music store, Mrs. Clark. Don't you remember?" I said.

"Yes, and I remember you never practiced, either."

"I remember you, Woodrow," put in the other femme. She was a bulky number with active eyebrows, fence-post legs, and dimpling smile. She waltzed over, gladhanded me. "I've followed your career with interest, as I'm the President of the Weevers Drama Guild. Last May we presented one of Victor Herbert's operas. I sang the leading role. I truly wish you could have been present."

"Likewise," I mumbled, masking divers shudders at thought of her heft in ingenue role.

Mrs. Marvella Bemis appeared to accept kayo in the cucumber derby with good grace, though. She continued to pump my mitt with one white glove, stated she'd had her share of ribbons, so share and share alike.

Unc was busy prying at the lid of the bollixed jar. "I wonder what might have been added to spoil—say." He blinked. "Come to think of it, Woodrow, where's your Aunt?"

Tate spaketh: "She said the heat in here was getting her, Pinky. She went to lie down a minute." He indicated in direction of entrances to Ladies' and Gents' in nearby wall.

Nodding, Unc unpried the glass lid, "Mighty peculiar. No odd smell. Just pickle aroma."

"But they'd never win looking like that," the deejay's blondie caterwauled.

"I repeat, 'twasn't me," said Mrs. Lulu Clark.

"Nor me," put in Marvella Bemis. "After all, since I have won nine blue ribbons, why on *earth*—" Whap! Simultaneous with oration, she dished out theatrical gesture which unfortunately banged her right glove against the jar Unc was grasping. Doll did impromptu terp routine trying to get out of way, but was too late. Scarlet since from the jug decorated her glove with deep stains.

"Golly, Marvella, I'm sure sorry," Unc said.

"Oh, don't fret, Pinkerton, it's an old pair." So saying, she peeled off both items, stuffed same in handbag. She must have cut her right thumb as she sported a Band-Aid.

"Land to Goshen, it's Woodrow!" Aunt Ellen appeared, all flustered and patting her gray bun and adjusting her specs. "If this isn't the most amazing surprise."

Following buss, I said, "Just in time for some boffo material, too. Don't forget, county fairs are still a big source of coin for vaude vets."

"Woodrow, must you use that shameful entertainment jargon? Especially when things are in such a stew? And—Woodrow! Where did you get that coat?" Sad expresh in Aunt E.'s optics indicated I was doubtless on the primrose path. Time to change subjects.

"Aunt Ellen, I really dig those nifty vitamin pills you sent me. I belt—er, take them every day."

"I should hope so, prowling around in dingy dens night after night the way you do. What's your Uncle up to?"

We departed stage center, then discussed mystery in low tones from the wings.

Aunt E. said, "Just look at Lulu Clark smile. I'll bet she was the one who did it. Oh, if only I hadn't raved about those gherkins yesterday. Now don't you raise your eyebrow that way, Woodrow. You may not put much stock in this back there among all your shimmying dancers and spicy-talking comedians that you're forced to associate with, but here in Weevers, a Blue Ribbon for pickles carries a lot of prestige."

"Zap! Plot perils prestigious pickle preem!"

"Woodrow, do you feel faint?"

"Just setting up a headline for—hey, what's up now?"

Posthaste I adjourned after Tate. Same was headed for spot where Unc was confabbing with young guy displaying Sam Browne, WELCOME TO FAIR VISITORS badge, large comb in shirt pocket, pompadour and sideburns all tonicked up, plus obtuse visage.

"Who's he?" I asked Tate, catching up. "He's posing like an R&R star."

"Beg pardon?"

"Sorry, rock and roller."

According to Tate, type was yclept Snooky Russell. He was the youngest Deputy Sheriff staffer for Unc's pal Gus Gumley and was allowed to earn moonlighting shekels as small-hours guard in Exhibition Hall.

"Snooky's all right," said Tate, "though a mite thick. Everybody in Weevers kind of laughs about his habits, too. They all know he's vain as a peacock."

"—pretty doggone tired," Snooky was saying as we arrived. He scowled, flicked non-existent lint spex from sleeve. "But I stuck around 'cause LeRoy here said you might want to ask me some questions."

"Appreciate it, Snooky. Were you on duty the whole night?"

"The whole night," said Snooky. "The heat in here was something fierce. Knocks a crease to pieces." He seemed pretty broken up about it, pointing to his trouser legs.

"Snooky, there are only two entrances to this hall, the ones on either side of the building at the ends of this main aisle. Now think hard. Did you see anybody come in or go out after closing time?"

"Not a soul come in. Some people did leave round 10:00. But it was just Floyd Bemis and the workmen helping him set up his booth at the last minute. They didn't go anywhere near the pickles."

This info was dispensed in somewhat absent-minded style, as Snooky was swiveling his head, beetling his brows, etc., etc., as though scanning premises for a friend.

Next question from Unc established that all the hall booths had been erected per sked on Mon. except the one belonging to Bemis. He was delayed until Tues. by a case of summer grippe. But Snooky said he was positive the sweet gherkins had not been doctored by the time Bemis and his bunch flew the coop, since Snooky was big on pickles and had passed the display at Fair foldup hour.

"After Floyd went home, Snooky, are you sure—nobody could have sneaked in here without you spotting them?"

"I set on a stool in this here center aisle, from which I could view both those doors which were wide open on account of the blasted heat, and nobody went in or out all night." Still doing the frown bit, Snooky had whipped out comb and passed it through his locks during foregoing reportage.

"And you didn't leave the building at any time?"

"I did not leave this here building at any time whatsoever. My orders were to stay put."

Unc sighed. "All right, Snooky. Thanks."

Tate said, "What next?"

"Well, LeRoy, I still have a hunch somebody did come in here and fiddle with those gherkins."

"But how?"

"That's just it, LeRoy, I don't know. Snooky saw nobody. He didn't go outside the building. He—hold on."

Unc developed that thoughtful, cross-eyed look. He did slow glom of entire hall. Followed this with a foxy smile.

"Woodrow, can you locate your Aunt and that pixilated pickle jar?"

I stuffed away my notepad and hoofed. Secs later, Unc held the jar, said to Aunt E., "Now, this jar still smells like pickles, but it looks like beets. I'm no great shakes in the kitchen department. I need some help. Here in Weevers, I don't expect the ladies have any peculiar, exotic chemicals handy. So can you think of anything simple and ordinary that

70

would turn pickle juice this color?"

Aunt E. rotated jar. "Land sakes, Pinkerton, I've been so flustered I hadn't thought about—oh. Why, yes. Food coloring would. Ordinary red grocery store food coloring. It wouldn't change the aroma, but it would change the color."

"Who'd have such around the house?"

"Most any housewife who fancies herself a cook. I have some."

"If you spill some does it stain?"

"It surely does."

Unc zipped off, all in pursuit. By exhibit table, Betty James was doing the hanky sniff, Mrs. Lulu C. was still registering beaucoup smalltown savoir faire, Mrs. M. Bemis was showing boredom with whole biz.

Unc said, "Marvella, you spilled some of the red juice from this jar on your glove. Could I please see that glove a minute?"

"Why, of course, Pinkerton."

With her right hand she pulled out glove, handed same over.

Unc did a thoughtful study of the glove's general appearance, passed it back.

"Why did you want it, Pinkerton?" said Mrs. B.

"Oh, I didn't actually want the glove, Marvella. I just wanted to check whether you were right-handed or left-handed." Unc shook his head. "Marvella, I'm surely saddened to say this, but there is nothing in the whole world worse than doing something unkind because of some silly notion about prestige or status. Life is just too blamed short for getting all knotted up over things which don't even exist in the long run."

"I dislike your tone, Pinkerton."

LeRoy Tate seemed to be doing a nervous-type soft shoe.

"Uh, Pinky, remember Marvella's brother is a lawyer. It wouldn't do to—uh—antagonize—"

"Calm down, LeRoy. Snooky, would you request those few folks watching down at the end of the aisle to step along? I don't think we want to make a broadcast." Per request, Snooky ditched his comb and carried out mission.

"See here, Pinkerton," said Mrs. B., "just what has my right hand got to do with anything? And what did you mean by those other remarks?"

"Though I regret to say it, Marvella, I'm sure your right hand is the hand you'd use to pour something into something else. Say, some red food coloring into a batch of sweet gherkins, knowing the awful color alone would knock those gherkins right out of the running."

"I've never heard such outrageous—Pinkerton, I told you several times I don't care a speck about the Blue Ribbon. Not a speck."

Unc leaned on the pickle table, giving out with the wrinkled-brow look. "So you did. However, I think that runs contrary to what the normal reaction would be from a lady who's won first prize nine years in a row. It strikes me that a life-long Weevers resident would kind of resent a newcomer stealing her laurels. Though it's true you've repeated over and over that you don't care, you're one of the leading lights in the Weevers Drama Guild, and we are all aware that means you have the ability to—as my nephew'd put it—thesp."

While dame began zing imitation of steam engine blowing valves, Unc continued to play it with max politeness.

"Of course, Marvella, what I just said is hardly grounds for more than suspicion, since Lulu Clark here is also a prize pickler, and she freely admits she was peeved. But certain other things suggest—oh, by the way, Lulu. Where were you last evening after ten o'clock?"

"Sitting at home on the front porch with Herman, if that's any of your affair, you old busybody."

Unc remained big in the restraint dept. "At home, eh? But your husband, Marvella, was down at the lodge playing pinochle for a good while after 10:30. I know, I was there myself. So nobody could have checked on whether you drove back here to the Fairgrounds."

"Of all the ridiculous, stupid, meddlesome—Pinkerton, I suggest you see a doctor."

"I'd a lot rather see what's under that Band-Aid on your right thumb, Marvella. If a person dribbled a little red food coloring on a thumb, which could happen since a person usually pours using thumb and index finger, it could stain. We all saw the bad stain it left on your glove."

"Unc," I protested, "that's too far out. She probably just has a cut."

"Could be. On the other hand, Woodrow, maybe you've misinterpreted the basic purpose of a Band-Aid. Now just what is that purpose?"

"To heal cuts or scrapes, natch."

"Woodrow, the purpose is to cover up a cut or scrape so that it'll heal itself. The purpose, I repeat, is to *cover up* a cut or scrape or something else—say, on the order of a red stain."

Mrs. B. twitched her right hand behind her back, realized mistake, did lotsa sputtering. However, poor Unc this time had left a blank which opened the way for a last-act bomb.

"Unc, Snooky swears he didn't leave the building."

"I dint," Snooky said.

"But Unc, he had to ankle outside in order for one or both of those egresses to be unwatched, so some party could sneak in and do what you just said."

"Woodrow, where I got into trouble was with the kind of careless way I asked my questions. Guess I'd better do it

73

again. Snooky, did you at any time leave this hall?"

"No, sir, I did not go outside of this here hall—not even once."

"But Snooky, did you at any time leave your *post?*"

"No, I did not—well, I mean, only—"

Before double-taking minion of the law could continue, Unc said, "Don't feel bad. You were telling the exact gospel truth the first time. Probably you've got into such a habit, no offense meant, you did what you did unconsciously. Or almost."

"What kind of tripe are you peddling now, Pinkerton?" said Mrs. B.

"Stop playacting, Marvella. Anybody who's been around Weevers a while—which includes you—knows Snooky likes to keep natty. Why, twice already this morning I saw him comb his hair."

"Can't do it proper without a mirror, though," said subject under discussion.

"Exactly, Snooky. I noticed just a while back you were kind of frowning and looking about for one." I'd seen that, all right, but like a dodo had figured object of optical search was a person. "What I'm saying is, Marvella came back here late last night, feeling pretty certain that if she hid outside, it wouldn't be long before you went to do the comb operation in the one type of place that is literally not outside the building at all, yet is without doubt completely cut off from the hall by a door, and like all such places, has a mirror as standard equipment. Namely that gentlemen's washroom plainly visible over there along that wall."

Did I feel bum! I'd spotted both doors when Tate said Aunt E. had gone to lie down and escape the heat.

Snooky beeted. "Heck, I didn't think that counted. I mean, it's not *out*side. I wasn't gone more'n a minute or so, either. And I didn't want to say nothing 'cause I wasn't supposed to budge from the stool in the aisle."

"Don't fret, Snooky. You won't get in Dutch. You felt guilty just now because you're a conscientious lad who believes in following orders. But you've served the cause of justice right well."

"*Justice!*" This from the guilty party who'd been simmering. "Blast you, Pinkerton. Blast you and your justice and your meddling! Did you think I'd stand for the floozy wife of a Johnny-come-lately taking away my position as—*oh!* Oh, my, where's Floyd? *Floyd!*" Entering Tearsville, she ankled.

"Take over, LeRoy," said Unc. "Now that the crime is exposed, I don't believe you need do more than bend the rule this once and allow Mrs. James to enter a new jar. Woodrow, let's stroll outside and I'll buy you and your Aunt Ellen a weenie."

After Unc had copped kudos from grateful platter-spinner's frau, plus more dirty looks from Mrs. Lulu who went to console Marvella, Aunt Ellen said, "Poor Marvella. She'll get all the punishment she needs from wagging tongues. What a spiteful thing to do."

Under the tent at the refreshment center sponsored by the Odd Fellows Ladies Aux., I presented Aunt E. with the giftie which I had fetched from the car.

"My, isn't this a pretty ribbon, Woodrow. And inside— land sakes, just look at it. Why, it's a—it's—well, it certainly is attractive."

"It's an ashtray," I said. "From Le Finkrat Club. Uh, that's a sort of 'in' bistro—I mean, I brought it all the way from—I thought it'd make a nice conversation piece—er—I mean I hoped—oh, rats."

Aunt Ellen said, "Woodrow, it's wonderful. Even if it does come from one of those wick—that is, from the Eastern seaboard. We folks in Weevers need to broaden our viewpoint. Don't look so downcast. You know how much you mean to your Uncle Pinkerton and me."

Big squeeze.

It sure felt good.

"I second that," grinned Unc. "I might even say that our pleasure at seeing you this canto is lofty, mighty, and wow."

"Woodrow! Cancel his free subscription the minute you get back to New York!"

Unc
Foils Show Foe

In-flight pix came to sharp halt as pilot announced midst midnight bouncings that a navigation gizmo had defuncted, resulting in letdown of big jet at airport I discovered was Cincy., O.

Plane was theoretically Gotham nonstopper, carrying me back from latest road stand for *GALORE, The Newspaper of Amusement.* But as it was already Sat. and I was not due in shop until Mon. ayem, seemed ideal setup for quick wheelover to Weevers, Ind., home grounds for my only relatives, who raised me after my folks passed on.

Same burg is located in hills north of O. River. Yearly vacations and side trips are pleasant changes of pace after nights spent lamping stars in saloons.

A toothsome airport chick skedded me on flight out of Indpls. late Sun. eve. Then I ascertained rental car was available. Before claiming, I went into the lounge for a quick cleanup, only to discover my shave bomb in emptysville. I would have to surprise Weevers kin sans smootho cheeks.

Midmorning Sat. discovered me tooling down Main Street, Weevers, in warm June sun. Quick pause and park revealed odd circumstance. My Uncle Pinkerton was not present in his hardware store. Also noted hand-scrawled placard in window flacking *Annual Rummage Sale!* being staged Fri. and All Day Today by Ladies' Aid of Presbyterian Church. Doubtless Aunt Ellen would be attending event.

I flopped back in car while groups of farm folks shopping ogled continental cut of my threads and cast glances askance.

Weevers has lofty suspicions of Insidious East Coast.

Wondering about Unc's whereabouts, I headed for Elm Street, location of big old white house belonging to Unc and Aunt E. On left I saw a large, gabled joint with neon sign frontmost. Recalled this was Unc's lodge hall. In the side parking lot spotted a County Sheriff's cruiser and Unc's old, straight-stick Chev coupe.

This promised mystery. Unc is considered a double-dome in Weevers—viz., he knows what blvd. *Lullaby of Broadway* is named after. Rural constabulary invariably consult him on matters criminologic.

I pulled in and ascended the lodge hall steps. A card inside a glass bulletin case read: *Saturday Night Only—STAR-STUDDED VARIETY SHOW! Tickets $1.50. Benefit Fluoridation Referendum Publicity Committee.*

Puzzling over unique teaming of music and molars, I was unprepared for sudden opening of door. Got glowers from middle-aged Deputy Sheriff standing guard.

"Sheriff Gumley says no newspaper reporters allowed until the trouble's cleared up, buddy."

"The name's not buddy, and I'm not exactly a newspaper reporter."

After beaucoup ogling of my strictly uptown wardrobe, he said, "Well, I know for a fact the manager don't talk to liquor peddlers on week-ends. Beat it, bub."

Luckily I espied Unc passing across corridor within. "Unc! Hey, Unc, it's me!"

In act of putting bandanna back into wash-pants pocket, Unc peered. "Good land! Woodrow! What on earth are you doing here? Otis, let him in. That's my nephew, Woodrow Ennis. You remember, my sister Nella's boy."

Deputy did goggle. "You're joshing me, Pinkerton. I recollect Woodrow Ennis when he was just a shaver shooting marbles in front of the courthouse. This fella looks like a Chicago sharpie."

"Tempus fugits, Clyde," I said but Deputy didn't flip over levity.

"My, Woodrow," said Unc as I bypassed guard, "I surely am glad to see you. I know your Aunt will be, too. She's over at the church rummage sale this morning, by the way."

Following Unc down long stuffy hall, I heard from chamber on left ahead a soprano caterwaul, as of young chick doing bathos bit. Unc was thinking of something else.

"By the way, Woodrow, the snapshot you sent in your last letter from San Francisco sort of upset your Aunt. Now I appreciate you have to visit nightclubs for your entertainment newspaper, but your Aunt was mighty worried by the picture of those girls wearing not much more than their good intentions. Also, they appeared to be gyrating some."

"Gosh, Unc," I said, "I thought Aunt E. would dig a scene of authentic SF discotheque dansapation."

"Unfortunately, Woodrow, your Aunt doesn't fathom the customs of the entertainment trades. Which is why you have to sort of shift mental gears when you visit Weevers." But he grinned and punched my shoulder. Pleasantry was short-lived, however. Caterwauling burst out afresh from room ahead.

"Say, Unc, what's that racket? And why the fuzzmobile parked outside?"

"Someone," said Unc with grim glance, "did a mean underhanded thing last night. Sneaked in here—well, I shouldn't say sneaked, exactly, he walked in and out bold as brass, and he—see for yourself."

He aimed mitt at big open doors on right, entrance to small lodge-auditorium. Rows of folding chairs were set up show-style. There were musical instruments, mikes, juggler's clubs, other vaude apparati on stage. The piece of equipment nearest the blacked-out foots was a large marimba, mostly colored green.

"Wow, that's a real smear job, Unc."

"Yes, somebody came in here last night and threw a quart or so of green paint all over Wanda Jean Finch's perfectly good $500 marimba. Ruined it for fair. Oh, we've got the culprit but he won't talk. And we don't know how he managed it. Worse, I'm pretty certain about who's really responsible, but I'm jiggered if I can figure out how to prove it. You know how Sheriff Gus Gumley is, Woodrow. A mite of mystery and he sends out for help. Namely me. This time I'm stumped. Well, let's see if Wanda Jean has calmed down any."

As we ankled for chamber from which the howls issued, I asked, "Is that musical gear for the variety show I saw advertised outside?"

"Yes, 'tis."

"But what's it got to do with tooth decay?"

Further eludication was prevented by our entrance into chamber where four persons were assembled. First was 7-yr.-old juve all dolled up in banana curls and sobbing heart out. Mother, a young jane, was attempting to console her.

Also present was older gent in Oshkosh B'gosh work togs. He sat in a chair pulled out in room's center. He had several stogies sticking out of his shirt pocket. He was scratching stubbly chin and looking vacant in gray cells dept. I pegged him as lodge hall handyman, harmless old coot named Luther Small. Standing over Small was fatty in Sam Browne belt who failed to recognize me.

"Pinkerton," cried Sheriff, "I won't stand for those fluoridation folks sending a hotshot lawyer in here to bedevil us."

"Woodrow, take off those sunglasses. Gus, it's my nephew."

"What's he wearing that sissified suit for?" Gumley retorted.

Was no time to comment on lack of knowledgeability of stix hix re notched lapels and side vents. Couldn't have anyway, as tot burst out afresh, wailing, "Oh, mummy, mummy, you promised I could play for the peoples tonight."

Gumley glared at his captive. "See what you caused, Luther?"

Old Luther had a guilty puss, but he was stubborn. "I—dint do nothin', and I'm not sayin' nothin' more."

"Now Luther," Unc said, "if somebody has bulldozed you into clamming up, you ought to realize that Sheriff Gumley here exerts a lot more influence, relatively speaking."

Luther Small scuffed work brogans on flooring. He looked trembly and scared, but he had plenty of ginger left. "Dint do it. If you think I did, where's the paint can, hannh? Where's the paint I shoulda had all over my fingers, hannh?"

He held up mitts, which showed no traces of green. I had my notepad out, scribbling away. Variety show tie-in possibly meant hotsy copy for *GALORE*.

Unc sighed. "Gus, I'm afraid he's got us licked. Are you positive your boys searched the lodge hall top to bottom?"

"Yes, Pinky, I am. No empty cans of green paint anywhere. And Luther didn't have nary a stain or smudge when Deputy Booth picked him up after he came out of the lodge hall at 11:30 last night."

"Oh, mummy," tot burst out, "I wanna play for the peoples, I wanna, I wanna!"

Young mom feverishly attempted to soothe offspring. "Hush, Wanda Jean, we'll get you a new marimba, I promise. You can play *I'm Putting All My Eggs in One Basket* another time. Oh, I wish they'd never brought up that awful fluoride business anyway. We'll come back later and see if the big thinkers have found the guilty person."

Mother cradled tot to bosom and team exited. Words "big thinkers" caused Gumley to sigh and Unc to shake his head in mystified way. Wanda Jean went baaw in distance. Door slammed.

"Psst, Unc," I said. "Fill me in?"

Unc nodded in his absent-minded way and said, "Gus, I want to have another look in the basement. That's where I ran into you-know-who Thursday night." Luther seemed to know who too. He gave a shudder like extra in Karloff pic.

"Luther's scared to death," Unc muttered after he had shut the door behind us. "And I know who's scaring him. But proving it is something else again."

I urged Unc to take it from the top as we tramped down into musty basement occupied by large workbench, tools, junk, oil containers, big coal furnace out of use now that June had arrived, and janitor's closet. I stood scrivening in my notebook while Unc gave synopsis of action thus far.

Two elements in Weevers were warring over a big issue—viz., whether to add fluoride to drinking water supply come Fall. Some locals were for it. Other, and more vociferous element, was equally strong against, considering it part of subversive plot to poison U.S. body fluids. Pro-fluoride folks had decided to mount p.r. campaign in local paper and on Radio Station WEEV. This took cash nut. Hence variety show, to feature terping, thesping, vaude acts by fluoride proponents and their small fry. However, very rental of lodge ball to this group had touched off brouhaha.

"We had a lively go-round at the lodge board meeting Thursday night. Those of us who thought there was no harm in renting the hall outvoted the others four to two. The one loudest against renting is the sanctimonious windbag I suspect has got Luther Small buffaloed—namely, our chairman of the Buildings and Grounds Committee, C. Harold Bixby. Remember him?"

"Think so. Premium pusher?"

Unc cocked an eyebrow. "In exactly what tongue are you speaking, Woodrow?"

" 'Scuse me, Unc. Bixby's in the insurance rack—business?"

"Right. He's not only anti-fluoride, he's anti almost anything you can name, from nicotine to *I Love You Truly* at weddings. I don't object to him being against things, mind you—that's his right. But I surely do object to his talking poor Luther into an act of vandalism designed to sabotage the fund-raising show. I know he did it—feel it in my bones. It's logical, too. Being chairman of buildings and grounds at the lodge, he can throw Luther out of a job overnight. And Luther, being Luther, couldn't come by another job very easy."

"Bixby against everything," I muttered, writing. "O. o. b. b."

"Beg pardon, Woodrow?"

"Optics of beholder bit."

Unc cast eyes heavenward, then gazed at old pine workbench upon which reposed tin lunch pail bearing initials LS scratched in side with knife point.

Unc stared at the initials, finally said, "Proving Bixby twisted Luther's arm so he'd throw paint on the marimba is only half the problem. Bixby has an alibi—tight as a drum. He was down at the rummage sale last evening helping his wife out till they closed. Then he and his missus invited some friends over till way past 11:30, which is when Deputy Booth caught Luther sneaking out of here. Gus Gumley made some phone inquiries this morning." Unc stopped running index digit aimlessly round and round brown ring stain left on pine surface. Puss glum, he wound up, "Bixby's alibi is solid."

"How come the deputy picked up Small? I mean, being handyman, doesn't he have the right to be in the lodge hall at night?"

"Yes, but his behavior roused Deputy Booth's suspicions. On the nights when Deputy Booth is on duty, he usually parks his car right across the street to keep an eye on Main Street. The lodge hall closes up about 11:00. Last night Deputy Booth saw nobody go in or come out after that hour until Luther showed up at 11:25. Luther seemed to be sort of sneaking into the building around the side, but Deputy Booth spotted him. And he recollected that Luther had been in a scrape a couple of years ago."

"What kind of scrape?"

"Luther got pressed for funds and dipped into the lodge cash box one night after hours. He got off that time because everybody in Weevers felt sorry for him. Last night Deputy Booth remembered the scrape when Luther came sneaking back out of here, exactly five minutes after he went in. Deputy Booth jumped out of his car and yelled to Luther, who jackrabbited off."

"Then what happened?"

"Oh, Booth collared him easy enough. And poor Luther, caught flat, bleated out a lame story. According to the deputy, Luther said he'd just come back for his lunch things, which he maintained he forgot. All right, said the deputy, then where are your lunch things? Well, Luther wasn't carrying anything at all, so it was pretty obvious he was scared, muddled, and saying the first thing that came into his head. So with Luther still yowling, they went back inside, just for a check. And there, all over the marimba, was fresh green paint, wet as a tadpole in a pond."

Possibility of *GALORE* copy under my Woody byline caused me to exclaim, "Socko! Unreel the next skein quick!"

84

Next skein was nub of other half of problem. To bedaub marimba, Luther had to have a can of paint. He was carrying nothing with him when he went into lodge and, as reported, nothing when he came out. Outer apparel consisted of just a skimpy jacket as it was a warm pleasant evening. No possibilily of concealing can on person. And there was not a stain or smudge of green on his hands.

"Now it certainly seems likely, Woodrow, that a man is going to spill just a spot or two somewhere on his person if he opens a can of paint and lets fly. But not Luther. Deputy Booth and his men searched this place all over. No paint cans or lids anywhere. Not in that furnace—not in the trash barrels out back—not even in Luther's lunch pail here on the bench. Not in any place big enough to hold an empty paint can. So where did Luther get the paint and how did he get rid of the can?"

Big sigh. Unc ran finger along edge of the workbench, where a half-dollar-size blob of dried green paint contrasted with light pinewood. Unc stared at green blob.

"I didn't notice that before. Wonder if Luther came down here last night and spilled some of his paint on the workbench getting the can open? Then where's the can? Oh, fiddlesticks. Come along, Woodrow. I spent enough time in this basement Thursday night, and I'm fed up."

So saying, he led march back upstairs. We looked into quiz chamber, discovered Gumley alone and morose in facial dept.

"Pinky, you got to come up with something. Luther absolutely won't talk."

"Knows he's got us over a barrel," Unc opined.

"How about a little rubber hose scene?" I suggested.

"In those films you are required to sit through for your work, Woodrow, maybe. But we folks in Weevers don't do things in that way. Your Aunt should be home from the rummage sale about now. She'll fix us some lunch. Gus, I'll phone you if I get a hot flash."

"Yow," I exclaimed. "Scheme snags tooth tuner."

"Has he drunk some intoxicating beverage, Pinky?" Sheriff said.

"No, Gus. A tuner is, I believe, a musical show. Woodrow is just composing another of those headlines in his paper's peculiar lingo."

Unc grinned, but sans heart. Many frixamples could be given of how Unc had saved local police bacon, and he was doubtless feeling current failure keenly as we took his Chev coupe out Elm to the digs.

On the way, per my request, Unc explained earlier reference to activities Thurs. eve. in lodge cellar.

Seems that after rent-or-not-to-rent vote, C. Harold Bixby had stalked out, refusing to sit in meeting any longer with "parlor pink named Pinkerton." Meeting broke up about an hour later. Unc, who is stanch Repub., was still doing slow burn over Bixby crack. He located Bixby in dingy cellar where "self-important frog" had gone to "make routine weekly inspection."

Unc filled in scene, picturing C. Harold Bixby as portly do-gooder garbed in size 46 blue pinstripe and size 13 shoes.

"There he was, leaning back against that workbench puffing a cloud of cigar smoke in my face and telling me to go jump in the lake. I said anybody who walked out of a meeting the way he did was a crybaby. But he just stood planted there with his elbows resting on the workbench and kept puffing away. He promised to make sure I was voted off the lodge hall board because I was a dangerous radical. I don't often get the urge to punch anybody in the nose, but I got it then, so I walked out."

"That's real gutsy meller material, Unc," I said as we swung in the drive.

"Now Woodrow, try to control your racy jargon. Aunt Ellen's home."

As we entered kitchen, Aunt E. turned, did double take and flustered bit, patting her gray bun and fiddling with specs. "Woodrow! Mercy on us, what are you doing here long before your vacation?"

Following buss and squeezes, I scenarioed stranding at Cincy airport.

"Sit down, Woodrow. There's cherry pie just coming out of the oven." Aunt E. paused for sad-but-loving expresh. "You look undernourished. Have you been consorting too much with those loose-living theatrical persons?"

"Been in Vegas covering a preem of a Blighty rocker troupe, Aunt."

"If I interpret my free subscription copies correctly," Unc put in, "that means he was attending the first performance of some English music group with soup-bowl haircuts."

Aunt Ellen pulled out her freshly heated pie. "Well, I do wish you'd go to bed a little earlier. Somehow it doesn't seem quite American rising at noon like you do. And that reminds me. That picture you sent of those girls dancing—was that in public?"

"Natch," I grinned. "Frisco diskery nitery."

"Oh, dear. And I still remember when you used to raise mushrooms in flats in the basement. You be careful, young man. Sleep under that comforter I sent you. Pinkerton! Are you falling asleep?"

Unc blinked, chin resting on palms, elbows on table. He screwed up his face in that thoughtful way of his. "No, I was just wondering what I'm missing. I think I've got all the pieces, yet I can't put them together. Meanwhile, C. Harold

John Jakes

Bixby is getting away scot-free, Wanda Jean Finch's marimba is ruined, and Gus Gumley can't make Luther Small talk."

Rapidly Unc described latest developments to Aunt E. as we attacked chow. He mentioned Bixby alibi.

"Well," Aunt E. said, "I can vouch that Harold Bixby was present at the rummage sale from seven until ten last night. He was helping his wife Grace the way he does every year. The place was packed, too. As for the Bixby party later, I wasn't invited. Grace Bixby is obviously mad as a hornet because of your row with Harold at the lodge. I met her at the door as she was bringing in some men's clothes last night and she cut me dead. Not that I care a fig. I must say Harold acted a mite peculiar too. He dropped in a while this morning and he was still acting the same way."

Unc dropped fork with clatter. "Peculiar? Explain yourself, woman."

"Nervous. Fidgety as a tick. He was watching the folks buying the dishes and clothes and books. This morning he kept whizzing around the church basement like an express train."

"Thunderation, that's it!" Unc jumped up, did nifty jig.

"Pinkerton! Have you got the St. Vitus dance?"

"Ellen, I see how he—oh." Unc's shoulders slumped. "I believe I have Bixby, but that's not enough. I still don't know how Luther hid the paint or kept his hands clean. Think I'll drive over and discuss it with Gus some more. Coming, Woodrow?"

"You bet."

Escaped house before Aunt E. could press extra glass of cow extract into my hand. As Unc drove, I recalled being out of shv. crm. He doubleparked at Atwater's Drug Store while I ran in. He seemed off in outer spheres when I slid back into seat.

88

"What's that you have, Woodrow?"

"Just the shave bomb I bought in the pill parlor, Unc."

"Shave cream. Drug store. My store! Right under my own nose all the time. Woodrow, quick! Park the car and meet me at the hardware store. I'm going to phone Gus. At last I've got that sneaky Bixby red—er, green-handed." Out he hopped.

Fearing Unc had really flipped this time, I ditched lather on car seat, parked per order, and awaited his return. I leaned against the hardware frontage while rurals gave the o.o. to tassels on my cordovans. In about 10 mins. Unc came racing up sidewalk, a bulgy paper sack tucked under arm.

"What's in the bag, Unc?"

"Something which absolutely had to be around the lodge someplace, Woodrow, even though I never actually saw it myself."

"What is—?"

"Let's not waste time. Gus Gumley will meet us at Bixby's. If I can crack Harold, that'll make Luther talk."

I wondered about nature of fade-out if Bixby was innocent as lamb and sued for false arrest. However, following Unc allowed no time for speculation. He plunged inside a first-floor office door featuring cornball copy—BIXBY INSURANCE, *"C. Harold" For Your Coverage.*

Overstuffed sec'y. babe did not immediately think I was with Unc, announced that presence of "hawkers" was discouraged. Unc said I was in party and was Bixby in back office? Babe started to say nix when Gumley arrived, puffing.

"Pinky, what in fire are you up to?"

"Just follow me, Gus. Don't announce us, Rosemary, we'll go right in." Unc pushed through swing gate.

With Gumley looking worried, me feeling same, we charged ahead into large office. Human mastodon in blue pinstripe of Ringling tent proportions ceased shuffling papers behind desk. Mastodon scowled while tiny eyes glared at Unc amidst lotsa flesh.

"Pinkerton, I resent your barging in here. I have nothing more to say to anarchists."

"But I've got a lot to say, Harold, concerning a mean act of vandalism rigged up to ruin the variety show."

"Oh, I did hear something about that," said C. Harold. "But only in passing. Say, who's this debauched-looking lad? Some egghead agitator?"

"This is my nephew Woodrow Ennis."

C. Harold clutched paunch. "Woodrow Ennis! He used to roll a hoop past here every night on the way home from school. He was clean-cut and wholesome. This specimen has obviously had his bodily fluids poisoned by the conspiracy which is now sweeping—"

"Be quiet, Harold," Unc said. "You have a right to your opinions, but when you start cat's-pawing poor Luther Small to spoil a show put on by people who happen to disagree with you, I get mad."

"Pinky," Gumley stage-whispered, "don't make rash accusations."

"Did you make that phone call, Gus?"

"Yes, but I'll be switched if I see why."

"Let me worry about that, Gus."

"Just a minute here," said Bixby, big sneer on map. "Do you propose to give me a lecture on fluoridation, Pinkerton? I suppose you think it's healthful."

"When I tender an opinion, Harold, I'll do it in the ballot box, not after dark using a poor fuzzy-witted janitor as a dupe."

C. Harold turned ripe red in jowl dept. Gumley looked petrified as Unc went on, "Specifically, Harold, I think you

90

decided when you lost the rent vote that you had to stop the fund-raising show. After you stalked out of the board meeting, I think you went home and got the particular can of green paint. Then you came back to the lodge with your scheme fully hatched. I think you found Luther Small puttering around in the basement, and you threatened to have him fired unless he helped out. That's when I came downstairs to give you what-for."

Premium pusher puffed in pump-organ fashion, "Nothing but a pack of outrageous—"

"Do me the courtesy of letting me finish, Harold. When I found you in the lodge basement, I think you were putting Luther through his paces—showing him what to do with the paint so he wouldn't get caught by leaving evidence behind. Folks in Weevers know you're against vice of every sort, as I mentioned to my nephew earlier today. You're against sin, gin, and also nicotine. And yet there you were Thursday night, leaning against the workbench and blowing cigar smoke in my face.

"It's my opinion you grabbed that cigar out of Luther's pocket and lit up when you heard me coming. You hate products of the weed. But Luther doesn't—in fact, he had some cigars in his shirt pocket this morning. You heard me coming downstairs, shoved Luther into the janitor's closet, sacrificed your principles, and puffed up a real smokescreen. I was so riled it didn't dawn on me then—you don't smoke but you had to Thursday night. Because, Harold, you'd been showing Luther how to use the paint. *And paint smells.*"

What a performance! I'd eye-balled smokes in Luther's togs pocket also, but failed to link same with earlier antinicotine fact stated by Unc. Bixby gnawed liver lips and rolled eyes as if seeking escape hatch.

Unc pressed on. "Further, Harold, in demonstrating how

Luther was to do the job you got some green paint on the edge
of the workbench. So you leaned against the bench kind of
nonchalant-like and didn't move the whole time I was there.
Otherwise I'd have seen that paint which I did see, dried, this
very morning."

"Then where's the paint can?" snapped C.H.B. "The way
I hear it, Gumley's boys couldn't find it anywhere in the lodge
hall."

"That's where we got temporarily snookered," replied
Unc. "Gus's boys searched every cranny in the lodge that
might have hidden a round, squat, ordinary-type paint can of
quart size or less. But like everything else these days, cans
have changed. There's another style of paint can for sale most
everywhere. You probably had one around home. I sell 'em
right in my own hardware store. I was reminded about it
when Woodrow stopped in at the drug store. Y'see, Harold,
I'm old-fashioned—I still use shaving soap in a mug. But
Woodrow here is modern. He buys those lather bombs.
Those spray cans. And today, Harold, *paint comes in spray
cans too.*"

"Of all the crazy—!"

"Tall, thin, round cans, Harold. With a nice, neat spray
nozzle that you just press. Hold a can like that far enough
away from you and if you're careful you don't get a single
drop on your clothes. Or even on your hands."

"But we didn't find any new-fangled aerosol paint cans
neither, Pinky," protested Sheriff G.

" 'Course you didn't. You didn't search in the right-
shaped place."

"In the what?"

"You said your boys looked in lots of odd places, like
Luther Small's lunch pail down in the basement. But they
passed up something else which I found just a while ago,

tucked way back in a corner of the janitor's closet." Unc waved paper bag.

"No fair!" I said. "We didn't look in the closet before."

"Now, Woodrow, don't be thick. I told you I didn't have to look. The evidence not only said what the hiding place had to be, but exactly what it looked like, too. We know Luther couldn't have carried it out, so it was just a matter of finding it. If your boys spotted it at all, Gus, they must have passed it up because of the shape problem."

Shaking dome vigorously, I said, "Beats me."

"Remember," Unc said, "the first thing Luther hollered when Deputy Booth caught him was that he'd forgot his lunch things. Luther was making up a story, all right. But he was blurting out the truth too, in a kind of slantwise way. He was guilty as sin, and, when he thought up that excuse quick, he also automatically thought about the hiding place of the evidence against him. Luther definitely said lunch things, *plural*. Deputy Booth even repeated it. Now Woodrow, what goes along with a packed lunch and, if it spills, leaves a brown ring like the one we saw on the workbench plain as day?"

"Yipes. Jamoko!"

"I guess you're trying to say coffee. You're right. Now, what one thing on earth holds coffee, but could also hold a tall, thin, round spray can of paint, and goes with a lunch pail—lunch things plural—as surely as eggs are the other half of ham?"

Presto! Unc whipped open paper bag and took out an old, battered qt. Thermos.

Bottle had red plastic drinking cup screwed upside down onto top. Unc unscrewed this, pulled plastic jug plug, then unscrewed top part of outside cylinder. He lifted off this smaller upper part, turned over larger bottom cylinder—and bingo! Out dropped not a shiny glass liner but a tall, round aerosol can of *E-Z-Glos Spra-E-Namel, #314 LEAFY BOWER GREEN.*

Bixby lamped can on carpet like it was tarantula.

"Neat fit," Unc said. "Nice hideout, too. Luther gets the paint out of the Thermos bottle, ruins the marimba, puts the can back for disposal later. And it almost worked, except for Woodrow needing a shave."

Right then Bixby zipped around from behind the desk, shaking fist. "You rotten, radical meddler—you still haven't got a nickel's worth of proof."

"Not here—no, that's right, I haven't."

Mother! thought I. Here's where Unc's carpet gets pulled.

"You admit there's no proof?" Bixby said, suddenly narrow in eye region.

Unc fielded fast. "I said I don't have any proof here, Harold. I have a notion the proof is over at the Presbyterian Church rummage sale. I phoned Gus, and he has a deputy looking for it now. I'm speaking of one blue pinstripe suit coat, the only kind you wear. This one probably has a green stain down around the seat of the coat—a stain you got leaning up against the workbench so I couldn't see the spill Thursday night.

"The way I figure it, Harold, maybe you didn't know how to get rid of that coat without rousing suspicion. You couldn't, for example, throw it in your furnace, or in the one at the lodge hall. This being June, and warm, and all furnaces shut down, anything burning in a furnace would be noticed right off. Or maybe you didn't realize right away that the coat was stained.

"I bet you sneaked the coat home. Then lo and behold, in typical fashion, as a lot of men with wives can testify, your wife went through your things yesterday, looking for rummage when you weren't around. She found the paint-stained coat and took it to the church. My wife saw Grace bringing in some men's clothes. The suit coat being in the batch would certainly explain why you acted, as I get it, so dang nervous at the sale last night. Why you watched to see who bought what. Why you went back this morning to see if the coat was still there.

"Because I guess you know, Harold, there isn't much of a market in Weevers for size 46 suits, not since Chubby Henderson moved away, anyhow. With so many people milling around, you'd have to wait until tonight—until the sale was over—to get that suit back and dispose of it. Taking one of your own garments off the rack during the sale would just have called attention to it. Yes, I'll wager you've been pretty nervous, Harold, waiting for that rummage sale to wind up so you could destroy the evidence we're going to use to make Luther Small confess."

Loud confabbing in outer office caused all parties to rotate heads. Deputy Sheriff bearing clothing item had entered premium pusher's premises. Even from inner office, green stain on blue pinstripe was highly visible.

Bixby wilted instanter. Gumley collared him.

"Come along, Harold. You should be ashamed of yourself."

"Second that," said Unc with nod.

"Take your hands off me!" Bixby jerked arm from Sheriff's grip. "As for you, Pinkerton—I hope you're satisfied, and will continue to be satisfied when the fluorides of which you are in favor poison all your bodily fluids. I'll get a lawyer. I'll fight this, don't you think I won't."

So mouthing, guilty party was taken away. Faithful sec'y. appeared ready to expire from shock.

Unc hitched up his wash pants, bent down, retrieved the paint can. He deposited same in paper bag again with parts of

Thermos. "Let's be going, Woodrow. I haven't put in a lick of work at the store today. I have several things to wind up before we go out to eat."

We ankled to street. "Eating any place special, Unc?"

"Yes, I'm treating you and your Aunt Ellen to cube steaks and all the trimmings at Hadley's Hickory Heaven before the show. I also have to pick up an extra—ducat, is it?—for you. I'll bet little Wanda Jean electrifies the folks tonight."

"But her marimba's kaput!"

"Oh, Wanda Jean also studies the novelty tap. She's a real trouper though only age seven."

"Unc, I thought tonight's gig had already done El Foldo!"

"What ever gave you that idea?"

"You mean the amateur show must go on?"

Eyes a-twinkle, Unc said, "Certainly, Woodrow. That's show biz."

The Girl in the Golden Cage

That Sunday started gray and didn't change. The early winter clouds piled up over the skyscrapers and just before noon, a cold windy rain began slashing at the windows of my apartment. I stayed inside, eating toast and drinking big glasses of milk and going through a western novel. I felt good—safe and peaceful. Business was at a low point, which came as a relief after a couple of hectic months; I got a kick out of doing nothing. My apartment sealed itself off from the rain of the chill day. A gunman stalked through the pages of my book, hunting the marshal. And every time the heroine made an entrance I saw the face of the girl I'd slept with last Wednesday night. The face was a rich, warm image for such a Sunday. It made the apartment seem even more secure.

I looked at the clock when the phone rang. Twelve twenty-one. I picked it up and said hello and all of a sudden, the gunman and the marshal disappeared and I heard the rain on the windows, sharp as a rattle of bones. "Johnny," a voice said. I'd heard that voice often enough to know it. Lt. Hans Broekman. Homicide. I didn't say anything so he went on, "Johnny, did you know a girl named Lorraine Perau?"

Past tense. That jolted me right down to the bottom of my gut. "I knew her," I said, wondering how he'd made the connection. Then I remembered. I'd given her one of my cards the first time I met her, a month before. But nobody was supposed to know that I knew Lorraine Perau. She wanted it that way. You see, Lorraine owned the face that floated warm in the middle of this Sunday gloom. Lorraine owned the face that belonged to last Wednesday night, and other Wednesday nights stretching back over the month.

"You have any connection with her, Johnny?" Broekman asked.

"That depends."

Broekman sighed. It was a habit; he tired easily. He had a wife who stayed up every night watching the late movies on TV, and besides that, he had insomnia. "A girl answering to the name of Lorraine Perau was found this morning in the Twelfth Street Freight Yards, inside a refrigerator car." He lowered his voice deliberately. "Somebody shot her to death."

The sickness hit me then, full and strong. In this business, you try to tell yourself that death is commonplace. But in the dark hours of the night you get to thinking. A human life ended. A miraculous machine broken. And when it's a girl you knew, a girl who came out of nowhere into a bar, who seemed afraid, yet who turned a handful of nights into something fine, the horror hits like a sledge.

"She had one of the agency cards in her pocketbook," Broekman said. "They didn't try to remove identification. You want to answer questions over the phone, or you want to come down?"

"I'll come down."

"We're still at the freight terminal. Twelfth Street." I stood staring at the dead phone. Finally I put it down and put on a tie. Black eyes watched me in the mirror. The gray hair said, Hood, you're thirty-one and you're a wreck. Lorraine Perau is dead and there won't be any more Wednesday nights. I wanted to call Romo Spain, but the big man, the brains of the agency was vacationing down in Miami Beach, wheeling his wheelchair along, cigarette holder sticking up jauntily from the corner of his blunt mouth as he eyed the girls switching their hips in the sun. Romo couldn't help me now. Someone had short-circuited the world, and it was turning cold and the life was seeping out of it and freezing me. I practically ruined my coupe getting to the terminal. I knew all the homicide boys on the scene. Broekman stood under a tin-shaded light, a sloppy, sad-eyed man with a fleck of tobacco on his lower lip. He was questioning the switchman who'd found Lorraine.

I stood in the doorway and lit a cigarette. The old switchman shuffled his feet and said that, Hell, he'd never have noticed if the refrigerator car door hadn't been open and there was this red high-heeled shoe sticking out.

Broekman said, "That's all for now." He turned around, knowing I was there. "Hello, Johnny. Fast trip." He didn't waste any time either. "What's your hook-up with the girl?"

I told him. How she walked into a bar and we talked. How we spent the night together, and several more nights after that, unknown even to Romo Spain. How she seemed afraid; how I never knew where she came from or where she went; how I somehow understood that if I tried to find out, I'd never see her again. How the only thing I did was look for her in the phone book and draw a blank.

"What was the name of that bar? The first one?"

"The St. James, on Dearborn."

He looked at me. A wind blew in from the freight yards, moving the tin-shaded bulb. Light-flecks showed in Broekman's weary blue eyes. "It's not a very pretty story, Johnny."

"For Christ's sake, Hans, who are you to pass on my morals? Who was she? Do you know?"

"Yes, I know. She wore a lot of makeup, thick pancake stuff. So I followed a hunch that she was in show business."

99

"Lots of women wear pancake makeup who aren't in show business."

"Lorraine Perau wasn't one of them." His eyes pinpointed, hard. "You're in cheap company, Johnny. She was a stripper at the Golden Cage."

His words cut me up inside. Sure, he was so tired he could hardly stand up, and the rain had soaked through his shabby suit coat but he said the wrong thing and I slammed him on the point of the jaw and brought a thin line of blood glittering out of his mouth into the glaring light. One of the homicide cops said, "Hey, damn you," and rabbit punched me so that I slammed against a crate and stood holding my head, watching the comets behind my eyes slowly trail away.

I looked up. I felt like a guilty little kid. "I'm sorry, Hans."

"It's okay, Johnny. This time. People get mixed up with other people and sometimes you can't judge how they feel." He took a pad out of his pocket and wrote something down. "I haven't got anybody to tag with her killing, but there's no sense in my trying to tag you. I guess I'm all finished with you."

"I'm not finished." He turned back to me when I said it. "I want the guy who put the gun to her."

His eyes hardened to little chips of blue ice. "No dice, Johnny. You weren't hired by a client on this one. I wanted to know your connection, I found it. If I want you, I'll call you. Otherwise, steer clear. We'll handle it all right."

"Okay," I said. He stared at me levelly and his face didn't change. He knew me well enough to guess that I was lying. But he didn't say anything. "I'd like to see the body, if it's still around."

He hesitated, frowning. Then he jerked a finger for me to follow.

We went out of the shed and down the platform through

the rain. The refrigerator car, with two cops on guard, stood about a quarter of a mile away. We tramped across the tracks and the cops opened the door for us. The refrigeration was off but the air still had a flat, frozen smell. The pipes were thickly frosted.

The bulk under the sheet didn't seem real. I lifted one corner and saw her face and it was enough for me. I didn't want to remember her that way at all, lips whitened and drawn. I wanted to remember the Wednesdays, the taste of our steaks, the tang of late fall air in Lincoln Park, the warm room and the warmer arms. Just a couple of people who met as strangers in a bar and wound up having something pretty fine.

I got out of there and drove slowly back to the apartment. The wipers ticked back and forth and I got to work, thinking. I had wondered about her, of course. Where she came from; what she did. But it had never been necessary to find out when she was alive. Now, it was necessary because she lay in a refrigerator car with all the strange frightened life shot out of her. I found the Golden Cage in a phone book. The far northwest side. I drove out there. A big house, an old one, decorated with neon and a doorman. I knew that Broekman had been right. On the poster outside were the words, The Girl in the Golden Cage. Above the legend, Lorraine in a bra and g-string looked out at me.

Inside, I ordered a steak sandwich and a drink and motioned to the bartender. "Who owns the place?"

His mouth looked like a steel trap. "Steve Lannes," he grunted.

That name I knew. I'd heard it in other bars, from men who got their cash outside the law. Steve Lannes had more than one club, plus a flock of rumors trailing after him. Steve Lannes had been mentioned once or twice in connection with call girls and making money from really heavy porn, which could sometimes pay off almost as well as a spot like the Golden Cage.

When the floorshow started, I saw what Lannes had done here. A yellow-painted cage descended on a chain from the ceiling and a big-hipped girl did a strip in there, high up, where everybody could get a good look. That was Lorraine a few days ago. But somehow it didn't ruin the memory of her. I knew her in a different way. I listened to the small combo grind away, saw the flesh of the big-hipped girl in the Cage sweating in the round yellow tunnels of the spotlights and it didn't make any difference. After the number was over, I left.

The rain was coming down harder than ever as I drove back toward the Loop. The wipers worked fast, and I made my mind keep up with them. I wanted Romo Spain, because he would have helped me. But I was on my own this trip. So I worked on it, sweated it out, and little by little, I got something.

Lorraine had been running, hiding when we were together, hiding from something on the outside. Now I figured a girl wouldn't hide from the fact that she took off her clothes for a living. To do that, she'd have to have to be pretty screwy, and Lorraine wasn't screwy. I reasoned that it had to be something bigger.

So what does a woman hide from? Sometimes from another man. That was the easiest answer. But it could have been anything. Maybe she'd poisoned her old maid aunt to get the family fortune. Romo would have looked over the possibilities and picked the right one, however obscure. Johnny Hood, the dumb leg man, took the obvious answer.

I locked the door of my apartment behind me. I turned on the light in the kitchen and got out two pints of liquor. I sat there, staring at the bleak unshaded windowpane with its dapple of rain. Tears. Black tears from a cold night. I lit a cigarette and opened the first pint.

I poured it down steadily, one drink after another. I thought about her. I thought about her face and her mouth and her arms on those Wednesdays that were real and yet as unreal as the fall smoke of burning leaves hazing the park where we walked. The rain kept raining. I kept drinking. And I saw her face, right up to the moment when I fell off the chair and hit the floor.

Morning brought a clearing sky. I climbed out of the sack about nine, feeling that the worst of the shock was over. I fried some eggs, drank a quart of milk and took the coupe down into the Loop. I parked two blocks from city hall and hoofed it over. The air had a sharp, cool tang down there in the shadows between the buildings. The movements of people in the crowd seemed crisp; alive. A girl in a green woolen suit that fit tightly over her body clicked by on high spiked heels. I looked away fast. I thought of Lorraine when I saw her.

The clerk in the marriage license office was a gray-haired old bird with a lardy belly and rear end, the kind that grew heavy when the city hall crowd stayed in power too long. I knew him. I pulled two tens out of my wallet and laid them on the fresh white page where the couples signed their names.

"I want to go through the records, dad."

He blinked and shoved his specs up higher on his nose and shook his head, as if to say, I shouldn't do this. Then one veined and mottled hand slithered over the page and clamped around the bills. The hand disappeared in his pocket. "What was your name again?"

I showed him my license. "John Hood. The firm of Hood and Spain."

"Oh yes, oh yes." He nodded vigorously and put on one of the smiles reserved for times when it was necessary to smile. "You've been here before. Well, you know your way around. Help yourself." He even did me the favor of opening the wooden gate in the counter.

So I got to the records. I broke out a fresh pack of cigarettes. I didn't know where I should start, so I picked a year ago, arbitrarily, and started backwards from there, flipping pages, discarding the endless names that meant a lot when they were first put down; names that meant loving and money and a house and kids but didn't mean a thing to me because I was looking for the name of a girl who was dead. When I finally found her signature, a week before Labor Day two and a half years back, I stared at it for a whole minute.

I had never seen her handwriting before. But there it was, small yet bold, as she had been. Lorraine Perau, twenty-four. I had her age, another unknown quantity. Slowly, I moved my eyes across the page to the spot where the man signed. Steven Aubrey Lannes, thirty-three.

I slammed the book shut and kicked the chair back and jammed my cigarette into my pocket. Now it fit together a little bit. She not only worked there, she lived with the man who owned the place. Somehow, I couldn't imagine her loving him. If she had, she'd never have let it go beyond a casual drink in a bar. With me, I mean.

Just as I walked out into the hall, I saw the elevator door open and I recognized Ted Fishlin, one of Hans's boys. I stepped into an open doorway, my back to the hall, ducked my head and lit a cigarette. Fishlin's steps cracked by. I turned and watched him go into the marriage license office. I ran for the elevator.

The cage seemed to take a year getting down. I shouldered my way out to the street and a woman punched me angrily with her elbow as I went by. I kept going. Hans Broekman of Homicide was right up with me, playing the hunches. His leg man was only about ten minutes behind me. Fishlin would talk to the old man, find out I'd been there, and probably discover the book on the table where I'd left it. Fishlin would go through the book. Then we'd be neck and neck, heading for the wire where Steve Lannes was waiting.

I unlocked the glove compartment of the coupe, took off my jacket and slipped on the .38 in the shoulder holster. The attendant gave me the eye as I drove out of the lot. I didn't pay any attention, swinging the car wildly into the line of cars. A gray sedan slammed on its brakes and somebody swore but I kept going.

I roared through the first light a second after it changed from yellow to red. I pushed down the accelerator, weaving in and out of traffic. Once across the river, I turned left into a bad section. The little bar was open, the sidewalk in front littered with papers. But Index Harry sat at his table in the corner, a wine bottle before him and his eyes bleary. I waved to the bartender and jerked a chair around, straddling it. Index Harry put down his book and offered me a drink. I shook my head. He brushed an imaginary speck of dirt off his threadbare but clean gray suit and sniffed. I gave him a ten. "Who is it this time?" Index Harry said, pouring himself wine.

"Steve Lannes, owner of the Golden Cage."

The cops would use the phone. Lannes wouldn't be at the club this early, and Broekman, for all his professional experience, didn't have a gold mine of information like Index Harry. According to the legends, the blotch-faced old man across from me had been a college professor, Phi Beta Kappa and Ph.D. before he started drinking, God knows why. Now he had only a photographic memory and unknown sources of information to keep him in drinks. But he knew the address, private phone and whereabouts of every big shooter in the city, from the mayor to the leading hoods.

"Lannes is not in town," Harry said. He sniffed again and turned a page of his book.

"Is that all I get for ten bucks?"

He drew himself up haughtily. "My mind commands a high price, Johnny. A man who knows Milton and the other great thinkers of the world can't be bought cheaply."

"How much more does it take?"

"Twenty-five."

As soon as I paid him, his mouth flew open and the words rattled out. "Lannes went to his home on Coldwater Lake sometime Saturday night or early Sunday morning. So far as I know he's still there. That's all I have." He sloshed more wine into his glass. He reeked of it. One carefully trimmed fingernail pointed to his book. "*Paradise Lost.* Wonderful poetry here, Hood. You should read it some time. Satan's by far the best character. The righteous ones are weaklings, and uninteresting. Which is frightfully close to the truth of life."

"Sure. Thanks." I walked away and left him as he got up, reeling a little, and started to recite poetry in a thick voice.

The new sun hit me like a ball bat when I reached the street. The gears grated as I swung the coupe around the corner, heading north to the state line, and Coldwater Lake just beyond. I was ahead now. Ahead in the race with tired Hans Broekman; the race to reach the man who killed Lorraine and the Wednesdays.

I ate lunch on the road, crossed the state line at about two in the afternoon and hit the little town of Coldwater Lake about four. The blowzy woman who owned the combination gas station, diner and general store, gave me cold looks and the directions to Lannes's place out on the lake road. She also informed me that Lannes had roared through town at nine a.m. Sunday morning in his powder blue Cadillac and hadn't as yet left. "They been havin' a party out at that house ever since, believe you me."

Steve Lannes celebrating. What? Lorraine's death? I bought a hamburger and a shake from the woman and sat in my car until sunset, going through another whole pack of cigarettes. Then I started the coupe and went bumping along the dirt road that led around the lake. Night came down, cold and hinting of winter.

The big expensive vacation houses bulked against the sky. All were dark except one, up ahead through the pines. Every light in that one was turned on. I swung off the road onto the shoulder, put out the parking lights, and closed the door quietly. I moved through the trees, tight inside, my coat hanging open. In spite of the temperature the palms of my hands were sweating.

The pine needles crunched under my feet. There the pines stopped, opening a vista of blue-black sky dotted with stars. I stopped too.

The house was a modern ranch, with plenty of picture windows. The curtains were closed, but every window glowed. By now my eyes were accustomed to the dark.

I heard a dance record from the house. My breath made little vapor clouds in front of my face. The cold crept into my bones. I waited. For what, I wasn't sure. I suppose I realized that I had come all the way up here knowing that Steve Lannes had killed Lorraine, and now there was a party going on and I was all by myself; stuck. Romo would never have let himself get into a mess like this. He would have known what to do. But Romo was on vacation, and Romo had never known Lorraine.

Abruptly, the back door of the house opened. I ducked deeper into the pines. For a moment a woman stood outlined in a yellow oblong of light, cigarette in hand. Then she closed the door behind her and came down a couple of steps. She walked over to one of the two cars parked behind the house, a Cadillac. She opened the door of the Cadillac, perched herself on the edge of the seat and dragged on her cigarette. I didn't know who she was, but she was alone, so I circled the cars and came up beside her.

"Hello there," I said softly, trying to act like I might be one of the guests.

She swiveled around and I got a good look at her as she drew on the cigarette again. Blonde, but the bottled kind; heavily made up face; lips thick with paint, drawn in a precisely edged line. She had big breasts inside a dark, tight sweater and her stretched-out legs were long and heavy. She stank of booze. She was too drunk to be surprised to see me.

"Hello yourself." She swayed in the seat. "Do I know you?"

"I don't think so."

"My name's Gert Carter. Have you slept with me this weekend?"

"I'm afraid not."

She waved her cigarette in the house. "You been in there?"

"Not yet."

"My God, it's a madhouse." She leaned closer to me and I smelled heavy perfume mixed up with the booze odor. "C'mere, I'll tell you a secret. Steve and those two boys of his have put me through the wringer. I ache all over. My God, I couldn't stand any more. I lost count. They're really celebrating but I just couldn't take it. I had to get out for some air. I threw up twice tonight, it got me down so." She announced it matter of factly. "Am I talking too much?"

"I don't think so. I'm a friend of Steve's. Are you a friend of Steve's?"

She grimaced, and something bitter flicked in her eyes for a second, then it vanished behind the bottled dullness. "Sure, I'm a good friend. A two hundred-dollar-a-night friend. Could you afford me?"

I took hold of her shoulder. "Are you one of Lannes's call girls?"

She made a maudlin face. "Sad, ain't it? The primrose path. Well, it's money. Steve wanted a piece for the party and he picked me. I don't get any pay. That's the worst of it." She shuddered. "My God, he gives me the creeps. He's inhuman."

"Look," I said, still keeping my voice down. "Tell me something, will you?"

"Sure. You're a friend. All you want to do is talk."

"Why was Steve's wife afraid of him?"

She laughed, loudly. I stiffened, afraid someone would come out. But no one did. "Everybody knows that. You ought to know that, being a pal of Steve's. That dumb little twist thought all he did was run nightclubs. She was married to him for two years before she found out he handled girls. Then she found out about the pretty pictures and books he sells, and it—well, it turned her. The dumb twist. She stripped in his club because she was his wife, and he's a funny guy with funny ideas and he liked to watch her, but she couldn't stand the other stuff."

"Did she threaten to tell the cops?"

"Oh, no," she said hoarsely. "Just told him she was leaving him. But it's the same thing. If she does go ahead and leave, she might talk about Steve's business. So I don't think she's going to be around much longer. You know how it is, don't you?"

"Sure, Gert," I said. "I know how it is."

Gert Carter didn't know Lorraine was dead. Gert Carter

had been brought along for the celebration; the wake for Steve's dead and now unthreatening wife. My guess said maybe the two boys Gert had spoken of were the actual killers. But they didn't matter. Lannes mattered. He'd given the order. I patted Gert's hand.

"Wait right here for me, will you? I want to go see Steve."

She grinned drunkenly and ran her palm over my cheek. "Sure. I'll wait. You're nice. I might even find some more strength before the night's over. Hurry back."

I said I would. I turned my back and took out the .38. I walked up the steps and opened the door. The music hit me. The lights glared. Down the hall, somebody shouted. An empty liquor bottle lay on the carpet in front of me. The air curled with blue smoke.

I closed the door. One of the boys came out of the kitchen carrying a drink. I grabbed the drink and gave him the .38 barrel along the back of his thick neck. I caught him with my free arm and let him down gently. I started down the hall.

The second boy came out of a door on my left, his face warped into a scowl. "Hey, Louie, for Christ's sake hurry up with—" His mouth flew open.

I grabbed his coat collar and pulled him forward and pistol-whipped him the same way. I let him bump as he went down, though. Good and loud. When I stepped around the door, Lannes was out of his chair. He got a look at my gun and sat down again behind the desk, outlined against another picture window. This one didn't have the curtains closed, and it looked right out on Coldwater Lake.

The room was a den. On the desk was an ashtray, topped by two plaster figures. I looked at them for a second and caught my breath. I looked at the photographs and drawings on the walls. And when I looked at Steve Lannes again, the greasy-haired head bulking out of the rumpled white-on-white shirt, the bulb eyes and the liverish lower lip, he seemed old, and goatish in a dirty sad way.

"What the hell are you doing in here?"

I pointed at the ashtray. "Lorraine didn't like that kind of stuff, did she?"

"Who are you?" he shouted, jumping up.

"John Hood. I'm a private detective. I'm looking for the guy who killed Lorraine Perau."

His eyes told me everything in an instant. They said, Sure, Lorraine didn't like it and she threatened to get noisy about it so my boys bumped her. They said, Sure, there's good money in stuff like that, and besides, I like that kind of artwork myself. They said, You must be the guy Lorraine was running around with. I knew it was some guy. She wasn't the kind to go off by herself for very long. All he actually said was "You're a pretty smart son of a bitch, aren't you?"

He tried to open his desk drawer. He got the Luger out and fumbled with it as if he didn't really know how to use it. I shot him. He fell over his chair and waved his arms and crashed through the big picture window and tumbled down a rip-rap slope into the lake. I walked over to the mess of broken glass and stared down. His head bobbed in the water like some kind of sputtering cork. I stood there while he drowned.

Then I went to his chair and sat down in it. I knew I was nothing but a dumb sap and Romo Spain would never have let me do a thing like this. Steve Lannes lay dead somewhere down in the lake. But it couldn't bring Lorraine back. It didn't erase the memory of her face, either. *As if it ever could, you goddamned fool. What were you thinking? What in Christ's name were you thinking?*

I shouted out loud. "I don't know. I don't know!"

Louie and the other boy got away, I heard their car start. I holstered my .38 and went back outside. I walked Gert Carter to the coupe. We drove back south toward the city. I stopped in a grocery and called Homicide long distance and told them what I knew. I hung up when they started asking too many questions.

Gert Carter talked on and on but I didn't hear. In Evanston I dropped her at an El station and made a promise to call her. Then I went to my apartment and got out two more pints. I didn't pass out this time. Broekman came through the door before that.

"Goddam you, Johnny. Goddam you for sticking your nose in." He glared down at me, looking tireder than ever. "This wasn't your business."

"I'm sorry," I said. "You want a drink?"

"No, I don't want a drink." He started pacing, letting out sighs and slapping his right fist into his left palm. He wheeled suddenly and stabbed a finger at me. "We got the guys who actually shot her. After you called, we staked out all the terminals. They tried to get a plane for Mexico City. A couple of dumb punks. They got scared and admitted the killing, but that doesn't make you any less guilty."

"No, it doesn't."

"I wish I could pin something on you. But if he's got a gun in his fist when we get him out of the lake, I don't know what I can do. I wish to God I could stick you, though. Wait till Spain hears about this. He'll burn your tail off. A dumb private cop trying to take over my job." He was jealous and sore, but he was right. I had gone over my head. And it wouldn't bring Lorraine back.

"What time is it?" I said.

"Dawn. Six-fifteen."

I had sat up all night. "I guess I better go to bed."

"I guess you better." He walked out and slammed the door hard behind him.

Romo got home a week and a half later. By then he knew it all; Broekman had written him a letter, airmail special delivery. Still, I had to go see Romo. I was scared, but I had to go. I rang his bell and waited. The voice roared, "Come in, Johnny."

He sat in his wheelchair, cigarette holder tipped up jauntily from the corner of his mouth. He had Broekman's letter on his lap. I could see the police department seal and the special delivery stamps. He wanted to let me know he knew the story, but otherwise he ignored the letter. I stood fiddling with my hat. "How was the vacation?"

"Exceptional. There's milk in the icebox. Pour yourself some."

I did. I fiddled with the glass instead of the hat. He stared at me. "Do you want a shopworn phrase?"

I nodded.

"Time," he said. "It will take time."

Silence hung between us for a long space. When he spoke again, his voice had softened. "You loved her, didn't you, Johnny." It wasn't a question. Something snapped inside of me, broke like a spring breaking.

"Yes," I said. "I loved her." I drank the glass of milk. I pulled up a chair. I sat down and told him how it was.

Tex

He walked out through the gates of Fort Sheridan with his dis-
honorable discharge in his pocket. Once free, he stopped along
the edge of the highway, set down the plaid cardboard suitcase
that contained some khaki underwear and a Gillette razor, and
lit a cigarette. A fin-tailed powder-blue El Dorado came roaring
down the highway, and slowed a little as a blonde girl with sunglasses and a silk scarf tied around her flying hair gave him an
appraising glance. The car shot on by, going south toward Chicago.

He raised his head and watched the car dwindle out of
sight. He had not noticed the girl, but the direction she was
driving made an impression on him. He ought to go back. It
was a long way, but he ought to go back.

Fixing this idea firmly in mind and concentrating on it, he
crossed the highway to the electric railway station. The hour
was shortly past noon of a gray, somewhat chilly day. Long
gray clouds were blowing down from Wisconsin and Canada.

In ten minutes the train of two green cars came along, and
he boarded it. He got off in the small suburban town of Lake
Bluff, because he spotted a Chevrolet agency as the train
came to a stop. He crossed the same highway that ran by the
army post and went into the agency, a blond boy with huge
shoulders, only twenty-one years old by the calendar. Forty
minutes later he drove out of the agency in a new two-door
sedan, maroon in color. The automobile smelled fresh, of
leather and metal. He headed west on Highway 176, humming a little tune. After several minutes he realized he could

no longer avoid the thought that was badgering him. He had
no reason to go south, all the long way back to Texas. No one
was waiting for him there. Nothing was waiting for him. So
when he came to the four-lane span of U.S. 41, the Skokie
Highway, he turned north toward the Wisconsin line, admit-
ting defeat. After a quarter of a mile he saw a car stalled by the
side of the road, and as he slowed down, he saw the trouble, a
flat left rear tire. A well-dressed woman was standing by the
rear wheel, twisting a pair of white gloves in confusion. He
pulled off onto the bumpy shoulder and climbed out.

"Can I help you?"

"Oh . . . if you would." The woman seemed close to tears.

He studied the situation. The car had evidently swerved
when the flat tire forced it off the road, and the right rear
wheel had dropped six inches over a ditch on the edge of the
shoulder. He took off his coat, asked the woman to put the car
in neutral when he gave the word, and stepped down into the
foot-deep gully. He braced both hands on the bumper,
called, "Put her in neutral," waited a moment and then
heaved. A muscle vibrated in his temple. The car rocked
backward a fraction; he grunted softly and heaved, and it
went up and over the lip with a crash of pebbles. He clam-
bered up again and wiped the back of his hand across his forehead.

He drew the ignition key and opened the trunk, saying,
"You got a jack?"

The woman said she didn't know, although he had the
trunk open and the woman was looking inside and the jack
was in plain view. "Here we go," he said softly, and went to
work. In ten minutes he had the spare on, and he handed the
keys back to the woman, who still sniffled and rubbed at her
eyes. She began to work at the clasp of her handbag.

"Please let me pay . . ."

"No, that's all right," he called, already behind the wheel of his own car. In the rear vision mirror he saw the woman drive onto the highway behind him. He lit another cigarette and began to hum again. After a while he managed to convince himself that the state of Wisconsin might be something pretty interesting to see.

At the end of three miles he felt thirsty. Nope, he said to himself. He drove past one roadhouse, and half a mile later, another. As soon as he started thinking about liquor, he began to notice the dismal gray clouds, and all of a sudden the discharge—which he had forgotten for a while—slipped into his mind again. His defenses crumbled. He saw gas pumps up ahead, and a sign that read *Billy's Cabins, Café, Dine and Dance.* He swung the wheel with a feeling of defeat. The tires crackled on gravel. He looked at his watch. Lord, it was already quarter to seven. No wonder it was so dark.

He went toward the café door. There were no other cars parked outside, and the dirty windows of the café were closed up with green blinds on which he could see blisters of paint. He walked inside and blinked a moment, for the light was poor. The only illumination came from a large lamp sitting on the back bar. The place had a few tables of flimsy wood, with chairs upended on top, and a space for dancing and a pinball machine lit up with drawings of girls in bathing suits. It was called Yacht Club. No one was at the bar. He pulled up onto a stool. He could feel it coming now. He had been nuts to think it could be any different. Why, he'd even expected Billy's to be a comfortable little spot. He didn't really have a concrete notion of what he had expected it to be, but he knew definitely what he hadn't wanted it to be, and this was it.

"Hey!" he called.

A door in one corner led into a small room which also had

tables. Out of his line of vision a pair of feet scraped on the floor.

The bar was old-fashioned, with a large mirror. He stared at the rows of bottles with their silver pour spouts and looked away. The end portion of the back bar was a writhing confusion of plaster of Paris statuettes, no more than three alike: stallions, kewpies, coolies, blackamoors. There was also a wire rack of postcards featuring cartoons about vacations and outhouses. The lamp that threw the only light stood among the knickknacks. It was plaster of Paris, too, larger than the others. It represented a Chinese girl, and the bulb came out of the top of her head. The light filtered through a bright red shade. The Chinese girl was dressed in a purple gown and held a gold mirror in front of her face. Her right leg was crossed over her left in a sort of figure 4, and in the triangle of the figure 4 somebody had stuck a card, now dirty and brown, marked $4.95. The bar looked cheap and nightmarish. He wanted to get out, but then the proprietor came from the other room and he felt embarrassed, so he stayed.

The proprietor was a woman, with a doughy face. She must have weighed three hundred pounds. She wore a dirty pink dress. He couldn't tell if she was pregnant or just fat. A large plaster which looked like a Dr. Scholl's was stuck on her gray-looking neck. The plaster matched her dress. He felt revolted. He wanted to run away, but he was pretty certain now this was the kind of place he belonged in. The woman came to a stop under a sign that hung on the top of the bar. It said *Kwitcherbelliakin.*

Still, he wasn't completely sure.

"Yessir?" said the woman.

What would it be? Only one, he said to himself.

"Bottle of Schlitz."

She opened a silvered cooler, uncapped the brown bottle

and set it on the bar. She also set out a tumbler and a black plastic ashtray, and he bought a nickel bag of Chesty potato chips. He opened the bag but didn't touch the beer. He ate a chip, and stared at the brown and gold Schlitz label. The woman went to the other end of the bar, sat down on a stool, and began to read a comic book.

Reluctantly he filled the tumbler with beer, watched the head rise, and drank part of it. He waited carefully to feel the effect. None. He swiveled his head and looked at the deserted room. The floor looked unwashed. From outside came the steady hiss of tires, as the traffic roared north and south. He drank more beer, feeling now that he would probably have another after this one.

Things began to slip back into his memory, answering his own question to himself of how he had gotten here. He recalled the farm in Texas, and the taste of dust always in his mouth. He saw his father and his mother, dusty people, the man in overalls bleached nearly white, with the buttons no longer a shiny brass color, the woman in a dress that had once been a color but was now gray. They always read the Bible at night, and he remembered how his father had whipped him with a belt, using the buckle end, when he came home from town one night when he was about twelve, and said he wished he could taste whiskey. He had meant no harm. He had been curious about the signs displayed in the windows of certain places, and he had just wanted to taste it. But sitting in Billy's and staring at the way the lamplight threw shadows on the Chinese girl, he could feel the tang of the buckle on his flesh.

One thing he had always had, strength. The huge shoulders. He never wanted to lick the other kids in grade school but he could do it if it was necessary, as it sometimes was. Then high school, and though he had a tough time with his subjects, he learned football. They couldn't stop him when

118

he was on the line. He remembered how the man in the linen suit had driven out to the farm his senior year, and pulled up in a late model Oldsmobile and talked his father into letting him accept a scholarship to the state university.

There he learned to drink for the first time, and heavily. And when he got drunk he wanted to fight. He failed three courses his first semester, and without letting his folks know, left school, and enlisted in the army. Once he had written home, but the letter had come back unanswered, so he wrote to a friend of the family who told him his mother and father had been killed in a highway accident while on the way to the state fair. In the army he played football, and they wanted him to box, but he wouldn't, because he had to be sober when he boxed, and then he didn't like to fight, or thought he didn't. He only fought when he got drunk.

The first bad time was in a bar in El Paso. Two other soldiers who had been in the place said he had walked up to three Air Corps lieutenants who were drinking martinis.

"You don't like me," the other soldiers said he said.

"Shove, dogface," they said one of the lieutenants said.

He remembered nothing. He never remembered, once he got heavily drunk. He had been drunk, they told him, and had broken the arm of one of the lieutenants before the MPs dragged him away. He got in bad trouble for that one, because one of the Air Corps lieutenants had a father who was a brigadier general in Washington.

In between the big fights, there were all the small ones in bars and barracks when he took on just one man at a time. The second big fight was in a bar in Tijuana, when a Mexican stumbled and spilled tequila on him. It was six Mexicans against him. When he woke up in the base hospital, he had two knife wounds in his side, but his buddies laughingly (and truthfully) said he had damn near killed every Mexican in the place. He got sick when he heard this, because he thought he didn't really want to fight.

The third time, two months ago, he had been in a bar in Highwood, near Fort Sheridan. Three master sergeants had been making loud remarks about his outfit. He didn't remember that either, of course, but learned the story afterward. One of the master sergeants died of a broken neck, and another, they said, would be crippled for life.

Sitting in Billy's, he remembered the whole road. Even the interview with the doctor who wasn't a regular doctor, Major Nevins. At this very moment he still could not make sense out of the questions, though he remembered some of them:

"Did you ever feel you hated your parents, subconsciously, because of the way they restricted you?"

He said he didn't know what subconsciously meant.

Dr. Nevins, who had a mustache and talked like an Easterner, smiled patiently. "Well, did you ever think that about your parents and not want to admit it to yourself?"

"I guess so."

"Can't you remember?"

"Well, I guess I did think that. I always wished they wouldn't read the Bible so much."

And then about drinking:

"Why do you drink?"

"I like to."

"Why do you like to?"

"Well, I didn't like to at first, when I went to college, but after I got in trouble, fighting, I just couldn't stand to think about what I'd done, so I'd take a drink."

"You drink to keep from remembering what you did the last time you got drunk?"

"I guess so."

"You're too strong, do you know that?"

"I guess I am strong, all right."

"If you were a weakling it wouldn't make any difference. But you've got shoulders like a bull. You broke Master Sergeant Preebie's neck with one twist."

"I don't remember that."

Because he had gotten drunk and killed the master sergeant, but couldn't remember, they had to discharge him. Dr. Nevins wanted him to go to a hospital, but he didn't want to, and Nevins said he couldn't force it because on the surface it was just drunkenness causing the trouble, and the inquiry board called the killing accidental, even though they had to discharge him for it. Now, sitting in Billy's, with the traffic all heading someplace out on the highway, he wondered whether he should have gone to the hospital.

"Let me have another beer," he said.

The woman put down her comic book and got the beer.

He felt a little lift now.

So that was where he had been. Now, where could he go?

Well, he knew, all right. He couldn't keep a job, not remembering he'd killed the sergeant, who was really a pretty good guy. He'd have to keep on drinking. He couldn't even be decent, or have a home. Outside of the army they put you in prison for killing someone. All of a sudden, he knew that he would probably one day be executed for killing someone. It was only a question of time. That's all. Just a question of time.

Now that he had finally admitted it, finally told himself the truth, things seemed a little easier. At least he didn't have any wild ideas about pulling out. He just couldn't escape it. That was the way it was. He didn't feel like fighting any more. But it was a matter of time.

The door opened and a man came in. He was not over five feet three, and wore a yellow T-shirt and a greasy hat. He had a small, pointed face. The fat woman said, "Hello there, Mr. Tod. Haven't seen you for a week."

"I'm always around," said Mr. Tod. "Gimme a bottle of Miller's."

He drank again. He'd kill someone again, sure. It must be in the cards. He was never meant to do anything else, and though he didn't exactly understand why it had to work out so, he accepted it now. No use fighting it. No use prolonging it. It was just a matter of time.

He drank two more beers, and slowly felt the edge of reality going dull. His watch showed eight-thirty. The door opened and a girl came in. He stared at his glass, hearing her take a stool near him. The fat woman said, "Hi, June."

"Hi," the girl said disgustedly. A car without a muffler gunned away outside. He turned his head slowly, curious, to look at the girl. She had brown hair and was very thin. She was wearing blue jeans and a man's white shirt, open at the throat and with sleeves rolled up. She had a narrow face and small breasts. She wasn't pretty at all. On the other side of her he could see Mr. Tod still sitting.

"Bourbon and water, will you?" June said to the fat woman.

"You sure got your dander up," said the fat woman. She poured the drink from one of the bottles.

"Oh, it's that Jim."

"Was that his car outside just now?"

"Yes."

The fat woman heaved a snort. "What did he do, throw you out?"

"No, sir, I *got* out. I'm through with him, he ain't worth my time. Stubborn. I wanted to go to the drive-in, but no," she mimicked acidly, "he wanted to go to his old stock car races. I got fed up. I told him to let me off."

"He always was stubborn," the fat woman agreed. June took a sip of her drink, shuddered, and glanced sidewise toward him.

"Oh, there's plenty more," she said.

He licked his lips. Well, why not?

He waited until the fat woman went into the next room on an errand. Mr. Tod walked over and began to play the pinball machine. The lights flickered across the ceiling, buzzers stuttered like machine guns, and bells pinged. He picked up his beer glass and walked toward the girl. He sat down next to her.

"Can I buy you one?"

"When I finish this one." She smiled. Her lipstick was a thin and crooked red line. Up close he could see she had hardly any lips at all, and had painted the lipstick up over flat skin.

"You from Sheridan?" the girl asked.

He nodded. "I got discharged today."

"Oh, you did! Where you from? Down South?"

"Texas.

"I'll bet they call you Tex."

"Yes, they do."

"Well, my name's June." She smiled again, making no pretenses.

After a moment he said, "Like to go for a ride? My car's outside."

"That maroon Chevy? That new one?"

"Bought it this afternoon."

"Oo!" She clapped her hands, then seized his arm. Her hand felt hot. "Listen, honey. Let me go to the little girl's room and fix my face and I'll meet you in the car. How about it?"

"Fine," he said, not meaning it.

He watched her vanish out a side door, and noticed how thin her rump was beneath the jeans. Then he remembered what he'd been thinking about when she walked in. Couldn't forget it for long. He looked around. Mr. Tod still worked the pinball machine. Outside the traffic roared, all going someplace. He shook his head. No go. In a year, or maybe ten, maybe twenty, he'd kill somebody good and that would be all. It was just a matter of time. He felt like he wanted to lie down and have a nice long sleep, where he could forget it all. He didn't want to live all those years out.

The fat woman with the plaster on her neck came back. He started for the door, thinking of the girl. They could go for a ride. She ought to know some dark side road. It was just a matter of time anyway, now or ten years from now, what difference did it make, except that he was tired and knew the score.

He walked back to the bar, past Mr. Tod, his mind made up. He brushed Mr. Tod's shoulder but the man didn't look around. He put his hands on the bar, feeling the wood, feeling worse and yet better. The woman had started to read another comic book, and she looked up. He said to her, "I want to buy a fifth of whiskey."

Little Man—
It's Been a Busy Day

I should have known better when I turned the downtown corner in my heap and saw the mob outside the joint. But you know how it goes.

No, you probably don't either. Probably you are a nice, average height, instead of a slightly underfed five foot one. Doubtless you have a respectable job, while I make my green when and as I can, on assorted errands and assignments. This has led the local blue boys to refer to me as a hustler. Actually I am just an exponent of good old American free enterprise. But try telling that to detectives.

In any case, it was a warm summer's evening and business had not been especially zingo of late. At my pad I could hardly turn around for all the unpaid bills. Visions of collection agents searching the city for my person bedeviled me. So I said phooey and decided to zip downtown and spend my last couple of shekels on some sauce at the cozy bar off the lobby of The Dayview Motor Inn, which is one of those plush drive-in-and-be-relieved-of-a-bundle-while-you-relax joints.

Motoring around the corner, I was unprepared for the sight of a couple of hundred teenage persons milling on the sidewalk outside the entrance to the inn's underground garage. Sense said, "J. Havoc, go home." But I was thirsty.

I honked the horn and turned in. There were sneakers to the right of me, bouffants to the left of me, and several haircuts on all sides which left some question as to the owner's gender. I rolled down the left window.

"Move it, kids. You're blocking the sidewalk."

A dolly shrieked, "That's their manager! I recognize him!" She fainted. Simply dropped below the heaving level of heads and vanished from view.

The youths pressed against my vehicle. I felt a rocking motion. "Wait a minute, wait a minute," I said. "You're damaging my acrylic lacquer finish."

"Mister," panted a youth with a bowl haircut, "twenty-five bucks."

"For what? Not running over you? Get out of the way so I can get into the garage."

Somebody on the right side of the car tried to open the rear door. I gestured wildly. Over the heads of the unruly youngsters who should have been home reading Longfellow instead of crowding the boulevards, I had espied two gentlemen in blue uniforms. They carried billies.

One of the cops was attempting to approach my car. A youth in a state of frenzy poked him in the groin with a guitar case. Blue-boy turned royal purple and forged ahead, shouting and flourishing his billy menacingly.

There were assorted jeers and catcalls about free speech. Meantime, the importuning youth who had tempted me with the offer of twenty-five was leaning halfway inside the car and explaining in more pants: "Twenty-five dollars if you'll pose as my father."

"Mine too, mine too, Basil," said his girlfriend, clutching his sleeve.

"We can't get into the hotel unless we have our parents along," Basil explained.

The right-hand rear door opened and went *ka-chunk* quick. I turned my head. The officer was standing out there. He had apparently slammed the door in time to prevent fourteen teenagers from jumping inside.

"Officer," I yelled, "get these under-age hopheads out of

my way! I want to go inside."

"Move, move!" the cop hollered at the kids. "This gentleman wants—hey! You ain't no gentleman."

The officer was lamping me through the windshield. His eyes glowed like pinball bumpers.

"I recognize you, Havoc. I've seen you at headquarters. What are you doing hanging around here with all these kids? Trying to work one of your con games?"

They think I'm a swindler just because I negotiate my way around the more rubber-like corners of the law. If you do it and attend church every Sunday, the chamber of commerce will name you man of the year. But it never works that way for me. I sighed and said a mental hell with it and leaned on the horn. Two more girls fainted but their boyfriends dragged them to safety.

The officer was trying to come around the car to my side. I was trying to figure out whether I should laugh, cry, or bang my head on the dash when suddenly a shriek arose:

"There they are, there they *are!*"

"Yow, yew, oh, oh, it's too *much!*"

"Who is it, who is it?" cried I, caught up in the madness of the moment.

"The Moles, The *Moles!*"

Then it all registered.

A large item in the paper that morning had announced that the latest of the culture assassins, a totally untalented duo of millionaire teenage singers, was appearing at a local arena for a one-nighter. Tonight. Of course the teenage idols needed a pad. And I had picked the pad to have a drink in. I thought enviously of the $28,000 advance ticket sales mentioned in the news and wished I had a bit of that cabbage for my overdue bills.

Whilst I was thinking all this, the teenagers surged away

from my wheels and down the pavement like a buffalo herd.

All heads craned upward. The shrieks became deafening. Being unable to see because my car was already halfway under the garage canopy, I could only assume that one of The Moles had burrowed out of his upstairs window and was favoring the crowd with glimpses of his—if I remembered the morning's photos—unshorn locks.

The roadway ahead was suddenly free of bodies. All the teenagers were exhausting themselves clapping and howling elsewhere. I stepped on the gas. "—don't let me catch you doing anything fishy around here," the officer shouted as I wheeled it into the garage ramp. Hanged for a sheep already.

The fluorescent-lit garage one level below the street was a silent, motor-oil-fragrant relief. I turned into a slot between two bigger boats and lit a weed. Maybe I could take the elevator up from the garage level and make it to the bar without running into any further presses of people. I climbed out. That's when I spotted her hiding in the back.

"Get out of there. Get out of there this damn minute!"

She did. She was a nicely apportioned dolly around sixteen, neatly dressed, with a fresh, wholesome face and straw-colored hair. The officer hadn't kept all the kids out of my car after all. She looked guilty as she scuffed her sneaker.

"You ought to be ashamed," I said.

"But the only way I can get in to see The Moles is to be accompanied by a parent."

"Where is your parent?"

"He's at one of his silly old meetings."

"What's your name?"

"Delilah Somerset."

"Well, Delilah, my name is Havoc, and I am old enough to be your father, which gives me the right to tell you to take a streetcar right home where you belong."

"Oh, please don't be square," she said with a sigh. "The streetcars stopped running years ago."

She looked me over. By looking down, natch. She was about 5'6" but from my point of view that made her an Amazon. At last she said, sort of sadly, "You don't look very fatherly. You're not big enough."

Did I feel like a jerko in my natty Brooks rig and porkpie, or didn't I? I did. Besides, she piqued my pride.

"Now listen, I look as fatherly as the next. Just because I'm not one of those big tall clowns doesn't mean I'm a second class citizen." Unfortunately it means exactly that all too often in a world peopled by giants. "Just for that remark, Delilah, I'm, going to take you inside and let you do whatever it is you want to do. But while you're hunting around for those musical troglodytes, I'm going to phone your folks."

"Gee, maybe you're not so square after all," she said.

"No," I said, "just thick-headed. Also a sucker for a nice-looking kid. Come on."

"You've got to understand how it is," she breathed as we hoofed over the cement toward the elevator. "You know The Moles, don't you? Surely you've heard their million-sellers, haven't you? Dreamy songs. There's *Yam-cram-bam*, and *Zip-snip-flip*, and *Ugg-bugg-chugg*, and—"

"Delilah kiddo, is your stomach upset? Such ungodly noises—"

"You're nice," she said. "What did you say your name was?"

"Havoc, Johnny Havoc. And if there's anything I hate, it's being considered a nice guy. I am not. I am a professional hustler after the green bills, one who—oh, never mind. You are a nice kid, Delilah. So I am going to spare your innocence the story of my checkered career. I'll ring up your parents right away and tell them to fetch you home before any of the chowderheads rampaging around this misbegotten piece of architecture knock you down and break your arm or—"

Blah, blah, blah. Havoc the Mouth.

I was still talking as we approached the steel doors of the basement elevator. Consequently I never noticed the two lads in the sharp suits lurking in a recessed concrete bay adjoining the Otis. All at once they hopped out into the glare of the fluorescents. Poor little Delilah grabbed my threads and squealed.

"Surely," I said, "neither of these is a Mole?"

"Perfect," said one sharp suit to the other. "A guy and his kid. Let's take him."

Judging from the lethal weapons which each carried, and which they now pointed at my person, they already had.

"He's kind of a squirt," said one of the lads.

"Now just a minute," I began.

"Shut up," said the other lad. He gave me an unfriendly whack in the side of the head with his gun. I reeled against the elevator door, whango. My elbow bumped the button. The elevator was not in use. The door opened instantly and I fell over backwards into the cage.

From flat on my pratt I regarded the lads as they manhandled Delilah into the box, thumbed the control button and stashed their cannons inside their jackets. One of the lads, a mean, razor-nosed, lanky specimen of about thirty, glanced down at me with considerable contempt.

"You can stand up, midget. But don't funny it up with any antics. Or else you and your little girl are going to be two very dead Moles fans."

"But she's not—" I began, and stopped.

Delilah's blue optics regarded my own with well-justified fear. And I realized that for all practical purposes, yours truly would have to play the pops role to the hilt. After all, I had gotten her into this by agreeing to take her inside. Up went the Otis and down went my spirits.

The two lads in the sharp suits watched the indicator panel above the door. The cage stopped at the first floor. A couple of business types attempted to thrust in.

"All full, Clyde," said the scrawny gunsel, and thumbed the button so that the business types had to leap back or suffer their paunches to be clipped by the closing doors. Up went the Otis once more.

I was developing a slow and steady burn. I don't like goons who refer to me as a midget or a squirt or something like that. The salt in the wound bit. I vowed I would have my revenge, even if there were no immediate cash return in sight.

I would have my revenge provided I kept on breathing. Delilah Somerset clutched my sleeve. I could feel the poor kid shivering.

"Aren't you sorry you ever bought all those Moles records?" said I.

I certainly was.

Ordinarily in such a predicament I would have attempted to fast-talk my way out. I am not known to do the sacrificial bit unless a chance of personal profit is involved. However, the presence of Delilah Somerset somewhat took the decision out of my hands.

Delilah appeared on the point of hysterics. Her teased locks had strands out of place everywhere. Her blue eyes displayed the beginnings of tears. I slipped my arm about her in what I hoped was a fatherly fashion. I felt somewhat silly, as I was the smaller. The gunsels didn't miss that. They snickered and rolled their eyes, which caused me to redouble my determination to hand them lumps if at all possible.

As mentioned, the leader appeared to be Razor-Nose, the

scrawny one. His partner was shorter, though still well over my height. This partner was the lad who had bonked me with the pistola. He was not much past his middle twenties. He sported a crew cut and a nasty mouth like a parenthesis mark pointed down.

Both lads were attired in what low-grade criminals of their mentality consider sartorial splendor. This year it was two-tone loafers and iridescent suits. I was not deceived by their mental numbness, however. They both had eyes with the shine of the sewer rat in them. Fracturing my bones or worse wouldn't bother them.

"Twelfth floor," said Razor-Nose as the Otis halted. "Everybody off."

The lads still carried their cannons in side pockets. We marched a short distance down the plush carpet. Then the stocky one unlocked the orange door to Room 1211. He jerked Delilah into the Hollywood modern chamber. I was about to follow when he gigged me.

"Not so hard with the gun," I said. "I have the arthritis."

"You'll have worse than that if you don't pay attention. Now you and me, we are going to get on the elevator and go up a couple of more floors. You are going to pick up my cues and nod every time I say something aimed at you, and if you behave just right we'll be back here in a little while. Then we'll let you and your kid go. We'll just tie you up and take off. What happens all depends on you. I mean, you better pick up the cues. Because if you don't—if you funny it up—your daughter is going to get hurt. Buster—that's my partner there—he'll see to it."

From the reptilian expression on Buster's round face, I was certain he would.

"What's all this about cues to pick up?" I said. "I don't even know the lines."

"You'll catch on to the bit quick enough," he said. "I can tell you're a smart little apple."

I wondered whether I could figure out a way to escape this jam. But I wasn't even certain about the jam's exact recipe yet. Maybe a few more minutes would provide the answer.

I said to Delilah, "Don't be scared, sugar. I'll be back soon. Do what this—gentleman—says, as long as he behaves himself. If he doesn't, remember the karate lessons."

It was a hopeless jest. Delilah still looked petrified as the door shut.

"What's your name?" I said to my captor as we headed for the elevator.

"God!" For a sec I thought he was suffering grandeur delusions, but then he breathed, "Listen."

"What?"

"Sirens."

"Sweetest music this side of *yawp*."

He booted me in the tail, down along the empty corridor to a hall window overlooking the street. He cranked open the casement-type window and peeked out as I nursed my backbone and a deepening grudge. Drifting up from the street came the yowl of a couple of police prowlers, plus an overriding chorus of teenage shrieks, oaths and clamors. My captor turned around, grinning.

"I was worried for a minute," he said. "But the cops are after the kids."

"What are the kids doing?"

"It looks like they're having a riot."

"Oh, is that all?"

More blue boys down on the pavement wouldn't do me a hoot of good up here. We waited for the elevator again. A fat old dame and her hubby came out of one room, gibbering about the decline and fall of the morality of American youth. The elevator arrived.

The couple started to get in. Razor-Nose jostled the old bag and hissed, "This is the up express." The door closed just as the dame pointed to me and said something about over-dressed, pushy adolescents.

"The Moles are on this floor," said Razor-Nose as the car hit fifteen. At the back of my skull a vague notion of what this clown might be up to began to percolate.

We stepped out into a hall identical with the twelfth. Razor-Nose prodded me around an L-bend. I espied a law minion posted with crossed arms and a weary expression outside a door marked Suite 1500. Razor-Nose sauntered along with his heater pressed into my side.

The cop glommed us suspiciously. I hoped he might be one of the types who had seen me raked over the hot fires at headquarters. Unfortunately it was soon clear from his expression that he'd never laid eyes on me.

Razor-Nose said winningly, "Uh, officer, I'm Mr. Brown, the assistant manager."

That put the copper off just long enough. He started to unfold his arms and Razor-Nose gave him the knee lift in the place where it smarts most. The cop cursed and doubled over.

Razor-Nose whacked him twice across the back of the neck with his cannon. The poor blue lad dropped. I pulled my punch in mid-delivery as the gunsel swung around, half crouched, his pistola pointing at me. He was very fast, I had to admit that.

"Nuh-uh, sawed-off," he said. "Remember the little dolly we got downstairs?"

I sighed. "All too well." Razor-Nose chuckled and whacked the door with his gun butt.

I don't know what I anticipated. Certainly not the trim

little feminine package who answered the door. I saw a cute face, wild red hair, dark eyes, plus charming hips and bust encased in, respectively, a smart skirt and frilly blouse. The morsel was also virtually my size, namely about five feet.

I had no time to allow my hormones to become overwrought. The dolly had a no-nonsense expression on her face as she said, "Officer, I specifically told you—no interruptions until it's time for the boys to leave."

"Howzabout this kind of interruption?" Razor-Nose exclaimed, brandishing his weapon.

The morsel paled. "Maury! Manny!" She started to back up. "It's some kind of hold-up."

"Shut up and stand out of the way." Razor-Nose gave her a shove that bowled her back inside the plush suite. He manhandled my threads, pushing me into the chamber. Then he followed and kicked the door shut with his heel.

"Well, well, ain't you two a couple of cuties?" he said.

The objects of his reference were The Moles, a pair of lads just finishing up a steak dinner from a room service cart. Both looked barely into puberty. They wore pleatless trousers, shirts with lace at bosom and cuff, and their hair down onto their shoulders in a mop-like arrangement. The injustice of it, I thought. Millionaires hardly old enough to shave.

"You don't have to wave a gun to get our autograph," said one, rising. He stepped past the cart, around a bass and snare drum set-up, and over a temporarily dormant electric guitar and amplifier decorated with what looked like golden fish scales. "Autographs for free as long as you got this far. Got your book?"

The nitwit extended his hand. Razor-Nose hit it with his gun and guffawed.

The youth's eyebrows shot up. "What did you do that for?"

135

"Manny! Maury!" the redhead repeated, standing up again. "He's dangerous."

"You bet your sweet banana split I am," said Razor-Nose. "My name is Spiggs, Al Spiggs. My partner, Buster Beemis, is in a room a couple of floors down, with this guy's daughter. What's your name, weasel?"

Evidently that was one of my cues. "Johnny Havoc, and I want the rest of you folks to know I had nothing to do—"

"Shut up, Hammock, I'll do the talking." Spiggs scowled at The Moles. "I seen you guys on Ed Sullivan's, and I think you stink. But I'm not familiar with you, doll-face," he added to the redhead. "Are you their mother or something?"

The redhead was no chicken. But neither was she pushing into Medicare territory. She showed some spark in her black eyes.

"If I must dignify a thug like you with an answer, my name is Harriet Taylor. I work for Exclusive Artists, the booking agency that handles these boys. Maury Johnson and Manny Cox, The Moles."

The big stars blinked like Tweedledum and Tweedledee, still baffled by it all. Harriet Taylor stepped forward, showing a feisty spirit. "Just where is the policeman who's supposed to be outside to prevent this sort of thing?"

"Sleeping," said Mr. Al Spiggs. "Like you will be if you don't play along."

"What do you want?" Harriet asked.

Spiggs sniggered. "What else? Money. I see by the paper that there's at least twenty-eight grand in the till at the arena. There won't be no concert at all unless I get every last cent."

Harriet Taylor laughed. "You've flipped. We don't get paid until the end of the engagement."

"Tonight you get paid before," barked Spiggs. "Let's get the deal straight. Like I said, my partner's holding this guy's daughter in a room downstairs. She's a typical teenager, y'know? A Moles fan. I'll phone my partner and tell him to lay off the minute you, baby-doll, start for the arena. Like right now. Then, you pick up that twenty-eight grand—"

"We always get paid by check," said Manny, or was it Maury?

"The Government gets most of it," said Maury, or was it Manny?

"Shut up," said Al Spiggs. "Tonight you get it in cash. I don't care what kind of excuse you make, doll. You just get the money and get it back here, and don't breathe a word to anybody. Meantime, me and Haddock here, we stick around. I'll keep my gun aimed at your two choirboys, and when you come back with the cash, I'll clear out. Then this guy's daughter goes free, and you make the concert scene. How does all that register?"

Harriet Taylor looked stunned. "Like a no sale. I'm sorry. Haddock?"

"Havoc," I said. "Johnny Havoc."

"Do they really have your daughter downstairs? Or is this part of the dodge?"

This was it. I could spill the bit and maybe save my own goose-grease, but not Delilah's.

"Actually, they do," I replied. "Room twelve-eleven."

A tense silence. All of a sudden a notion hit me as to how I might get enough of an edge to untangle this mess before it became worse.

Harriet Taylor was studying me and my height, which so nicely matched hers. She probably thought I was some married john, the dullsville type. I desired to disabuse her, but that could wait. I thought I saw a flicker of belief on her face. I was certainly trying to look sincere as hell whilst adding, "Yes, my daughter is in that room. And she's in danger unless you cooperate. This bast—uh, this guy stuck that gun on us in the parking garage downstairs."

Maury or Manny plucked fretfully at his shoulder-length locks. "This is awful. First they tear your clothes. Next they fight over your airplane ticket stubs—"

The other longhair sighed, looking equally scared. "Sometimes I wonder if all the money's worth it."

"Listen," I said to Harriet, "do what he says. They'll mangle my daughter if you don't."

The redhead bit her lip again. "We don't want any kind of a scandal. But that's not really what counts." She looked at me dead level. "What counts is your girl getting hurt or not. To have her hurt wouldn't be worth all the cash in the world. Not to me, anyway."

She swung around to Spiggs.

"All right, you vermin. I'll get my coat and take a taxi to the arena. But the boys had better be here, safe, and this man's daughter too, when I get back. On my way out I want to verify the story. I want to see the girl you say is being held in twelve-eleven."

A blouseful of goodies and brains too! I could have kissed her. Al Spiggs hesitated. I picked it up fast.

"Spiggs, let her check. That way we know she'll go through with the pick-up of the money, and my daughter'll be safe. Call your partner through the switchboard and tell him she's coming, so he won't get nervous."

From the corner of my eye I gauged the distance between the trap drum set, the bass drum of which was decorated with a sketch of a mole with a bowl haircut, and the window of the suite. It was open on the warm night and the lighted downtown. Below, sirens caterwauled and jolly teenagers rioted briskly.

While Manny and Maury exchanged petrified glances yet

again, Al Spiggs toyed with his pistola, wigwagging it back and forth as though thinking. Finally he shrugged.

"So go ahead. Check on the little girl. But if you pull anything down on twelve, broad, you'll lose some very valuable clients."

He sidled over to the phone table and asked the operator to ring 1211.

"Buster? This is Al. Yeah, it's going perfect, yeah. Only there's this redhead who's going to fetch the cash, see. She wants to double-check whether—you *sneaky little s.o.b.!*"

Thus cried Spiggs as I made my move.

He'd been talking hard into the mouthpiece. That, plus watching me, Harriet and The Moles, caused his eyeballs to flicker hither and thither, as he couldn't survey us all at once. I jumped just as he was glancing over to the pair of millionaire musicians.

I ran doubled over. But I wasn't aiming for Spiggs, which startled him even more. I whanged against the drum set, ripped two big shiny cymbals off their uprights and scaled them one after another out through the open window.

"Get your souvenirs!" I cried, for no extremely good reason.

Spiggs leveled his cannon as I zigzagged all over the place to keep from getting perforated. "Now you get it! Not you, Buster. They're jumping me—"

Spiggs yowled this last into the phone, which was just what I didn't want him to do. God knew what frightful atrocities the other hooligan would perpetrate on poor Delilah now.

But I had more pressing worries. Spiggs' gun erupted. I hit the ivory carpet. Harriet Taylor cried out. Manny and Maury crawled behind the couch, bleating.

Spiggs's slug shattered a picture on the wall. Glass stung

the back of my neck as I ripped the snare drum off its stand. I sailed this straight at Spiggs. Whammo!

The chrome drum rim contacted his forehead and his gun arm flew up in the air. His finger jerked. The gun exploded. A shower of plaster came loose from the ceiling, falling down over us like snow.

Spiggs recovered fast. He aimed his heater at me. I picked up the bass drum. From behind the couch, Manny or Maury waited, "No, no! Mother gave me that drum!"

Through the open window came sirens and the roar of renewed pandemonium. Doubtless the flying cymbals had landed. I let Al Spiggs have it with the bass drum.

The drumhead burst. A chrome fitting gouged him in the eye. The big rim knocked a front tooth loose. By that time, I had kicked the drum aside to leap on him. The only trouble was, the goon hadn't let go of the cannon yet. I had a thrilling glimpse down its muzzle.

"You'll get yours, you rotten little midget!" His trigger finger whitened.

No time for ceremony. I gave him the toe of my shoe under the chin. His head snapped back against the wall so hard a crack appeared. More plaster fell from the ceiling. Then Spiggs sagged unconscious, blood trickling out one corner of his mouth.

Panting, I picked up the heater. It made me nervous. I never carry a rod because I am not licensed as one of those kind of operatives. I jammed the rod in the pocket of my Brooks rig, snatched up my porkpie and aimed for the door, yelling to Harriet, "No time to waste. Delilah's in trouble down on number twelve."

The redhead rushed after me as I ripped down the hall toward the fire stairway. Just at that moment the elevator door opened.

Blue everywhere! Police boiled out. In the forefront was the officer who had seen me earlier, down on the street. He had a nasty gash on his forehead. In one hand he clutched a cymbal.

He was saying at the top of his lungs, "That's right, sir. I definitely recognized that shyster Havoc."

"Am I glad I was on duty when the riot call came in," boomed a voice which caused me to shudder. "I've been waiting for a chance like this to nail that little unprintable."

It was my nemesis, Detective First Grade FitzHugh Goodpasture—long nose, spaniel eyes, thinning hair, plain clothes and all. His moist cigar worked with frantic speed in his eternally glum mouth.

He screeched to a stop outside the elevator.

"There he is! Why, I'll bet he's the one who threw the cymbals out the window. Havoc, you nearly hospitalized this officer. The other cymbal cracked the windshield of my car. You're under arrest. Put your guns on him, men!"

Thus arose my dilemma.

Faced by half a dozen armed blue boys all panting for my blood, and dogged by grim visions of what Buster Beemis might be doing to poor Delilah, I had to choose and very fast indeed.

Better I should have had to cut my own throat, as the saying goes. There wasn't any choice. Detective Goodpasture would only lock me up and refuse to believe my story. The delay could be fatal for Delilah. Of course things would probably be fatal for me if I got into any further trouble with the police. But that bucket of water wasn't quite as hot as the one on the twelfth floor. At least not yet.

"Move in." Goodpasture cried, wildly lapping his arms. "I don't know who that girl is with him, but they're probably in cahoots. Watch him carefully. The bum is as tricky as a—"

I seized Harriet Taylor by the elbow and propelled her around me with an ungentlemanly shove.

"Detective Goodpasture, meet Miss Taylor. She's Liz's fourth cousin."

The poor redheaded cutie was off balance. She collapsed against FitzHugh and made him stumble. He banged into the officer with the cut and the cymbal. This worthy also went off balance and in the course of his flailing, struck one of his comrades in the nose with the cymbal's edge.

There was a *whaaang*, assorted curses, oaths from FitzHugh, a flurry of petticoats as Harriet Taylor tumbled atop half the force, and I shot like the proverbial bat for the fire door, hoping against hope Delilah was still all right.

By the time I'd raced down one floor, FitzHugh and his minions were charging after me.

I zipped along fast as my undersized legs would carry me, caroming off the walls at every turn. As I hit the landing midway between twelve and the floor above, I could hear FitzHugh bellowing, "After him! This time we'll make the charges stick!"

The oversized brogans of his troops added a thundering emphasis.

Panting, I pulled up just inside the fire door which opened on to twelve. The door had a glass panel at eye level. Your eye level, not mine. I craned up. Like a snippet from a surrealistic flick, a face whizzed by on the other side.

"Delilah!" I yelled.

Instantly her alarmed face was replaced by the puss of Buster Beemis. Apparently he was hustling her down the hallway to the elevators. Buster saw me. His eyebrows elevated. I then got another appetizing view of the front end of a pistol. Buster aimed at the window and fired.

Now once in a while my less than heroic stature can be a boon. It was then. The small window exploded inward at me, a Niagara of glass. The stairwell filled with a cannonading thunder. The bullet would have removed my head, fired at dead-on range as it was, had I not instinctively stopped craning and bounced back down flat on my heels. The slug blasted over my head and ate a round hole in the cinder block wall behind me.

I counted to five, which was all the time I could afford. The law minions were falling all over themselves coming down the stairs one flight above. I rolled my shoulder and hit the door's panic bar.

As I tumbled into the hall, I dragged Spiggs' cannon out of my pocket. An elderly maintenance person in blue coveralls quivered against the wall opposite. He was posed beside a small, wheeled cart carrying several buckets of soapy water and a couple of mops with heads made of foot-long twists of black yarn.

"Don't shoot! I'm eligible for a pension in six months!" he piped as I swept the hall with the muzzle of the rod.

Tomblike and empty as my hopes for saving Delilah, that hall was. I ran down to the bank of elevators. Over the right-hand one, the indicator was flicking downward. I watched the dancing green light move from right to left. It had to be Beemis, with Delilah in tow.

How would he try to escape? The lobby? I thumbed the call button for the adjoining car. The one I was watching stopped at the mezzanine. A second later the elevator I'd called arrived. By that time FitzHugh and the minions were boiling in from the stair.

"Stand still, Havoc," Goodpasture warned. "You're finished."

"Or washed, up, as the case may be," cried I, taking two

giant steps and giving the wheeled clean-up cart a push with my right foot. The detergent juggernaut started to roll.

"Watch it, watch it for God's sakes!" Goodpasture bellowed, trying to dodge back out of the way.

I leaped for the elevator, whose automatic doors had opened and were closing again. As they shut with me inside I had a fleeting glimpse of the clean-up cart striking Goodpasture at the calves. Buckets flew. Gobs of suds erupted. Goodpasture's right foot went into one pail of the stuff. Then the scene was mercifully hidden by the closing doors.

Down and down went the elevator. I wiped my forehead and hoped the coppers wouldn't think of trying to stop the cage with the call button.

Fifth floor.

Third.

Second.

Mezzanine coming up. I wrapped clammy fingers tight around the butt of Spiggs' cannon as the elevator sighed to a stop. I hit the Door Open button with my free hand and held it down. I heard a familiar voice cursing somewhere. I peeked out warily.

Both sides of the hall were lined with an assortment of small shops. All were dark except for the drug store and the barber shop. Inside this latter, another lonely maintenance person was sweeping the floor under the white glare of fluorescent lights.

Further down, I espied Beemis. He was attempting to jimmy open a metal door which led, I presumed, to a fire escape. Beemis clutched his cannon in one hand and Delilah's wrists in the other. This meant that he was forced to work with elbows and knees, no easy task.

"Damn thing! Damn thing's jammed—"

Limp as an unset hairdo, Delilah Somerset spotted me over Beemis's shoulder. I tried to whip up the gun muzzle to indicate silence. Too late.

"Oh, Mr. Havoc!"

That put the grease on the griddle, okay. Beemis turned around and gaped. He whipped up his cannon and fired. I darted back inside the elevator as the slug spanged off the jamb.

Beemis's head swiveled like a lighthouse beacon. I swallowed hard and headed out for him, crouched over.

He wanted sanctuary. He dragged Delilah with him, diving into the first available open door. It happened to belong to the barbershop.

"Which way out of here?" he yelled at the petrified maintenance person.

"Ain't any way out of here, mister," the kid yelled back, cowering against the wall. I slid up past the shop's big windows and crawled inside. I went on all fours behind the first big barber chair, a black vinyl and chrome monster which fortunately hid my small person. I held my breath.

"Havoc?" Beemis wheezed like a vacuum cleaner. "Havoc, I know you're in here. Either I walk out free and clear or this sweetheart I'm holding gets plugged."

He sounded both scared and desperate. I couldn't decide whether he'd carry through on the threat or cave in, so I tried a little psychological warfare.

"You'd better not hurt her. I kid you not. The police are in the building. Right now they're on their way down here to—"

Blammo! Beemis fired. The slug hit the top of the chair behind which I was crouched. The chair revolved under the impact of the bullet, and I nearly got decapitated by the whirling brake lever that projected a good foot from the chair mount.

As the chair spun round and round I decided I had to pull a dodge. Up on the counter behind the spinning chair I noticed a hot lather machine. I slipped off my left shoe and flung it against the shop's opposite wall. Beemis fired another shot in that direction. The moment his gun blammed, I was up and hoping to mercy the hot lather machine was charged.

The machine was equipped with a sort of long, flexible hose that was attached to the box proper. I hit the machine's *On* switch but instead of turning it right off again like barbers do, I left it on and whipped the hose around. At the back of the shop Buster Beemis huddled against the wall with Delilah pulled up tight as a shield. When he saw me, he slid his gun hand forward around her waist. I aimed the hot lather hose and prayed.

A long, gobby squirt of the stuff sailed through the air and hit him in the map. Buster exclaimed in rage. His gun hand jerked. Another shot cracked the counter mirror inches from my right ear.

"Run, Delilah," I hollered. "Kick him in the shins and run."

That was all she needed. She gave it to him hard with the old step-on-the-foot gambit. Face covered with lather, Beemis let out another piteous cry as Delilah elbowed him in the ribs. He doubled over. Delilah dodged into cover behind the nearest barber chair. Racket in the corridor filtered into the shop.

Trying to sound tough, I said, "Put the gun on the floor, Beemis. I mean it."

I had Spiggs's gun in my right hand and the hot lather hose in the other. I'd neglected to turn this latter off, with the result that the area between me and the rear of the shop was filled with piles of the stuff. I heard footsteps clomping into the shop entrance. I didn't turn around because I was watching Beemis. Suddenly he lost all his fight.

"Oh damn it," he said, "I shouldn't of listened to Al. I should of gone on collecting my unemployment insurance. Okay, okay, I give up." He threw his gun into a mound of hot lather building up on the tiles.

"Hands up, Havoc," exclaimed a voice to my rear.

Now this so startled me that I spun around. And of course so did the hot lather hose. There was Detective Goodpasture, pistol in mitt and soapsuds still clinging to his garments. A long, gooey stream of hot lather arched through the air.

Guess where it landed.

"Oh you little *bastard*. Oh how I wish this were a police state. Then I could tear you apart the way you deserve!"

I was attempting to turn off the hot lather device as the law dogs surged around Goodpasture. One of them paused long enough to offer his chief a hanky with which to wipe off the white mess covering Goodpasture from eyebrows to foulard.

Delilah came limping down the aisle toward me. I smiled at her while I reclaimed my tossed shoe. In truth, there was no damn thing in the world worth grinning about.

"Did he hurt you, Delilah?"

"Well, he twisted my arm a few times, but—" The brave little smile cracked. She leaned against me, sobbing. "Oh, you're the bravest man, Mr. Havoc. You saved my life. I should have stayed home tonight and done my homework like Daddy said."

Goodpasture pulled us apart in a most ungentlemanly way. "He is not a brave man. He is a rotten, peace-disturbing, no-good crook, and I'm going to put him away for life. All right, Havoc. Take your sticky little hands off that girl and stick 'em straight out in front of you for the cuffs."

"FitzHugh," I said wearily, "your cigar has gone out."

So it had. It had hot lather all over it. But that didn't

147

matter to him now. He was wrestling with a pair of manacles that he was about to slap onto my wrists.

"Stand back, Miss. This man's dangerous—"

Delilah wiped away tears. "He is not. He's very courageous."

"Courageous! Why, the things I could tell you—but never mind. What's your name?"

"Somerset, Delilah Somerset."

Then she blinked back a few more tears, as if she had just remembered something. She stepped defensively to my side. "Officer, I said my name is Somerset."

"I don't care if your name is Princess Ziggaritz of the Aztecs, this guy is going to jail, and if I have anything to do with it, he won't get out until—uh, what was that name? *Somerset?*"

"My father is Harve O. Somerset," Delilah said with what I must admit was an air of cool menace. "The chairman of the Citizens' Police Procedure Review Committee."

"Oh yeah," I said. "They review the cases of officers accused of brutality."

"Oh my God in heaven," said Goodpasture.

"Detective, oh Detective!"

We all turned. Into the lather-smeared shop waltzed this managerial type with a flower in his lapel and his hair rumpled. He also sported a neat black eye. Right behind him came Harriet Taylor, whose face was whiter than the lather all over the joint.

It was white with fear.

All of a sudden, what had begun to look like a rap well dodged took its last, worst turn. The managerial type piped: "Detective, I'm Mr. Carrothers, the assistant manager. What have you been doing? The riot out in front has gotten completely out of hand. Those—*youths* are ripping up the potted plants which we installed in tubs on the sidewalk at great expense and—and now, this phone call—"

Harriet Taylor pushed a lock of copper hair back off her forehead and shoved Carrothers aside.

"What this dithering fool is trying to say is that my boys— two fine, decent young kids—are going to lose their lives if somebody doesn't do something. That gangster who had us at gunpoint woke up."

I groaned. I had totally forgotten Spiggs, sleeping up on fifteen. Harriet flashed me a desperate glance. Then she said to Goodpasture: "Mr. Havoc here took Spiggs's gun. But Spiggs says he's got a knife."

"He does," said Beemis. "A real pig-sticker."

Harriet went on, "He phoned the desk just a minute ago. He's got Manny and Maury and he's taking them down in the elevator to the garage. He said if he couldn't get his car out of here, and get away with nobody stopping him, he was going to knife one or both of the boys. Kill them. He said if he saw a single policeman with a gun, one of those boys would die."

A sob cracked her voice. "Somebody say something! Manny and Maury are my responsibility. I don't want them hurt."

With scant hope, I said, "Probably he's bluffing."

Up piped Buster Beemis again, limply in custody of two officers: "Al ain't kidding if he says that. He'll shoot 'em if he says he'll shoot 'em."

Everybody's eyeballs swiveled toward Beemis. From the sad expression on the hood's map, it was plain that he was telling the truth.

Harriet Taylor glanced down at the ball watch pinned to her blouse. "He'll be leaving the fifteenth floor in another two minutes."

Now I could see that the two rock-and-rollers were more

than simply a meal ticket to her. Her eyes filled up with tears. "Look, he told me the time specifically so nobody would get in his way. Don't everybody gape! You may not like the kind of music the boys play, but they're just *kids*. Nice kids. There's no telling what that monster will do if he gets out of the hotel with them. He might take them to some deserted place and—and—" She covered her face.

With a sadistic flourish, FitzHugh Goodpasture flicked a gob of hot lather off his cheeks. He peered at me malevolently.

"All right, Havoc. You started this. Finish it. The gunsel said he didn't want to see any cops. We'll take his word for it. We won't let him see any cops if it might get those boys killed. We'll let him see somebody else."

Goodpasture indicated the open shop door. "You're such a big fat hero, you pull the chestnuts out of the fire. Go save 'em."

"But—" I began.

Then I happened to glance at Harriet Taylor. Her eyes were practically dead level with mine. Those dark eyes were tear-loaded, and full of hope, too. I think the dolly actually believed I could do it.

Still, she gave me an out: "It really isn't Mr. Havoc's responsibility, officer. After all, he and his daughter—"

"Why, she isn't his daughter."

"She isn't?"

Goodpasture waved. "My God no. I have no idea how they got mixed up together, but this little hustler is a bachelor. And unless he can pull this one off, I swear I'll put him away for ever and ever, Review Committee or no Review Committee."

"FitzHugh," I said, "you're just trying to throw your authority around."

"That's right, I am."

"You're dodging your duty."

He worked his lather-doused cigar from side to side in his jaw.

"Maybe. But maybe I'm also making a crazy kind of sense. You see, Havoc, strange as it may be for you to believe with your warped little mind, I don't want the deaths of those two kids on my hands either. All I've got to work with is my boys. Spiggs will spot them right off. But I've got you. So it's got to be you."

Mother, what a twisted turn of fate!

Behind the animosity, the I'll-eat-you-for-breakfast glare in Goodpasture's eye lurked, I do believe, a hope that I might be able to pull it off. Harriet Taylor had given me the same sort of glance.

Now she looked somewhat baffled by the revelation that Delilah and I were not relatives. She consulted her watch nervously. Her voice sounded harsh in the silence:

"He'll be starting down now."

An insane but typically Havocian plan suggested itself. Quickly I briefed Goodpasture, who was forced to suffer the humiliation of agreeing to follow my orders.

I instructed him to have his lads watch the elevators and note which cage descended, ostensibly containing Al Spiggs and his prisoners. Then, in half a minute, the coppers were to pile aboard the unused cage and direct it to the basement level. At that point they were to hold it in the basement, with fifteen hands on the Door Closed button. They weren't to spring that door until they heard me yell. I headed for the barber shop exit.

Goodpasture said, "While all this is going on, Havoc, where are you going?"

"Probably to the funeral parlor."

Everybody certainly had a peck of faith in me. I merely had

leaden sensations in my mid-section as I headed for the nearest broom closet.

When the problem is unconventional, unconventional solutions are called for, right? Such as the seeking out of the maintenance closet on the mezzanine floor.

Inside of it, amongst the buckets and the bottles of floor wax, I discovered what I needed. Namely, one of those mops I had seen earlier, the kind made of foot-long twists of black yarn.

Hastily I unscrewed the wooden handle and with the mop head tucked beneath my arm, I hotfooted for the stairs to the lobby.

As I banged down the risers, a frightful pandemonium assaulted my ears. All available personnel of The Dayview Motor Inn, together with a number of blue boys, had linked arms inside the glass doors and were attempting to withstand the pushing, shoving, driving assault of several hundred jolly teens who were still engaged in good, clean rioting outside. The teens were determined to push open the doors and enter.

Even as I watched, interesting items whizzed back and forth outside the doors. Those zany kids were throwing things such as a police car fender, three feminine undergarments, and the remains of the trunk of one of the motel's tubbed shrubs, of which Carrothers had complained.

All the persons attempting to hold the doors fast from inside had their backs to me. Consequently, no one inside the lobby saw me pop into view and strike a pose on the staircase. I draped the mop atop my skull in a reasonable approximation of the hairstyle of The Moles.

Then I started waving to get attention.

One teenager pushing against the glass spotted me and began pointing.

I tossed up both my hands and waved harder. "Hi, hi there, fans! Hello, hi!"

Through the glass screams arose.

"Ooooo, *ooooo,* it's Manny!"

"No, no, it's Maury, I recognize the dimple."

Several of the linked-arms defenders turned their heads. They looked horrified, especially when I made a sweeping, grandiose gesture that pantomimically said to the hopped-up youths, *Come on in!*

Against the response of the youths to that invitation, no flesh and blood could stand. The doors bulged inward. A desk clerk piped up in panic that his cholesterol couldn't stand it. Then the dam broke.

A bouffant-hairdo dolly dodged under the linked arms. Another slipped through. Another. The howling increased.

A blue boy was toppled, cursing. I waited until the first of the charging throng was halfway across the lobby. Then I grabbed the stair rail and vaulted over.

I landed with a jolt on the stairs that led down from the lobby to the basement meeting room area. The kids came caterwauling after, crowding, pushing, shoving, squealing.

I zipped around a corner. Ahead, a small green illuminated sign over a door displayed an arrow and the word *Garage.* I headed for it, stumbled, and experienced a moment of panic as, behind me, six dozen open-jawed teenage faces loomed, hands stretched out questing for a piece of my hair, suit material, flesh or what have you.

Scrambling up only inches ahead of the pack, I shouldered open the steel door to the garage. I darted behind a cement pillar and ditched my mop by throwing it away.

The kids boiled into the garage. Headlights flared. Around the end of a row of parked cars whizzed a battered sedan. The kids poured into the aisle.

"Where'd he go?"

"Where'd Manny go?"

"No, no, it was Maury, I want a piece of his T-shirt."

Behind the windshield of the sedan, the blurred, bleary face of Al Spiggs peered out. Instead of police minions, he saw scores of wildly shrieking youths blocking his path. He slammed on the brakes. That's when I jumped from behind the pillar and whipped open the door on his side.

I had a quick glimpse of two dark, trussed forms on the floorboards in back. Spiggs's jaw hung down as he surveyed the teenagers gathering to charge the car. Then he recognized me as I grabbed for his neck.

His eyes went nasty. His right hand snatched up a knife lying on the seat beside him. He whipped his right hand across. The knife came arcing straight for my face.

There was one thing to do. I hurled myself backward out of the way of that flying blade that would rip me open if it connected. Spiggs leaned half out of the car to slash me. His arm stretched out through the space between the front edge of the door and the doorframe.

Wham, I kicked the door shut hard.

Spiggs squealed. The pain from the closing door made his fingers open. I kicked the fallen knife under the car, jerked the door open and let Spiggs have it in the puss with all the power in my arms.

"Midget, huh?" *Kapow.* "Shrimp, huh?" *Slammo.* Without his lethal weapon, he had practically no fight, and I had plenty stored up as a result of all of his insults. I was clobbering him royally when I felt portions of my Brooks jacket beginning to disappear.

"Save me two inches, Florence!"

The teenagers were upon me.

154

"Goodpasture!" I bawled. "Goodpasture—*now!*"

What it amounted to was a rescue mission, as I had planned. But those who got rescued were myself and Al Spiggs. The ones from whom we got rescued were those happy, fun-loving American kids. Before it was all over, fresh reinforcements arriving from the riot squad restored order with a few whacks on the collective noggins. I barely had a loincloth left to cover me. Al Spiggs was down on the floorboards in the front seat of his car, weeping and begging piteously to be taken off to a nice, restful cell.

The funny thing was, the kids never discovered The Moles in the back of the car.

Perhaps that was because they were too busy ripping my garments to shreds, not to mention those of Detective Goodpasture.

Who started the rumor circulating in the melee that FitzHugh was The Moles' musical arranger I, of course, do not know.

Of course . . .

Washington and A. Lincoln stared patriotically down from beneath glass in the otherwise undistinguished green-painted cubicle that FitzHugh called home. "I want to thank you for saving my daughter," said Harve O. Somerset.

He pumped my hand while I attempted to reciprocate and untangle my paw from the sleeve of a bathrobe that evidently belonged to a six foot ten inch center on the police department basketball team. In the crook of Harve's other arm, Delilah beamed, safe again.

"I want to say that this little guy really swings," said a rather pale-looking Manny. Or was it Maury?

"I want to second that," said the other one, whoever the hell he was.

155

"I want to thank you personally too, Johnny." Harriet Taylor pressed up against me in the crush of reporters, photographers, and gawking bulls who had seethed into the office following our arrival. Sweet little Harriet. A delectable morsel just my size. And she let me know, hormonally speaking, that she got the message.

She bussed my cheek and whispered, "And when I say I want to thank you personally, I mean personally. At the motel. As soon as I get the boys safely tucked in their room after the concert." Her dark eyes sparkled with a wicked promise.

"I want to say it will be my Freudian pleasure," I said.

"I want to take up lettuce farming," said FitzHugh Goodpasture sourly.

Not, I will admit, without some reason.

The Man Who Wanted to Be in the Movies

George Rollo stepped away from the mirror and surveyed his scrupulous grooming. His hair was neatly brushed back, his suit freshly pressed, and his maroon tie with the white polka dots was artfully knotted. His face was almost eclipsed by the carefully planned sartorial perfection.

George Rollo was in love. He happened to be in love with a young woman who received his attention with reserve. But he went right on pursuing her, doing anything within his power to win her affections. Because of her, he dressed carefully.

He picked up the expensive box of candy secured from the drug store. He was able to afford a large box because he was a pharmacist in the drug store and could get the candy wholesale.

He locked the door of his room soundly behind him and clattered down the stairs. On the second landing a young and rather pretty woman with big amber eyes stood leaning on the doorjamb, next to a sign that announced, *Yolanda Fox, Licensed Thaumaturgist, Helpful and Benevolent Spells of All Types.*

"Hello, George," she said warmly as he came banging down the stairway.

"Oh. Hello, Yolanda, how are you?" His voice was strained, absent.

A large furry white thing rushed past the girl's legs and began lapping affectionately at the young man's shoes.

"Down, Faust," Yolanda said sharply. "Come here."

The familiar, who resembled a large and pugnacious bull

dog with amber eyes quite like the girl's, crept back to a position at the side of his mistress, whining helplessly.

"Going out?" Yolanda asked yearningly.

"Yes," George replied in a nervous tone, "with Mabel."

"Oh." Sadness dropped like a curtain across her face.

"Well," he said nervously, "well, I guess I'd better be going."

He hurried off down the stairs. Yolanda caught a glimpse of the candy box and her amber eyes narrowed with faint jealous anger.

Faust growled, displaying bulldog teeth.

She shrugged then, as if winning out against an impulse to injure George, who shot a hasty glance at her from the bottom of the stairs just as she returned to her apartment.

Out in the street, George shivered. He knew Yolanda liked him, even though he had a distinct fear of witches. Even white witches licensed by the State Thaumaturgy Board. They could only conjure helpful spirits or make hexes to ward off illness. The law said they could do no more, but George was certain many of them had darker, half-forgotten powers.

He put Yolanda from his thoughts and hurried on down the street.

Miss Mabel Fry sat in her dirty armchair, surrounded by piles of magazines. Their glazed covers blanketed the rugs, made colorful landscapes even in the small dinette. The walls of the apartment were covered with pictures of male movie idols wearing hound's tooth jackets or holding a golf club or smiling at starlets.

The doorbell cracked with a noise of sad disrepair.

Mabel reached for another peppermint, shoved it into her red mouth and went on reading her magazine: *It's the Simple*

*Home Girl For Me, by Rodney de Cord, Rising Young Parafilm
Star.*

The doorbell cracked a second time.

Mabel lifted her large body and moved disconsolately to
the alcove. She opened the door and said in a bored manner,
"Oh. George."

"Hello . . . uh . . . Mabel."

He burst eagerly into the room, presenting his candy. She
accepted it with mumbled thanks. She was a perfume clerk in
a local department store, but she didn't much like the idea of
accepting candy from an ordinary druggist.

"Where are we going tonight?" she asked, slipping into her
coat.

"Anyplace," George replied casually. "There's a fine concert at the Music Hall."

She ignored him. "The Royal has a wonderful new picture, *I'll Slay My Love*, with Todd St. Bartholomew. He's so
masculine. When he played a private detective and slapped
Lona Lawndale in *Bodies to Burn*, I just couldn't stand it, it
was so thrilling."

George didn't argue. "Anything you say," he mumbled.

As they walked to the theatre she babbled about the latest
gossip from Hollywood. Who was marrying whom. Who was
divorcing whom. Who was in bed with whom when who came
home with who's perfume all over him. George listened with
resignation.

Mabel waited under the glaring lights of the marquee
while he bought the tickets. She rolled her eyes ecstatically at
Todd St. Bartholomew staring belligerently from the poster,
gun in hand. A caption balloon from his lithographed lips announced, *I'll Slay My Love*.

As they passed through the door, Terry Silver, the aging
owner of the theatre, waved to Mabel.

"Evening," he called affably. "Next week we're showing *Husbands and Paramours* with Michael Yarven."

"Ooooooo," Mabel exclaimed loudly. "How wonderful."

She allowed George to take her hand as they approached the main aisle. Just then a young man in a bright red sport coat sauntered over.

" 'Lo, Mabel," said Bertie Wallen.

George swore in a whisper. Bertie Wallen was a bit actor on local television shows. He dressed and looked like a movie star.

"Thought I might find you here," Bertie said to Mabel. "Got big news. Friend of mine in Hollywood just wired me that I should fly out there right away. Metropole wants to test me."

Mabel squealed with delight.

George stood by impotently, glaring at Bertie as if he were a liar.

"Like to see the wire?" Bertie asked in broadly humorous tones.

"Sure, Bertie," Mabel cooed.

"Come on out to my car. Only take a minute."

Mabel started away, then turned to George. "Be a sweetie and go inside and wait for me. I'll be right in. The usual seats."

He started to protest feebly, hesitated, and stumbled into the auditorium. He found the customary seats, saving the adjacent chair for Mabel.

For two hours he sat woodenly, alone, watching Todd St. Bartholomew consuming quarts of alcohol and being pounded by assorted mobsters. George rather enjoyed the picture. One of Hollywood's better character actors, a man named Tab something or other, played a kindly old judge. George liked Tab whatever-it-was, although he doddered a bit. He must have been at least seventy-five.

He had a sympathetic rugged face. He did not impress George as a professional lover.

George tapped on Yolanda Fox's door at eleven-thirty that evening.

The door opened after a moment and she invited him in, surprised and pleased. Slipping out of a black robe and erasing a chalk pentagram from the floor, she turned up the lights.

"Just practicing a hay fever prevention spell," she explained. "Pollen season coming on."

He sank down on her sofa, staring moodily at the floor. Faust nuzzled his leg.

"Yolanda," he said as she bustled out of the kitchen with two steaming cups of tea, "you're the one for me."

She almost dropped the cups. Quickly she set them down and hurried to his side. "Oh, George . . ."

"Yes sir," he added gloomily, "you're the one to help me get Mabel."

"Oh."

Her face smoothed out. She seemed quite calm. She served the tea and inquired in a helpful tone, "What can I do?"

"I love Mabel Fry. I'll do anything to make her love me. But she . . . well . . . she likes movie stars. Isn't there any kind of a spell to make me lucky?" He paused, deliberated and plunged on. "Can't you get me into the movies?"

"I don't know," she answered, thinking.

"I'll pay anything," he offered. "That is, anything I can."

"It won't be necessary to pay me," she replied carefully. "I'll be glad to help you. In fact, I think I can get you into the movies tonight."

"You can?" He was startled.

"Certainly." She picked up a valise, began to stuff it with the paraphernalia of demonology. "But we must have the right atmosphere."

"Atmosphere?"

"A theatre. The Royal is near. I guarantee that before morning you'll be in the movies. Come, Faust."

They hurried through the dark streets.

The Royal was a mound of shadow, closed for the night. The street was relatively deserted. Only a drunk reeled from a cocktail lounge opposite the theatre.

"Sssssh," Yolanda cautioned, finger to lips. "We've got to get inside."

They crept through the vacant lot adjoining the theatre. Before the brick wall, Yolanda halted and made several passes in the air, murmuring something about Asmodeus. A cold wind shoved George forward through gray fog.

He looked about. They were in the middle of the darkened theatre lobby.

Faust yipped with satanic glee. His large amber eyes glowed with strange delight. Yolanda's eyes glowed in the same fashion. George didn't notice.

They made their way down one aisle of the auditorium. Above them, the screen was a formless patch of silver-white.

Yolanda opened her valise, pulling forth her black robe. She lit two small braziers that gave off pungent fumes. She drew circles on the rug, remembering all of the bits of black magic the law had forced her to forget.

George watched the screen in fascination, because if Yolanda proved successful, he would be up there, and soon!

Yolanda moaned and waved her hands in the air and chanted. The braziers smoldered with oily bronze fire. Faust capered up and down the aisle, barking. And then Yolanda tapped George on the shoulder. Her face was illuminated by some unholy light.

"All right, George," she whispered. "Here you go."

He was strangely lifted.

Yolanda erased her marks, put out her braziers, repacked her valise and departed. Faust cavorted behind her, bulldog face aglow with strange humor.

For a long time George Rollo didn't know what had happened, or where he was. If this was the way to get into the movies, it was certainly a peculiar way.

When he tried to move his hands or feet he found it was impossible. Legs too. That is, he amended in his thoughts, he would have been, if he could have felt his arms or legs.

Everything was strangely dark. Then suddenly it was as though a curtain had been swept away from his eyes. He saw rows of white staring faces. Two of them belonged to Mabel Fry and Bertie Wallen. It began to dawn on him just what Yolanda had done. Blinding lights hit him. He screamed.

The only sound that came out was a ruffle of drums and a snatch of vaguely familiar music.

He wasn't George Rollo.

God in heaven!... he wasn't even a man. He was flat... and from one end of him to the other, in gigantic letters, he said IN CINEMASCOPE ...

Dr. Sweetkill

For three weeks Nick Lamont heard nothing from Wilburforce. For three weeks he drank too much, stayed out too late in the Soho clubs, and stared with eyes that grew more gritty with each successive hung-over morning at the credit notices piling up in the day's post.

Then finally, one drizzly evening when Nick had touched his last friend for a few pounds, he was forced to hang around the flat because he was broke. That was when Wilburforce rang him up.

"Kemptons Luggage has a little task for you, Nicky," Wilburforce said. Kemptons Luggage was a shadow firm in a shadow office. It was the cover behind which Wilburforce and his counterparts in British intelligence farmed out their nasty work to free-lances like Nick. "Of course, this is rather a take-it-or-leave-it proposition."

Nick Lamont kicked one of his expensive calfskin lounging slippers halfway across the room at the grate. He wished he could smash his fist into Wilburforce's white and narrow face.

Take it or leave it. Did the bastard think he could do anything except take it after the Tenderly mess? He was nearly washed up in the trade as it was.

"I'll meet you," Nick said after a moment. "Five tomorrow at the usual place?"

"Sooner. Luncheon." Wilburforce mentioned a posh grille. "Actually, Nicky, I didn't think you'd hesitate as long as you did. I'm glad to hear you're so enthusiastic about working again."

Nick Lamont's dark-burned face turned white around the edges of the lips. "I haven't said I'd take the thing. I'll listen."

Wilburforce clucked. "Try to control that red temper of yours, please. You're hardly in favor. If you want to keep on working for the firm, you'll pick up our little—ah—sales errand and relish it."

Nick's epithet was short.

Nick had made dozens of pleasant acquaintances among the British in his years in London. Not friends, really. You never could afford friends in the trade. But Wilburforce was another case. Wilburforce disliked Americans. He disliked reasonably competent Americans like Nick even more. Nick had done some jobs well. But now Wilburforce had no reason to conceal his antipathy. As a result of the blunder in Gibraltar, Nick's stock as a free-lance was sharply down.

Wilburforce said: "Am I to interpret that filthy language to mean you are interested?"

Across the flat on the writing desk lay the bills. Nick wanted the new silver-gray Jag so badly he could taste it.

And there was Tenderly. Tenderly, and the gun in Nick's hand in the frowsy little room upstairs over the restaurant.

"I'll be there tomorrow," he said.

"When you arrive," Wilburforce said, "try to be civil. This is not the state of Ohio, Nicky. Nor are you the muscular hero athlete who can dictate his own contract. We shall be writing the contract this trip, and you shall accept our terms, or none at all. Good evening."

Cursing, Nick slammed the dead phone down.

He walked to the windows opening onto the terrace. Rain dribbled down the glass. When he turned round to fix a whiskey-soda from the liquor cabinet, he passed the mantel mirror. He avoided glancing into it. He knew what he would see if he did; a big, husky man now turned thirty-five, and a little heavier than he should be.

But flat in the gut. Hard. His hair was still wild, curling black, though it was turning a little gray around the ears. Occasionally his hands shook when he put a match to a cigarette. But the eyes still had the old temper-spark on occasion.

While the London rain pelted, he drank three whisky-sodas and then fell into bed, hoping for no dreams. He wanted to sleep soundly, in preparation for meeting Icy-Guts, as Wilburforce was called behind his back.

But he dreamed.

He dreamed intensely, vividly, yet disjointedly. There was the stadium in Ohio under a crisp purple and gold late afternoon sky. The stands thundered. Women's faces shone here and there, red with screaming. Suddenly, just before he made the field goal he heard an amplifier roar, *"Nick the Kick does it again!"*

Yet at the dream-moment when his foot should have connected with the ball and sent it sailing between the uprights, he was in the room in Gibraltar.

Nick had been flown over to bring back one Wing Commander Saltenham, who had, according to the evidence, been jobbing copies of an air defense network alarm system to a notorious middleman on Gib. Wilburforce's section wanted Saltenham quietly withdrawn from circulation, in order to subject him to extended interrogation at a country estate discreetly maintained by the section in Kent. Along with Nick had gone one of Wilburforce's own operatives, an aging, modestly attired clerk type named Arthur Tenderly.

On Gib, Nick ran Saltenham to earth in the room above the restaurant. The Wing Commander was bouncing a bawdy little girl with Moorish eyes and nothing on except several cheap rings. Nick threw her out, aimed his pistol at Saltenham and told him they were departing via a special charter flight that would take off shortly.

Tenderly had knocked, entering with hardly a sound. The plane was standing by, he reported. Saltenham knew he was finished. Fear coated his cheeks with acrid sweat. Yet he had guts.

Either he would be carried out dead, he announced, or he would not go. In other words, Nick would have to use the gun. Saltenham was snide about it, too. In a physical go, even with two against one, the Wing Commander promised to knock their jawbones down their throats. He looked as though he meant it. And he had one advantage—his correct guess that Nick Lamont and Tenderly had no orders to kill.

That didn't prevent Nick from going at the man with the raw sight-end of his pistol. He charged in, trying to counter-buffalo the suspected spy with a slash of the muzzle. Arthur Tenderly disapproved of Nick's gambit. What he didn't know was that Nick had, regrettably, lost his temper under Saltenham's snide needling. Tenderly chose the moment to intervene. He seized Nick's arm to prevent serious damage being done by the rather notorious American.

"I'm running this and I'll run it my way," Nick shouted, trying to shake Tenderly's pale, small grip off his forearm. In that moment, as Nick gave his right arm a wrench to free it, the pistol, off safety, exploded.

The Wing Commander tried to escape through the window. Nick pumped one bullet into his right calf because it was already too late to do the task without a racket. Forty-five minutes later in the naval base hospital, Arthur Tenderly died of a gunshot wound from the first bullet.

After Nick had returned to London with his prisoner, his stock had plunged. He was questioned, requestioned and finally cleared. But the phone failed to ring—until tonight.

And now, in the tortured dream that brought him wide

167

awake to hear the midnight toll of bells, he somehow still saw Tenderly at his elbow. The gun had exploded. Tenderly was falling back, aghast. Somewhere an announcer thundered, *"The Kick does it again!"*

Two more drinks managed to send Nick back into a dull, thick slumber.

At 11:30 the next day he took a cab to the Castlereagh Grille. Smoking in the cab, he tried to think back. Where had he gone wrong?

He had started out fine in college. All-American. Some said he was the most powerful, accurate kicker ever seen on a football gridiron. Then came the Army. A stint with Intelligence. He didn't lack brains, and he preferred to be of some damn use, instead of playing ball for one of the base squads.

His Army record hadn't been bad. Afterward, he had no trouble landing on a pro club. For three years The Kick made them stand up and yell themselves silly.

Meanwhile a taste for good living built and built. It included liquor. The liquor unlocked the temper—and that led to the awful night he wrecked four rooms in a hotel. After the team failed to renew his contract, he drifted to Europe. He'd grown to like a fast, expensive life. And rather quickly he found a way to earn money.

For a time he sold his services to the Allies: NATO, the French secret service twice. Then he was invited to London, with a pretty good guarantee of income as a free-lance. The work was sometimes dirty; the trade was never clean. But he enjoyed the cards and the wine and the girls the money bought. So long as he checked the temper, he was all right.

Then, in Gib, one wild swipe of his arm had exploded a gun and killed a man. And the phone hadn't run for a long time.

Well-dressed in a Saville Row suite and an expensive rain-proof, Nick climbed out of the taxi in front of the Castlereagh Grille. He hurried inside. He didn't look like a man who was up against the fact that his luck had run out. But in the trade, you kept a hard face.

Three flights up, down a corridor and through a succession of small private dining rooms, he came to the elegant, thick-walled chamber with steel behind every inch of patterned wallpaper. Here executives of Kemptons Luggage now and then met for "conferences." Here, by a dim little table lamp that threw a shadow of the senior agent's bald head onto the wall, Nick lunched with Icy-Guts.

Wilburforce picked at his chop. "Because of the Tenderly business, Nicky, you damn well may never get another assignment." He smiled. He had a gold tooth, which glowed. "Unless you take this one."

"How much is the fee?" Nick felt sarcastic. "Half the usual?"

"Twice," Wilburforce said.

Nick's scalp crawled. The jokes were over.

Thrusting aside his willow-patterned plate, Wilburforce began to speak in his flat, dry manner.

"You will be assigned a target which is a perfectly legitimate and prosperous chemical corporation near Munich. Chemotex Worldwide G.m.b.h. Some of our lads working in the East, on the other side of the Curtain, have come up with the news that while the factory is indeed legitimate, its department of basic research—a separate ring of the home building—is in fact a thriving laboratory doing research on nerve gas and bacteriological agents."

"Who runs the outfit?"

"The firm's director is Herr Doktor Franz Staub. We suspect he's sympathetic with the East and that, at very least, the secret laboratory has his tacit approval. But he's small fry.

169

The laboratory's director is much more important. His name is Yonov." Wilburforce glanced across the spotless linen, pointedly. "Dr. Genther Yonov."

An ugly memory ticked in Nick's mind. "I saw a dossier a year ago. The Athens thing. Something he'd sold. A compound. They had a code name for him."

Wilburforce nodded. "Yes. Dr. Sweetkill."

A long silence. The shadow of Wilburforce's head loomed malignantly.

"Dr. Sweetkill, the seller-to-all," he said at length. "Pacific yet ghastly death available on the open market. Almost uniformly, he seems to sell to the East. A filthy man. We understand Yonov has delivered to the East the formula for a new, quite deadly nerve gas code labeled Pax 11-A."

Nick lighted one of his cigarettes that cost twice as much as the ordinary kind. "And I'm supposed to do the old formula-stealing bit?"

"Already done," Wilburforce replied. "By our lads in the East. The mechanics needn't concern you. We have Pax 11-A, right enough. But now we have another signal from Top Planning. The Yonov gas and germ factory is to be destroyed. Blown up, obliterated. This will represent a considerable setback for the other side. Years, perhaps. And you, dear Nicky, win the choice assignment. You are to penetrate the basic research laboratory within the Chemotex headquarters, and finish it off."

Slowly, Nick blew out smoke.

"How do I get in? Knock politely?"

Once again Nick found himself amazed by the thoroughness of Wilburforce's preparations. Despite being a bastard, the man was good. There would be a six-week training period in England. During that time Nick would be melded into the personality of Nickolas Lamont of Ridgefield, New

Jersey, a young man with an impeccable record in international sales for a leading U.S. chemical firm. No relation to the American football player who enjoyed some vogue a few years ago, et cetera. N. Lamont had been hired by a man in the U.S. who was on the payrolls of both Wilburforce and Chemotex. N. Lamont would work for Chemotex in its legitimate international sales operation, and would, on a date not far away, travel to Munich to take over his new post. He would be trained by Chemotex, at factory sales training sessions.

"We have the papers, we have the photos, we have everything but the man," Wilburforce said. "We even have your wife for you."

One of Nick's black eyebrows hooked up. "Wife?"

"Chemotex Worldwide treats its sales staff rather royally. She will be traveling with you, all expenses paid. She's one of ours, of course. And she will not be with you," Wilburforce added rather nastily, "to gratify your sexual appetites. She will be there to aid and assist you in handling the necessary details. You could do it alone, but a wife provides a better cover for a man your age. How you get out of the factory after you set the explosives—indeed, how you even get in to set them at all—is your affair." Wilburforce leaned forward. "Do you still want the little task, Nicky?"

Nick was cold in his mid-section. He tried to check his temper. "You hope I do."

"I hope you do. You're a smart, cheeky so-and-so. Lots of flash and brag. And there's Tenderly. He was one of my best. A lifelong friend. I hope you want it."

In the private, protected, sealed and guarded dining room, all Nick Lamont could think about was a ridiculous stack of unpaid bills. For his guilt there was no specific symbol. It was only a feeling, heavy on his mind, never concrete except in dreams.

"I want it," Nick said. "And I'll come back in one piece."

Wilburforce dabbed his lips with a napkin. "That's doubtful. But I'm delighted you accepted all the same."

Six weeks later, on another of those dim, wet London afternoons, Nick Lamont met his bogus wife at the airfield. He had seen photos of her while he was in training. A round-hipped, slim-waisted, high-breasted girl with a pretty, though not beautiful, face. She had been trained separately. Once Nick inquired pointedly about this unusual procedure. Wilburforce fobbed him off with a reply that made no sense: the less dilly-dallying between the two of them while in training, the better they'd learn their lessons.

She wore a lavender suit, a small, wifely hat, and very little makeup. Her diamond rings sparkled. She had a crisp, athletic stride, a pink mouth that suggested passion.

"Hello, Nicky darling," she said, kissing his cheek.

"Hello, Anne." His smile was easy. "Couldn't we have a more wifely greeting?"

"I think not." She said it softly, but with a perfect smile. Something in her eyes bothered him. It was something hard and direct, which made him stop paying attention to the rather choice way her firm, high breasts thrust out.

He'd looked forward to this part of the trip even if the rest of the excursion promised to be grim. She was a damn fine-looking girl. He'd hoped they might act husband and wife in more than name. Now he was doubtful.

"I've checked my luggage aboard," the girl told him. "Including the cameras."

In the noisy, aseptic terminal, Nick chilled again. The cameras were explosives.

They strolled toward the boarding area. "You don't seem overjoyed to see me," Nick said.

"Didn't Wilburforce tell you my real name?"

"No, just Anne Lamont."

"It's Tenderly." She paused, faced him. She stared directly into his eyes. "Charity Tenderly. I know what happened in Gib. He was my uncle, you see. We were both in the trade. I know his death was technically an accident, so I'll do my utmost to see that this job is a smasher." Her smile was bright and hollow. "I do want to make sure you succeed, you know."

Through the terminal came the mechanized scream of a BOAC jet taking off. Charity Tenderly—he was going to have a hell of a time thinking of her as Anne Lamont—walked a few steps ahead of him. She smiled again over her shoulder, as if beckoning for him to hurry. There was a red fury in Nick for a moment, which he quickly quelled. Then came a vast, fatalistic depression.

In the assignment of this girl to be his partner he sensed the hand of Wilburforce at work.

Destroy the factory.

And himself.

Below, the picture-book prettiness of a Germany that looked unreal and untroubled gradually came up to meet them. They would land in Munich shortly. Nick tried to open the conversation again, meeting the difficult subject square on:

"Look, I know I've got a reputation for a temper but—"

The hostess was passing in the aisle. For her benefit, Charity interrupted, "Why, darling, I've grown used to your temper in all the years we've been married."

Nick's fingers closed on her wrist. "Don't play smart games. What happened was—"

"Final." She said it looking him straight in the eye. "A

bullet. My uncle. But it's over. We don't want to be harping on it, not on airliners, not anywhere."

Nick momentarily forgot caution. "Why the hell did you come on this trip?"

Charity Tenderly grew quite serious. All malice was gone. "Because this kind of career—your career—is important to me. I do what I do—well, darling, not for cash, that's for certain."

"Then it's going to be all business?"

"Let's not argue, shall we? We'll be forced to stay in the same room. But there will be separate beds."

Nick scowled. The seat belt sign came on. Charity Tenderly said nothing more, only stared thoughtfully out the aircraft window.

A small reception and dinner party was scheduled for them at the colorful but rather touristy inn located in the tiny village not far from Munich. They had reached the inn via a limousine waiting at the airport courtesy of the Chemotex management. The Chemotex works itself was several kilometers from the city, and one kilometer beyond the inn. That evening, Nick and Charity dined by candlelight in company with Herr Doctor Franz Staub and several other executives of the firm.

The dinner was excellent. Nick avoided wine, concentrated on dark beer and told a great many American jokes. Dr. Staub, an ascetic figure in a narrowly cut suit and small, gold-rimmed glasses, dry-washed his hands and nodded, pretending to understand the humor. Charity was seated between two of the sales executives who directed the European operation. She acted properly wife-like.

They were seated in a private dining room with a glass wall that overlooked the winding inn driveway. Shortly after the dinner began, a chauffeur-driven Mercedes arrived. Its occupant came in to join the group. She was tall, shapely, wearing a billowy out-of-season print dress and a large picture hat. Nick, a shade fuzzy with beer, was introduced.

"Permit me to present Fraulein Judith Yonov," said Dr. Staub.

Nick took the woman's hand briefly. Under the shadowy hat, her eyes were luminous, challenging. They were dark brown above a strong nose and full, brightly made-up lips. He judged her to be about 30. She had a low voice, pale cheeks. She seemed to wear a great deal of makeup. She did not remove her hat, even though the private dining room was dim.

"This is the young salesman from America?" Judith Yonov said in lightly accented English. "How pleasant."

"Your father—" Nick began. "I've heard the name. Research director, isn't he?"

"Yes. I am most regretful that he could not be here to share the occasion. But his projects—and Herr Doctor Staub's insistence on Chemotex competing vigorously in the world market—keep him laboring late many nights, I'm afraid."

Up his backbone Nick felt another oppressive crawling sensation. The daughter of Dr. Sweetkill. She reeked of Chanel. There was something eerie about her.

"I've heard among the competition in the States," Nick said, still trying to sound off-hand, "that your father has led Chemotex into some interesting basic research areas. I'd like to know more about that, Fraulein Yonov."

Was he pushing too hard? Across the table Charity's glance was a brief flicker of warning. Dr. Staub clinked his spoon against his demitasse, laughed politely.

"Ah, my dear young Herr Lamont. How fascinated you

Americans are with all things new. Actually, the nature of our basic research program is a rather closely guarded secret. If I may put it as tactfully as possible, I am afraid that new employees are not permitted access to that area of our operations. Indeed, we must insist upon heavy security to protect our patents and processes, as well as work in progress. In any case, I'm certain you will be kept quite busy learning our current commercial line, and selling that in the U.S. markets."

Judith Yonov pushed one of the candleholders slightly to one side, in order to get an unobstructed look at Nick.

"Perhaps, Herr Doctor," she said, "if Herr Lamont is truly interested in product development—and he is one of the family now, so to speak—" There was a pause. "Perhaps I might talk with father and we might arrange a tour."

"The rules forbid—" Staub began.

"We shall see," Judith Yonov interrupted. Staub flushed, silent.

The smoke from his cigarette burned Nick's throat. It was plain to see who in the group had the clout. But he hadn't liked the shrewd, luminous glare of those eyes from beneath the big hat. He wished her face were not so heavily shadowed. The party was spoiled. He was sitting across the table from the daughter of a mass murderer. A concertina played a bright air in another room.

Had Wilburforce triple-crossed him? Was he somehow part of a game, the rules of which were known to every damn one of them except himself? Or had there been a leak during preparations?

Judith Yonov had been baiting him. Or had she? Did she *know?*

Presently, as dusk fell over the spectacular scenery outside, the party broke up. Nick would report to the Chemotex works tomorrow to begin training, Dr. Staub said. Pleasantries were exchanged all around. The sliding doors of the private chamber were rolled back. Judith Yonov excused herself and disappeared, presumably into a powder room.

Charity—he could not think of her as Anne, though he had no difficulty calling her that in public—was still chattering brightly with the executives. Nick discovered he was out of cigarettes. He left the room to buy some.

Going through the door to the inn lobby, he noticed a big, thick-shouldered man with a shaven head and a splayed nose. The man was emerging from the main taproom. He wore a dark uniform and highly polished boots. He had several inches on Nick, who was by no means small, at just over six feet.

The man walked unsteadily. He halted and blinked toward the party breaking up. He had a chauffeur's cap clutched in one hand. His eyes were small; he reeked of beer.

Nick crossed the lobby, purchased his cigarettes and was just turning round when he heard a quick, brittle exclamation of alarm. He knew the voice. Charity!

He whipped around fast. Several of the executives had gone to fetch their hombergs from the check rack. Charity had apparently walked into the lobby to wait for Nick. The big chauffeur had stumbled against her. He was standing close to her now, an idiot's smile on his lips.

"I think you've had too much to drink," Charity said.

"Nein." The heavy man stroked her forearm. "American lady, *ja?* Very pretty. Looks pretty, feels pretty—"

Charity glanced past him, and her eyes for once were something other than cold. The man had her cornered. Nick crossed to her quickly, touched the man's shoulder.

"Beg pardon, but she's not for handling."

"Don't put hands on Rathke." The big man slobbered it, scowling.

"I'll put hands on anybody I damn please. Get away."

"Very pretty, very nice," the man called Rathke said, squeezing Charity's wrist. The girl made a face. That was all it took for the Lamont temper to crack.

His mouth wrenched as he punched Rathke hard twice in the belly. Rathke stumbled back, more surprised than injured. Nick's arm ached. His knuckles hurt. The executives began to jabber. Staub bore down on them.

Thoroughly drunk and furious because of it, Rathke planted his big boots wide and swung a huge, flailing punch. It caught Nick's chin, spun him just enough to unbalance him and set off the red fury in him in earnest.

He went in fast. For a second or so, Rathke punished Nick's belly with big, brutal fists. Then Nick got through the man's guard, counter-attacking the beefy German face with four fast, vicious punches. One of them slammed Rathke against the wall, brought a dribble of blood and a wild bellow of rage out of his mouth. Rathke lunged for Nick's throat—

In between the men there was a swirl of print fabric.

Judith Yonov spoke curtly in German, ordering Rathke to control himself. Rathke lowered his hands. He swiped his mouth with his uniform sleeve.

Nick's tie was askew and he was breathing hard. But he was pleased, because he'd caught a glimpse of Charity's face. She was irritated. He interpreted it to mean she was secretly pleased.

"Rathke, *Nein!*" Judith Yonov exclaimed as the chauffeur made up his mind and shoved past her. Nick's head ached. Afterward he wasn't quite sure what had happened but he believed Judith Yonov reached into her handbag, then touched her hand to the bare flesh of Rathke's left fist.

The man stopped. He blinked again. He took one more

faltering step. With an audible swallow, he put on his cap. Blood made a thin red tracery down from the corner of his mouth.

"I do extend my deepest apologies for my chauffeur's behavior, Herr Lamont," Judith Yonov said. "He is under strict orders not to touch alcohol. But I cannot watch him constantly."

Now the executives pressed close, apologizing in turn. In a moment Judith Yonov and Rathke had gone. But not before Rathke glanced back once with a black scowl.

Nick guessed that Rathke had been subdued by some sort of needle prick. A Dr. Sweetkill special? Very likely. What a nice poison-flower Fraulein Yonov turned out to be.

As the party ended at last, Nick Lamont quietly cursed himself for the burst of temper. He might have handled it another way, though he couldn't think of a good one off-hand. As he shook hands with Herr Doktor Staub and the others, he noticed Charity watching him again. Not quite with approval, but without animosity.

That was worth it, he decided—that single look. Worth it even if Rathke did remember, caused more trouble and— God forbid—endangered the mission.

Charity said nothing about the incident as they went upstairs, however, and they slept in separate beds.

Two evenings later, Nick got a measure of satisfaction when Charity at last mentioned the fight. Earlier they'd driven into Munich in a sea-blue Volkswagen the factory had provided for the length of Nick's training session. After a good deal of beer, a sumptuous meal and some reasonably friendly if inane talk, they returned to the inn around midnight.

Nick flopped down on his twin bed. Charity stepped into

179

the bathroom and closed the door. He lay sprawled, his shirt speckled with cigarette ash as he squinted through the smoke at the black beams of the high-ceilinged room. In his mind he went over what he'd learned about Chemotex in his two days of classes.

He was being taught the company's products, its pricing policies, its distribution, and he had a notebook crammed full of scribbled facts. But the lunch periods had been more illuminating, because during those times he'd gotten to see more of the facilities. He dined in the company cafeteria with the various sales executives who were his tutors. Today Herr Doktor Staub had lunched with them too. Nick's mind was drifting over the lunch talk about research—Staub had been guarded, as usual—when the bathroom door opened.

Charity walked out. She was applying a pink comb to her hair. Nick tried a whistle. He got little response except a nod that indicated the bathroom was his. Still, this was curious. On their first two evenings Charity had appeared ready for bed clad in hideous baggy striped pajamas of mannish cut. Tonight she had put on a black sleeping gown, lined so as to be opaque, but short. Her calves were tanned and attractive. The gown's front fell precisely away from the ripe, high sharpness of her breasts.

"Don't get notions," she said. "I ripped the pajamas." With her back to him she began to hang up her daytime things.

Nick grinned. "Oh, here I thought it was the softening up for the kill."

"That's not particularly funny. I don't care to see anyone killed."

With a twist of his hand, Nick flicked ash into a tray. "I meant the romantic kill."

Charity's auburn hair shone by the dim lamps. "That's

rather presumptuous of you, Nicky darling." The *darling* was acid.

"I thought so, too."

"Oh, you did?"

"Yes, but I'd like to know your reason."

"I didn't ask to have my honor defended the other night."

"Aha." Up he came off the bed, pointing a finger. "You're still thinking about it."

"I am not thinking about it. You're trying to imply I owe you something which—"

"Did I say that?" he cut in. "You said it. Been bothering you, has it?"

Charity flung back the coverlet of her bed. "Since we're getting so damn psychoanalytical, why did you tackle that big, vicious creature?" Charity raised her feet, bending her knees to slip her toes beneath the covers. The brief black gown's hem fell away for a second from the gently curving bottoms of her thighs. The view was exquisite, painful and over virtually at once.

"Was it," she continued, "just another case of the Lamont temper breaking out of bounds?"

"Listen, maybe I felt he shouldn't paw you. Did that occur to you?"

"Yes. But I really think it was guilt. Thanks anyway."

And, with a yank of coverlet up over her bare shoulder, she turned her back toward him.

Nick closed his eyes. He saw it all again. The room in Gib. Tenderly's pale face wrenching as the accidental bullet drove into his breastbone and brought death and surprise to his failing eyes. Nick jumped up and stamped into the bathroom, where he slammed the door and ran the tap loudly so it would disturb her.

When he came out again, yanking the knot of his pajama bottoms tight to secure it, he made a quick round of the room as he did every evening, checking for hidden listening gear. Even though Charity was sitting up watching him, he avoided her eyes.

Finally he crawled into his own bed, reached for the light. Across his outstretched arm he looked at her. Strange, drawn lines pulled down the corners of her warm, pink, mouth.

"Nick, that was a bitchy thing for me to say. About the guilt, I mean."

"Forget it."

"No, really. You've a tough enough job ahead without me complicating it. I do understand why you hit that filthy boor. Just to be decent. There's not much forgiveness in me. I apologize. We're none of us perfect. I had a bad marriage, I ruined—well, forget that. But do accept my thanks. Also the promise of truce. Nick?"

"Truce." He snapped out the light immediately. He didn't want to look too long at the black-wrapped swell of her breasts above the coverlet, nor speculate on what tiny but definite change had come over her.

She settled down with small murmurs and rumpling bedding noises. Nick smoked one more cigarette, staring into the dark. He tried to concentrate on what he had to do.

His sales training wouldn't last forever. The Chemotex research wing had to be destroyed. The gear was in the wardrobe, as part of their luggage. He had to transfer it to his attache case. Use it. By God, he would, and go back and shove a fragment of Chemotex's blown up steel up Wilburforce's damn behind.

He would come back.

After another 12 days, at the beginning of the third week,

Nick Lamont had learned enough—or all he could. He was ready to move.

A means of entrance to the basic research wing had to be found. This he'd learned early. He'd been studying the problem since.

The headquarters building of Chemotex Worldwide G.m.b.h. presented a face to the one main access road. That face was all tinted blue glass and aluminum. Structurally, the building resembled the crossbar of a gigantic letter T. Running straight back from the crossbar was the basic research wing. It was three floors high, exactly like the main headquarters section. But all the doors leading into it from the main building were guarded during the daylight hours, alarm-rigged at night, and were, in any case, made of thick steel.

So far Nick had not even seen Dr. Genther Yonov. But he saw many of the scientist's white-coated research associates. They had their own private, treed and sodded exercise park at the bottom of the stem of the T. They checked in and out through a rear gate in a high, electrified fence. Their cars were parked in a small, separate pool alongside a secondary road that ran off the main one and serviced the rear compound.

At noontime the scientists lunched in the fenced park much like highly educated animals. Other employees from the main building, as well as from the nearby but separate manufacturing buildings, lunched in the regular cafeteria. And so far as Nick could tell, there was no fraternization between those who labored for Dr. Sweetkill and all the rest.

At another lunch, Nick commented on the unusual arrangement.

"Necessary, necessary," Herr Doktor Staub replied, munching. "Here in Germany, as in your United States, industrial espionage is not unknown. Thus we must guard our most precious commodity, our brainpower."

And crawling bottles full of bacteria for Eastern stockpiles?

Staub's explanation made commercial sense, though. The security even included the extra precaution of having the entire factory hooked into a master fire and police signal system that connected to the two municipal services in the nearby village. Penetration looked next to impossible until the night Nick became aware of Rathke's evening habits.

On a crisp Monday morning he was ready.

He packed his attache case carefully. A small but potent automatic pistol was concealed inside a dummy text on chemical engineering. One rectangular side of the case now contained jellied explosive layered between thin metal. Nick sweated as he carried this to his sales training class and gingerly opened the case to take out his notepad.

A pair of sales engineers lectured at him all day. By evening, Nick was used to handling the case. Shortly after the works closed, he checked out the gate and walked down toward the regular employee car park.

The sun slanted low. The sea-blue roof of the waiting VW gleamed. Nick bent down to tie his shoe. Charity had been picking him up at the factory all the past week. Now, directly opposite the VW, Judith Yonov's Mercedes was parked.

Charity was leaning from the window of the VW, directing a sunny and seductive smile at the driver of the Mercedes, Rathke. The man stood by the left front fender of the smaller car, a witlessly pleased expression on his thick face.

One of the sales engineers who'd lectured Nick that day emerged from the gate. Nick used the man's presence as a pretext for a question. When they had exchanged goodnights, Nick turned around.

Sweat trickled down the back of his neck into his collar.

He clutched the attache case handle and walked between vehicles leaving the car park, to the VW. The Mercedes was pulling away along the secondary road, going around the rear of the gleaming headquarters toward the research wing.

"How did it go?" Nick asked once the VW was in gear.

Charity headed back toward the inn and the village. Smoothly she downshifted in the factory traffic. "I must look the perfect bored wife. I didn't think it would work at all. But the poor beast evidently has so few brains—anyway, I was parked there as he drove past. I hailed him and apologized for your behavior at the party. At first I think he was very suspicious. Then he smelled the gin I drank before I left the inn. When I petted his hand and gave him the smile, I knew I had him. But it was crawly, touching him. He's an absolute brute."

They were speeding down the twisting road between fragrant pines. The peaked roofs of the village, gilded with sunset, appeared ahead. Nick felt obliged to say "Sorry to force it, but I was beginning to get desperate. Rathke's the key. The Yonovs live inside the research wing. He takes care of them, so he can get in and out. It was a damn godsend when I got to noticing that he came back tanked from the village every afternoon about the time the factory lets out. Have you set it up?"

Charity's pink tongue touched her coral-painted lips, nervously. "Yes, for this evening."

Nick was conscious of the keen of the wind past the car. "How?"

"I'm just to be walking somewhere on the main street after dark. He thinks I'll be waiting breathlessly because I have this fixation about large, powerful men with black boots." She shuddered. Before Nick could say anything else, she swung the wheel of the Volks sharply.

The small tires skidded on the shoulder, shooting gravel backwards. The sedan slowed to a stop. Other factory traffic streamed by, going downhill to the village and the sunset. They were cool sitting in the shadow of great soughing pines. Quite unexpectedly, Charity gripped Nick's hand.

"I haven't forgotten my uncle. But don't let Rathke hurt you."

Startled, Nick hooked up his eyebrow again. "Does it really worry you?"

"Damn it, don't be flip. You're a decent sort. Maybe a little flashy and—oh, I don't know what's got into me. Is it living in the same room with you every night for two weeks running? Or—damn you, stop staring." And her arms, rough with the chic tweed of her suit jacket, came round his neck and her mouth came up firmly against his, moistening as her lips parted.

Nick thought, *This is idiotic. You're liable to be dead.*

But as he kissed her two things hit home hard. One, he'd grown fond of her. Two, in some strangely chemical way, the same thing had happened to her regarding him. Somehow it made what he had to do this evening all more frightening.

Yet for a moment it was all swept away as he wrapped his arms around her in the shadowy car, hugged her hard while her mouth opened and she kept murmuring between deep kisses that she was a bloody fool who ought to know better. Nick touched her left breast. He felt it shudder, harden beneath the fabric of her suit. She pulled back suddenly.

Her eyes were bright with an amazed passion she could hardly believe herself. With both her hands she clasped his big-knuckled right one to her breasts.

"I'm crazy for you, Nicky." She was almost crying. "Damn fool blunder, isn't it? I hope you come back. Please come back. Please."

Then she tore away, almost angrily. She drove fast back to the village.

On one hand, Nick felt pleased that it had happened. On the other, he wished it hadn't. Having it happen made him all the more conscious of the attache case jouncing lightly between his knees, layers of leather containing layers of steel and layers of steel sandwiching between them the jellied explosive he must use tonight.

The chimes in the village church rang half-past nine.

Nick waited in a dark place as a shadow in the center of the dim street—Charity, walking—turned. The shadow was outlined by the sudden brilliance of headlights.

The auto slowed. Charity walked over, white-faced in the leakage from the lights. Smiling, she leaned toward the driver's side of the Mercedes.

Attache case in one hand, Nick glided from the shadows. He raced the distance to the Mercedes, yanked open the door opposite the driver and slammed inside. He shoved the automatic pistol against the side of Rathke's muscled neck.

"Drive to the factory or I kill you right now."

In the dash light glow, Rathke's lumpy face became by turns baffled, then dimly comprehending, then enraged. Charity quickly backed away from the side of the gently humming car. Rathke cursed low, not too stupid to have failed to understand the betrayal. His immense right hand speared out through the open window.

Nick ground the muzzle deeper into the man's neck flesh.

"Pull your hand back."

Rathke did. Charity was by then out of range.

"Either start this thing going or you're all done right here."

Rathke turned his head slowly, hatefully, toward Nick. Then he faced front. He engaged the automatic drive lever.

187

Charity floated out of sight. Were there tears shining on her face? Nick dared not look around.

He changed the position of the gun so that it prodded Rathke's ribs while the Mercedes shot past the limits of the tiny village and up the winding road into the pines, toward the death works.

Perhaps the prospect of death made him euphoric. At any rate Nick found himself speaking in a fairly relaxed, conversational manner as the Mercedes ground smoothly up the twisting mountain road. "Now let me make one or two things clear before we hit the grounds, because unless you understand me, you'll try something and there'll be trouble. If there's any trouble, this car is going to crash and you're going to get it right along with me. Understand?"

No answer.

"I said understand?"

Rathke's peaked cap threw shadows far down over his face. His lips twitched. *"Ja."*

"I know this much. You work for Yonov. His quarters are in the research wing. So I figure you know how to get in without triggering the alarms. If there's an alarm, one goddam jangle of a bell, or light—anything—all you'll get for your pains is your brains smeared over the dash. If I don't do anything else I'll pull this trigger. It's all business between us as far as I'm concerned. Living or dying's up to you."

The brutish mouth worked at the corners, as if Rathke was bright enough to feel contempt for what Nick had said. It was not all business from Rathke's end. He hadn't forgotten, or forgiven, the fight at the inn.

Nick had, though, because he had so much else to think about. For the first time in weeks, or months, or years, he didn't give much of a damn about a new Jag or anything except getting back to Charity. And now that it mattered, he had to work doubly hard to keep the tension-edge out of his voice, the nervous spasm out of his gun hand. Those who theorized that there were no frightened men in the trade were fools.

Ahead, the bonnet lamps of the Mercedes brushed across the high crosshatching of the electrified fence. Rathke made a tentative reach with his left hand for a small red button on the dash.

"What's that?" Nick said.

"Automatic signal. It will turn off the electricity and open the fence. We drive through when it opens."

"It had better do that and nothing else." Nick gestured with the gun. "Go on."

Rathke's finger pressed the red stud. Somewhere under the bonnet, an electronic device hummed. Abruptly the massive gates in the high fence began to swing inward like a scene done in slow-motion. The Mercedes slid ahead along the service road.

The gates passed on either side of Nick's field of vision, then the black of the lawn where the research workers exercised during the day. The Mercedes rolled up to a rear door in the three-story building. Two bluish florescent lights in an aluminum fixture over the door cast a ghastly glow. Nick had to risk passing through the lights.

"Out, *bitte*," he said mockingly. The night had grown chill. The pine smell was stingingly sweet. Rathke climbed from the car, then straightened up.

"Do you know how to get inside with no noise?"

"*Ja*, I know."

"You'd better."

The chauffeur fished in his smartly tailored black uniform blouse. He produced a pair of aluminum keys that he jingled. Nick nodded for him to proceed. The attache case weighed heavy in his left hand.

Rathke slipped the first key into a lock, twisted. He withdrew the key, inserted the second one into a lock immediately below. Nick was trying to listen, watch, take in more than human senses could. At any second Rathke might be planning to trip some alarm.

Using his shoulder, Rathke nudged the glass and aluminum door inward. A long corridor stretched into a vista of metal walls with pastel-colored office doors shut on either side.

"The pilot plant area," Nick said. "We'll go directly there."

"Then this stairway—we go up." Rathke led the way.

Footfalls had a hollow, eerie ring. Dim service lights burned in the stairwell. Inset in the walls Nick noticed one of the black pull-toggle devices he had seen in the main plant. The fire and police alarms were connected to the village . . .

On the third floor Rathke went down a hall identical with that on the first. It seemed endless. More of the black pull-toggle alarms were spaced at intervals. Ahead, a metal door brightly lacquered in red loomed. It bore Keep Out warnings in German, English and French.

When Nick asked whether the pilot plant lay beyond, he received a grunt in reply. The big chauffeur pushed the panic bar and the door swung open. Rathke moved ahead, onto a steel-floored gallery with a rail. Below, for two stories, there was emptiness crisscrossed with a weird tangle of glass piping.

Nick was starting through the scarlet door when he realized the wrongness of it all. The pilot plant tanks, distillation apparatus, centrifuges, were two floors down. Rathke had chosen to bring him to the third level—the catwalk went all the way around the big chamber as another did on the second level.

He was through the door now; and Rathke was midway between the door and the rail. Nick broke stride as the notion registered that it was all wrong. This brief hesitation was what Rathke had counted on. Too late, Nick realized that the chauffeur's mind was less spongy than it seemed. For even as Nick noted the arrangement of the pilot plant—huge windows; the chemical piping swooping up and down like big glass arteries in which colored liquids flowed—Rathke turned and rolled his shoulder down and came charging in to kill.

Nick tried to keep hold of the attache case and get off a shot at the same time. Rathke's shoulder hit him violently at the waist. The attache case dropped, slid away on the catwalk floor. Rathke lifted hard, up and over in one immensely powerful lunge. Nick tumbled down the man's back—straight at the rail and the drop, and death.

Wildly, he shot out his free hand. He caught the top of the railing, grappled for purchase. His arm was nearly wrenched out of place as it took the whole brunt of his body dropping. But he hung on by his left hand, cheek smashed against the rail's middle rung.

Rathke threw his cap away. He wiped his sleeve across his upper lip. He smoothed the front of his uniform tunic and walked toward the rail. His great black boots gleamed as he came on, nailed heels going *clang-scrape, clang-scrape* with each step. Nick lifted his right hand with the automatic pistol in it. He hurt from hanging there, two floors above the concrete of the pilot plant floor. His face contorted as he tried to steady his trembling right hand, aim between the railing rungs.

The chauffeur leaped, closed thick fingers, twisted the gun loose. He threw it, clanging, on the catwalk floor. Sweat formed on the palm of Nick's left hand. The left hand began to slip.

"Is the American growing tired?" Rathke said. He drew out something that suddenly doubled its length with a *snick,* and shone bright blue. "Tired of holding on, *ja?*" Rathke pointed the knife blade at Nick's bloodless left hand clasped around the rail. Nick struggled to get his right leg up. He managed to do it, giving himself a little extra support on the catwalk's edge.

Rathke kicked his foot away. Nick nearly dropped again. His shoulder took another bad jolt. "Perhaps we release the fingers with a cut, one at a time," Rathke said. He brought the knife down toward Nick's middle finger knuckle. The blade edge touched skin, broke through, went down to bone.

Nick bit his tongue to keep from yelling. Every bit of power he had left went into the frantic surge as he again brought his right foot up to the catwalk edge, tore his left hand back, out from under the knife, away from the rail. For a moment he held onto nothing.

Then his grappling right hand caught the rail. With his left he reached up, caught Rathke's white collar, one quick, powerful jerk at the point where the chauffeur's tie was knotted. And suddenly Rathke was pitching over, his eyes showing terror as he sailed over the rail, past Nick.

Rathke seemed to spiral slowly. Then his head struck the concrete and burst.

Something hurt Nick's ears. A deep, throaty sound. As he dragged himself over the rail and knelt on the catwalk, gasping, he realized that Rathke had yelled as he went over. Yelled in wild, frantic fear. How loudly?

Loudly enough. There were footfalls somewhere on the second level.

Nick could barely move. But he had to move. He crawled

forward and picked up his gun. On his feet at last, he headed for the service stair to the main floor.

He was recovering a little from the shock of the fight. The footfalls had stopped. Had he imagined them? As soon as he set the timer on the explosives, he wanted out of the plant. He wouldn't be able to get much beyond the exercise yard before the explosives blew, however. And there were night guards in the main building. They would surely catch him in the open. Some diversion might help. He had to plan that now, and then move very fast.

He stopped at one of the black wall toggles. Police or fire fighters from the village would create the right kind of diversions; keep the guards busy and give him a chance to escape. Nick reached up and pulled the toggle. He hoped the alarms really rang in the village.

He went lurching on down the iron steps and out onto the pilot plant floor. Overhead the glass pipes full of liquids—and several contained smokish gasses, he saw—soared and crisscrossed so that he moved through a weird checkerboard of shadows. He ran panting past Rathke's corpse to a central point on the floor, knelt, unfastened the snaps of the attache case.

"That will be quite all, Herr Lamont. *Quite all.*"

Nick twisted his head around. He'd been watching the corridor entrances at the back end of the research wing. Now he saw that the voice came from the opposite side: an almost wholly shadowed doorway on the second level, on the side leading into the main building.

At the railing was a woman in a dressing gown. He recognized Judith Yonov. Beside her, gaunt, in an old maroon lounging jacket with black lapels, holding a pistol, was Dr. Sweetkill. It was Dr. Genther Yonov who had spoken.

He was a tall, slope-shouldered man, mild of face and affecting a tuft of beard. "Our apartments are on the end of the wing through which you entered," he said as he headed toward the stairway. Judith followed. "We decided it might be prudent to circle around and approach from a different direction. Poor Rathke's yell carried. Be so kind as to throw the pistol to the floor. Then stand back from the briefcase."

Feeling weary and defeated, Nick obeyed. Judith Yonov's voice was stridently sharp, bouncing back and forth across the pilot plant as she followed her father down the stairs:

"From the beginning it had the smell of a penetration."

"Pity we had to lose Rathke to verify it," Yonov said. The two came toward him. Judith Yonov came only part way, however. She stopped, standing in the shadow of a tall mixing tank. Dr. Yonov appraised the disheveled Nick.

Stroking his long scholar's nose with his free hand, Yonov said, "I am aware that you triggered the village alarm connections. All doors from this area are now locked, so the police cannot enter. Still, they will be here. Their vans move rapidly. They should arrive at the back gate shortly. I have already decharged that gate. They will have no difficulty getting in to the yard."

Nick's head pounded. What was there to say, or argue about? Yonov had him.

The man called Dr. Sweetkill was in his late fifties. He looked bright enough, but there was an odd remoteness in his deeply set brown eyes. Nick sucked in long breaths. Why was Yonov so casual about the police arriving? Had he fixed them? Not all of them, he couldn't have, that wasn't possible. Nick would try talking his way out. Stupid idea, but what else was there now? The gun was gone. The attache case lay open several yards away, near a centrifuge recessed into the concrete floor.

Dr. Yonov stepped around Nick, instructing him to turn

so as to keep his face toward him.

"Who you are makes little difference, though we may learn that presently," he said. His thin free hand reached up to a vertical steel pipe that rose through the floor. A big but delicately balanced wheel with four metal spokes spun at his touch.

Through one of the glass pipes overhead, a whitish fume of smoke went crawling. Then it twisted and leaped as blowers took over.

"For the moment," Yonov went on, "it's quite enough to say that we have long anticipated a penetration attempt. Obviously they have sent us an amateur. Ah, you're looking at the wheel. Well, out there—" The gun waved toward the high windows which overlooked the night-blackened exercise yard. "—out there we have an underground valve system. We frequently employ it to test our experimental gasses on small animals in the open air. When there are no humans—no staff members relaxing, of course," Yonov added with a stilted chuckle. "What you see going through that tube is now being pumped down through conduits and up again through the valves scattered in the grass. If I no longer have the required cover for operating in this facility, then I might just as well leave it in grand style, wouldn't you say so, whoever you are?"

"Red light," Judith Yonov said from the shadow. "Coming up the road fast."

"The gas mists quite easily," Yonov went on. "They'll not see, feel, taste or smell it until they're in the midst of it. I have not tried this special compound on small animals—or any animals. It will be interesting to note what happens."

Red light whirling, the police van screamed up to the gate. Armed men opened the gate. Others followed the first pair across the lawn. Before any of them had reached the halfway point between the fence and the building, they dropped,

195

white faces distorted, ugly.

Over the seven incredibly still bodies the revolving van light washed waves of red. Nothing else moved.

"Satisfactory," Dr. Yonov murmured. "Yes, satisfactory." He smiled. "And now, dear friend, we turn to you."

Dr. Genther Yonov stroked the ball of his index finger up and down the side of his nose for a meditative moment. Nick's mind was dull, thick, struggling for some way to live, some way to even the wretched odds. Judith Yonov had not stirred from the shadow of the chemical tank. She acted as if she were afraid of the light.

Yonov gave his gun hand a slight twist. The gesture seemed to indicate that he had made up his mind.

"First," he said, "we had best cut off the gas flow into the yard, else we shall have half the neighborhood dead." He moved to the upright pipe, spun the delicately balanced wheel again. In the act of turning back he suddenly seemed to move much faster, dancing across the concrete to hit Nick's head viciously with the pistol muzzle.

Nick tried to fend off the next blow, right himself, grab Yonov's gun. Yonov kicked hard, a high, telling kick to the small of the back. Off balance, Nick skidded across the concrete floor. Suddenly there was nothing beneath him but a great, round circular darkness. Primitive panic clogged his throat. Everything dropped away.

He hit hard, with a whanging sound and a cold, nasty smack to the side of his head. He sprawled on the bottom of one of the great stainless steel centrifuges whose upper rims were flush with the concrete floor.

He shook his head, crawled to his hands and knees. The shadow of Yonov fell across the mirrored interior of the sunken centrifuge. Nick gauged the distance up to the concrete floor as hardly more than four feet. But his arms and legs felt heavy, useless. He had to jump. He had to get up, get out of this sunken silvery dish—

He came up on his feet, reached for the lip of the centrifuge. Yonov gave another of his little waves with the gun. "Judith, please?"

A rasping click somewhere. Suddenly, beneath him, the slippery steel floor seemed to revolve. The centrifuge was spinning.

Nick was slammed, hurled around and around. Each time he tried to stand he was thrown down. Yonov's shadow flicked past, and past again.

Nick felt like he was in a fun-house device, crazy, laughable, but he couldn't stand up, or grasp the concrete lip now because force kept him pinned to the wall.

Somehow Yonov's voice penetrated. "Now, Herr Lamont, before I increase to the next highest r.p.m., perhaps you will tell me for whom you are working."

Around and around everything went, sickeningly. Yonov's shadow was the only constant, black across Nick's field of vision every other second. Each time he tried to stand he was thrown back to the outer wall, revolving more swiftly now. Or was that all in his head?

Above him, a blue shiny object glimmered. Yonov's voice alternately dinned and faded. "You are traveling slowly enough to see these objects which I am holding. Empty ten-gallon chemical vessels, glass. I propose to drop one, then the next, then the third. Then I propose to throw a control which will slide the steel cover outward from its recess, completely covering you. I think thirty seconds with the cover closed and the glass flying will make a nice blend of blood and pain. Then I propose to slow the machine down again and you will have the opportunity to tell me who assigned you here."

197

Around and around . . . The bell-shaped glass vessel was recognizable to Nick because Yonov's words had made it so. Nick could imagine the bits of shattered glass being whirled outward like deadly darts, at his cheeks, his wrists, his eyes.

"Say welcome to the first of the glass, my spy friend," Yonov said.

Glass shattering. Tinklings, crashings. There was a loud, flat report mingled with the noise. Nick was still pinned against the wall of the spinning centrifuge. Only a moment later did he realize two peculiar things. The centrifuge was slowing down. And Yonov had vanished from the rim.

Dazed, Nick swallowed hard. The centrifuge came to a full stop, revolving one last time past the body of Dr. Sweetkill.

The scientist lay on his back. His mouth was open. His eyes were huge, fixed on the piping overhead. Blood bubbled out of a hole in his throat.

That had been the report Nick had heard. A shot. The glass laboratory vessels stood unbroken; Yonov hadn't dropped the first one. Nick's sweat-blinded eyes finally found the source of the breakage—a large lower pane in one of the pilot plant windows.

And threading a path through the glass, wrapped in an old tan trench coat that bore rips from where she'd climbed through the window, and looking pale and frightened, but with a small wicked gun in her right hand—

"My God," Nick said. "My God, Charity. My God."

"I—I thought they had you in here. I couldn't see clearly. I shot twice at the window first, to break it."

Out where the red van light still revolved, bells jangled. "The alarms," Nick said. "The breaking glass triggered the plant alarms."

"I had to come after you," she said, her words overlapping. "You'd told me about the police and fire bells connected in the village. I was walking—just walking in the street, worrying about you and—" She fell against him. After she had buried her face for a moment, she drew back. "The police alarm rang in the station. I heard it from a block away. A van left. I came too. After I ran all the way up here, I saw all those men lying out there. All dead. I thought they would have things in control. I saw Sweetkill through the window. They do teach us how to fire one of these accurately, you know. It's part of the training."

Nick Lamont swallowed a long, delicious breath of air. His temples had stopped hurting. Things had settled into reasonable focus.

"Then we can get out of here. We can—"

"Not as you think," came her voice from the shadows. "No, not as you think. The young lady's back presents a splendid target. She will please put her gun down, and turn."

Nick stared past Charity, who was frozen, trying to see in the mirrors of his eyes the source of the feminine voice. Nick's gut iced again. He'd drawn a hand that looked like a lucky one, but now there was a trump. Yonov's fallen gun had been retrieved by the girl who came walking from the shadows.

Charity's fingers whitened on the trigger of her own weapon. Nick shook his head, reached down and pried her fingers apart.

"I'll throw the gun off to the right," he said.

"Yes," said Judith Yonov. "Then the young lady will please stand to one side."

This Charity did, as Judith Yonov came all the way out of the shadow.

The strong nose, the full figure, the lipsticked mouth were

as Nick remembered them. Then, his mind created a beery image of a young woman hiding under a picture hat. This woman was not young. Turkey-skin, all wrinkled and reddish, showed at the throat of her robe. Her hair was dyed. Her makeup laid a hideous pink-orange patina over pale skin. She was not pretty, and she was at least Yonov's age.

"You needn't stare," she said. Nick heard false teeth clicking. "I am not his daughter. I am his wife. But there are certain reasons why it was better for me to remain well hidden under large hats, in dark places." A quick glance at Yonov's red-throated corpse betrayed her contempt. "You might say I was his guardian. I was his contact, his link with the East, you see. I am the one who gave him a cause, a purpose for his work. Except for the affection the poor idiot felt for me, perhaps you Englishers—I suspect that's what you must be since the young lady has the sound of it in her voice—as I say, but for me, he might have sold you his little bottles instead. Well, I am not so fond of the theatrical as he was. I shall do this quickly. But with pleasure."

Again the eyes flicked bright and fanatic at the dead Sweetkill. She added: "I did not care for Genther personally, but it was my duty to care for him. He was valuable. You have destroyed that value. I am duty-bound to finish what he began."

Nick heard the alarm bells still ringing, jangling in the night. He heard male voices, guards, shouting off in the direction of the main building. The guards hammered on the steel doors, unable to get in. On the floor, perhaps a yard away, lay the attache case. *I wonder if I can?* he thought.

His mind went back. He heard a thunder of a hundred thousand voices on a Sunday afternoon under an Ohio sky. He had to try; there was no other way. Up came Judith Yonov's gun muzzle. With a wide sweep of his arm, Nick threw Charity out of the way and did the run.

His right foot came up with less speed but as much fluid power as in the past *The kick! The kick!* they were screaming somewhere. His foot connected.

Judith Yonov's gun flamed; the shot missed. He had kicked the attache case hard but it seemed to slide forward slowly. Actually the case flew. It struck Judith Yonov in the left calf, not hard, but enough to distract her. Her gun hand jerked. A second bullet went upward.

A glass pipe burst, began to leak viscous greenish fluid that smoked when it hit the concrete. Then, before Nick could stop her, Charity was past him, screaming like no civilized woman should scream.

Judith Yonov tried to shove her back. Charity clawed, pushed. Judith Yonov went tumbling into the centrifuge. Charity saw the case skitter and gave it a swift kick, almost as an afterthought. It fell into the centrifuge.

Charity moved fast, a blur of hate, of foul words. Her nails broke as she punched and punched at the centrifuge control box. With a whine, the centrifuge began to spin.

Now guards were battering at the steel doors with what sounded like sledges. "Damn fool," Nick shouted at Charity. "The spin of that thing may detonate in the case—"

His chest hurt. Time was pitifully short. He quit squandering it and bowled broadside into Charity. *"Run!"*

They tore their clothing and their flesh getting through the shattered window. The dash across the field of dead policemen was nightmarish. Nick had to pick up Charity when she faltered. He carried her bodily out through the open gate. Then the night tore open behind them in one blinding, thundering red detonation that hurled them forward half a dozen yards, onto their faces. On his neck, Nick felt the heat of the death works dying.

★ ★ ★ ★ ★

"What a mess," Nick said.

He was panting so hard, he was barely able to speak. "What a damned indescribable mess." He dragged tired hands over his clothes. They were covered with sap, quilled with pine needles. He and Charity had run parallel with the winding road, all the way down to the village, while the fire vehicles passed.

The inn was empty. All the staff and guests were out in the narrow street, watching the furnace-hued sky. He and Charity had got in via the back stairs. Now, in the sanctuary of their room, Nick shot the iron bolt.

Heavy and tired, he sat on the bed, saying again, "A mess. We both look like things off the garbage heap."

"But we made it."

Charity's words came out as a squeak. She tried to laugh about it. Nick scowled. He scowled because her tan trench coat was an untidy collection of blood spots and sap stains. She looked sick, wretched, tired—and happy.

He said the first thing that came into his head: "That was a stupid thing—"

Disbelief, fury sparked in the girl's eyes. *"What?"*

"Killing the Yonov woman. Going crazy. It was a callous, dirty thing."

"Are you so blasted tired you don't know what you're saying?"

"You murdered her."

"Who told you this was dancing class, you son of a bitch?" Tears streamed down her cheeks, coming fast as she balled her fists at her sides. "I seem to remember a man named Tenderly in Gib. A man you killed, and here I'd got it into my head that maybe I had to forgive you and now you pull this."

She sank down. "Don't you know why? Don't you know

202

why I did it?" Slowly she lifted her head to look at him. She was no longer crying out of anger. "Because, Nick, I wanted you to live, not her."

He let out a long breath; relief came. An end to the guilt. Understanding seeped into his fatigued mind. He went toward her and sat beside her. New shiny-bright Jaguars no longer existed. Even Wilburforce hardly seemed worth bothering about.

Charity kissed him, hungrily. He tried to show her he understood, and wanted her. He reached and fumbled at her clothing. When he had her round breast cupped in his fingers, feeling the warm rising life of it, there was no longer a need for fear.

"The local police, Nick."

"Tomorrow."

"But—"

"Old Icy-Guts will fix it."

"I still worry that—"

"Please shut up."

They fell back together, tired, but ardent. Soon the antidote was there for both of them. The curtains of the inn room had been drawn tight when they crept in, so they saw no more of the red light of burning in the German sky that night.

The Siren
and the Shill

Dan Wilde scratched his head for the second time. He reached across the table for a cigarette, shoved it into his mouth and got it lit without taking his eyes off the piece of paper. Angie's handwriting, all right. *I want to get something settled. And this time, no dodging me. I'll meet you at the truck.* No signature. He was supposed to know who sent it. Well, damn it, he did. Angrily, he crumpled the note and flung it into the wastebasket. He glanced at his watch. Fifteen minutes to twelve. He grabbed his leather jacket off the chair, flipped out the lights, and went out of the trailer, down the steps to the south end of the midway.

Clay Brothers' Carnival lay like a Christmas tree on its side: a quarter mile of spangled lights and color. A ceaseless hum of voices, a constant thud of feet on sawdust that rose to a minor roar. The Ferris wheel went plunging down, and a girl's pleasured scream cut the night. The calliope wheezed away with *The Eyes of Texas*. Dan moved past the frame structure where a long gasp arose like a gust of wind, in accompaniment to the roar of the motorcycles. Hell's Motordrome.

Bells on the shooting gallery were clanging away as some amateur marksman demonstrated his skill. Hawkers peddled their cotton candy, their red hots, their plaster dolls spangled with glitter. Dan kept moving, a big heavy-set man of around thirty. People glanced at his ruggedly cut face and instinctively moved out of his way. This was his, Dan Wilde's show. He ran it, he kept it bringing in the money. One more season like this, and he'd have the desk job he wanted so badly. General Manager of Underwood's United Shows, of which the carnival was only one unit. Dan liked the idea, but he didn't smile. Angie was kicking up a fuss. Clay Brothers' was a business, nothing else. Everybody did their jobs like robots, at Dan's command. When people stopped acting like robots and started acting human, getting personal affairs tangled up with business, Dan clamped down.

He wondered how much he would have to clamp down on Angie. They had a more or less binding agreement that they would be married. But they never talked of it. Dan refused to consider a wedding until he got the desk job and the security it brought. He managed to keep himself going, just another efficient robot, without getting his affair with Angie all mixed up with business matters. But her note disturbed him. Maybe the personal element was rearing its head. He didn't want to think about that.

He walked on through the crowds of the midway. Emmanuel Fedderson, the barker for the Hawaiian Nights pitch, caught Dan's eye over the heads of the mostly male audience, raised his cane, nodded slightly. But the round button mouth in the center of Fedderson's chubby face kept right on working, emitting its stream of nasal talk, promising delights on the inside for only a quarter, rhapsodizing over those hula honeys, those lovely ladies from the sunlit sands of Waikiki. Dan waved back and stopped at the rear of the crowd, hands thrust in his pockets.

". . . and now," Manny exclaimed, "as just a sample of what you're going to see on the inside, I'm going to bring three of the little ladies out here. Three beautiful belles from the enchanted islands, featuring our own Miss Mawani Ba'ya, an authentic Hawaiian princess doing her celebrated Love Hula. Come on out, girls." The phono needle scraped and a recording of an electric guitar boomed out over the crowd. The curtains behind the platform parted and the girls came dancing out, bumping their hips generously. Bubbles on the left, Harriet on the right. And Angie in the middle.

Dan allowed himself a grin. She really put it over. With a dark wig and dark makeup and her trim little body sunburned a deep nut-brown under the imitation grass skirt and halter, she looked authentic enough. Her maternal grandfather, he knew, had been an exporter and importer in Hong Kong and had married a Chinese woman, which may or may not have accounted for the slight teasing tilt of her dark eyes.

Under the wig, though, was ash blonde hair. As the girls went into their routine, Dan caught himself noticing her figure. The shapely legs and pert sturdy breasts. She was a re-fined broad—wouldn't work in a smutty show. But she had the assets, and she took a kind of impish pleasure in holding herself aloof from male admirers. Tonight, though, Dan saw a new seriousness in her face. Her lips were parted in a smile, but her eyes stared out over the bald heads with a faraway emptiness.

Dan grew conscious of someone at his elbow. He turned. Chick Morrison stood there, in his usual flowered sport shirt and black slacks. He, too, was deeply tanned, well built. Hot-tempered blue eyes stared up at Angie's undulating figure. Chick had crew-cut blond hair and thickly-muscled arms. "Cool tonight," he said to Dan. "Wish I had a jacket."

"Relax, Chick," Dan said. "You don't have to make small talk."

"If she was my girl, I'd be damned if I'd let her get up there where all these old duffers could eye her."

"It's business," Dan said. But he saw that Chick's atten-tion was riveted more firmly than ever on Angie, or Princess Mawani Ba'ya, as Manny had named her in his far from au-thentic knowledge of Hawaiian names.

This Chick was a funny one, Dan thought. Ex-college boy, ex-Marine, ex-everything. He'd picked up some money somewhere and signed with old man Underwood to run the concessions in the carnival, under the name *Independent Amusement Enterprises.* A fancy name for a hard-headed kid who ran clean games and got a good rake-off and guarded his property with all the jealousy of his fiery nature. Chick had replaced a more crooked outfit of concessionaires, and brought a certain degree of peace to the midway.

He was a shill, Dan admitted, but a damned good one. He egged the customers on. He banged away at the shooting gallery and knocked over all the clay rabbits through his experience with firearms in the Marines. He always spilled the milk because he was once a farm team southpaw with a shot at the majors. He could come up with the right guesses on the wheels and horse race games ninety percent of the time because he'd been a math major before he got restless and quit college. A clean honest shill, who liked to talk, liked his work, and had a personality marred only by an intense, jealous protectiveness of what was his own. He liked Angie. He'd told Dan that. If he ever got her on his team, he'd be just as jealous of her as he was of his concessions.

Manny wound up his spiel, the girls danced back into the tent, and the crowd started its expectant surge forward toward the ticket booth. Saturday night. They'd be working for a long time yet.

Dan started to say something to Chick when he noticed a flurry of movement in front of him. A skinny rat-faced guy in a threadbare suit bumped against a bald-headed man and apologized. Dan grabbed the skinny man's shoulder, spinning him around. He snatched the wallet from the guy's hand and tossed it to the bald man.

"Get off the lot," Dan said quietly.

207

The skinny man's mouth curled nastily. He kicked Dan in the shins and twisted. A knife blade gleamed suddenly, throwing off the glare of colored lights. "Son of . . ." the man hissed, lunging. Dan grabbed the man's arm and snapped it across his knee. The man howled. Dan belted him in the stomach and he went reeling backwards. Chick Morrison grabbed him and smashed his jaw with an uppercut every bit as powerful as Dan's blow. The pickpocket seemed to sprout wings, rising upward until he slammed back down onto the midway. He picked himself up and scuttled off through the crowd. Dan retrieved the knife, closed it, and put it in his jacket pocket.

"Guys like that are a pain," Chick said, wiping his hands on his pants.

"It's a hell of a job, trying to run a clean midway," Dan agreed.

"Hey, how about having a dog with me? I'd like to talk."

"Okay," Dan said as they began to walk. Chick seemed very formal now, very businesslike. Dan sensed that some kind of trouble was on the way. Trouble that would be a lot harder to handle than ordinary two-bit grifters and pickpockets.

Chick said nothing until they got their dogs from the nearest stand. Dan ladled on the mustard and took a bite. He swallowed the bite and said, "Well, what's the topic for tonight?"

Chick didn't look away. "Angie."

"She knows how to hula, all right."

"Quit kidding around, Dan. You know what I mean. I want to know the score. Are you two going to get married?"

"Someday, yes," Dan said. "But I don't see where that concerns you."

"It concerns me because I like Angie." Chick's eyes got

that funny, glazed look, and Dan sensed that he was getting angry. Well, let him. Better to squelch the trouble before it got really bad. "You don't say boo to her half of the time," Chick went on, "and it seems to me that a guy who treats a girl like that has no right to put his brand on her. What I mean is, either say it one way or another—you're either going to get married, and I don't mean just talk about it, or she's up for grabs." He grimaced. "That's not such a good word, I guess, but you get the meaning."

"Yeah," Dan said evenly, "I do. I also think you'd better keep your nose out of it, Chick. What I do is my own affair."

"Suit yourself. You run the show, but you're nothing but a big adding machine. So you'll have to get ready to move over. I'm taking Angie."

"Like hell you are."

Chick grinned. "Try and stop me. You've got so much to do figuring out percentages and cutting corners, you haven't got time for anything else. You haven't got a chance, buster."

Filled with sudden anger, Dan tried to shift the dog awkwardly from his right to his left hand. He wanted to throw a punch, but while he fumbled clumsily with the bun, Chick brought his left hand down sharply, slapping the dog away. Mustard splattered on Dan's hands. "And don't try any rough stuff," Chick said, "or you'll get it right back." Before Dan could bring his fist up, Chick was gone, disappearing into the crowd.

Dan stood there for a moment, angry and confused. A pair of high school girls and their dates snickered as they went by. Shamefaced, Dan got out his handkerchief and wiped off the mustard. He cursed softly. Not only did Angie have to bother him tonight, but Chick Morrison, too. And Chick could be real trouble. If Chick got hold of an idea, if he once got a purpose fixed in his mind, Dan knew that all hell couldn't blast

209

him loose from it. Dan slapped his fist into his palm and started to walk, not noticing the crowds and the lights any more.

The finely oiled mechanism named Dan Wilde was no longer running efficiently. He found himself angry, and that wasn't good. The whole efficiency of the carnival could slide right out from under him if he didn't watch himself. He could lose Angie, he could lose old man Underwood's faith, and he could lose every chance he'd ever had for that desk job.

He moved in a kind of haze as the night wore on. He gave orders, took care of minor matters instinctively. By the time most of the marks had drifted off to their beds, minus a good deal of their money, he knew what he must do.

About two-thirty the work gangs began to strike canvas. The lights went out and the tinseled wonderland fell apart at the seams. The big trucks ground their gears and spewed out their loading platforms. The performers and concessionaires packed up. Under the dark cover of night, the carnival stirred like a living organism, getting ready to move.

Dan was in the trailer, counting receipts and making a record of them, when Manny Fedderson came in, shuffling his little stubby legs. He poured himself a cup of coffee from the pot on the hot plate.

"Had some more trouble with the cats tonight, I hear. Dorman almost got himself killed."

Dan finished his work, put the cash box and ledger in the squat black safe, slammed the door. "I didn't hear anything about it."

Manny peered at him curiously. "Dorman and his wife are going at it worse than ever. You know how mad he gets. He takes it out on the cats. Rajah got tired of having the blanks go off in his face and tried to chew a hunk out of Dorman. He just got out of the cage in time."

Dorman was a stocky, foreign-born man who handled two lions and a Bengal tiger named Rajah in a show at the other end of the midway. His wife, an acid-tongued slut, told fortunes. They fought constantly. Dan couldn't remember having been down that far this evening. It bothered him. He was thankful when Manny changed the subject, but he knew by the look on the older man's face that Manny sensed something out of place in Dan's behavior. Everyone in the show knew that Dan was everywhere, every night. Tonight he'd slipped. It wouldn't be good if word got around. He had to be careful. It made his determination to stick to his decision about Angie stronger than ever.

"You got the jumps, boy," Manny said abruptly.

"What?" Dan said absently. Manny pointed. Dan looked down and saw that his hand that held a cigarette was trembling.

"I said you got the jumps."

Dan stood up. "So I've got the jumps, what the hell difference should it make to you?" He stalked to the trailer door, ignoring the puzzled, half-pained look on Manny's face. He slammed the door behind him and inhaled a deep breath of the cool night air. *Get hold of yourself, Wilde. You can't crack. It's not that bad. Just hold on.* After a minute, he stopped trembling.

When the the trucks finished loading, they lined up in a long column at the edge of the grounds, headlights glaring yellow through the black night. Reluctantly Dan headed toward the front truck. He went around to the left side, opened the cab door, climbed up. Manny usually rode with him. Tonight Manny wasn't around.

A cigarette glowed orange. Dan turned on the ignition. The motor roared to life. All along the line, he could hear the other motors starting. Finally he turned toward her. "Hello, kid," he said. He kept all feeling out of his voice.

He saw her face in the cigarette glow, breathtakingly pretty. Blonde hair now, the phony wig gone. A firm honest face that belonged around kids and a bright kitchen. He knew it, but he couldn't bring himself to give it to her. Not yet. The machine had to keep running, or everything he'd ever worked for, dreamed of, would be down the drain.

She said nothing. He leaned out the window and waved. The big truck started forward, bumping over the field until it hit the highway. The caravan headed west, through the small town and into the dark rolling country beyond. The headlights sent yellow shafts into lonely blackness. Dan fumbled and got a cigarette lit for himself.

"I got your note," he said. "You've got something important to talk about, I guess."

"I want to talk about us, Dan." Her voice was soft, a trifle sorrowful.

"Well." He tried to laugh. It was no good. "Let's have it then."

Her hand touched his arm. "I've been thinking a lot lately. We just seem to drift along from day to day, getting older. I know we have an agreement, but . . ."

"We agreed to get married when I got the desk job," he interrupted.

"But why do we have to wait?"

"Because, damn it, I want to quit this business. It's a second-rate way to live. Sometimes I like it but I don't want my kids to grow up inhaling sawdust and getting a diet of pop and hot dogs."

"But we wouldn't have to wait . . ." she began.

"Look." He twisted the wheel, swung the great truck around a curve. "We've hashed this all out before. Have you got anything else to say?" That was Dan Wilde the machine talking.

"Yes, Dan," she said, her voice was pitched low. "Either we do it now or we don't ever do it."

He knew she was waiting for him to break because he loved her—knew that she trembled on the brink of something dark, with all her faith held in her hand. Knew, and somehow forced himself not to care.

"All right," he said. "I guess that's the way it is. I want that desk job."

No hysterics, she was too good for that. Nothing but a faint muffled sob and her head averted so that he couldn't see her face in the green glow of the dash. "I'm going to sleep, Dan," she said. "We open in Crystal City Monday and . . ." Her voice quavered, broke, but she got control after an instant. "And it's a long way."

The concrete ribbon ran ahead of them, swallowing up towns and sleeping people and peaceful houses. Dan tried to keep from thinking about Angie, the good times they'd had since he took over the carnival after the war. They had seemed right then. He turned to her suddenly. "Angie—" She mumbled in her sleep.

He repeated her name. She opened her eyes. "Have you been talking to Chick Morrison?" he asked. Still half asleep, she didn't understand. He repeated his question and she seemed surprised, the way people do when your momentous statement means nothing to them. She said she hadn't and Dan felt foolish. "Okay, sorry." But she would be talking to him before long. Word would get around.

When a gray dawn spread over the east, the caravan pulled in to an all-night truck stop. Dan sat by himself at the counter while the crew jammed the booths and tables, talking loudly and laughing. Manny slid onto a stool beside him. "You look tired," he said.

"Now listen . . ." Dan began.

Manny raised a hand. "Don't start on me, Dan. I'm just making an observation. Crystal City's a big town and we'll have a tough week. Lots of marks. You ought to sleep." He stirred his coffee, staring into space with studied carelessness. "Wiskolski could take over the trailer and I could drive lead and you could sack in. Just a suggestion."

Dan smiled thinly. "Sorry I snapped like that. You're right. Thanks." He got up and walked out of the restaurant, aware that the people were watching. He risked a quick glance toward the booth where Angie sat. She was bent over her coffee, in earnest conversation with Chick Morrison. Neither one looked at him.

Dan stepped outside into the gray morning. He felt cold, hollow. He lit a cigarette and tossed it away after the first drag. He walked rapidly down the line of trucks, opened the door of the trailer, and walked over to the bunk. He took off his jacket and flopped on his face.

Forget it, Dan, he told himself. *A kootch dancer and a high-class shill. They'll make a great pair.* But somehow, it was no good. He was asleep before the trucks began to roll.

They hit Crystal City mid-afternoon Sunday. Dan, feeling rested after a long sleep, though no more satisfied with things as they were than he'd been the night before, was driving the lead truck. They rolled down the broad main street, largely deserted except for a rash of bicycles in front of the movie houses. Turning left, they passed through a residential section. The streets dozed in sun-dappled shade, big elms arching their branches to form a green canopy. Comfortable looking houses sat well back on spacious lawns. Dan saw men and women on the porches eyeing the trucks. No doubt disturbed by the sight of a carnival clattering down their street on Sunday, Dan thought.

Bitterness gnawed his thoughts again when he realized that Angie probably was seeing those houses with their respectable owners sipping lemonade on their porches, and wishing that she could do the same. Maybe she'd get what she wanted from Chick Morrison.

A kid on a bicycle came down the street toward them and Dan honked the horn, taking pleasure in the jarring noise that disturbed the peaceful afternoon air.

The Crystal City fairgrounds lay dusty in the heat. Banners and placards welcomed you to the County Fair, to begin Monday. A few people had already arrived, setting up stands for the livestock and foods displays. The trucks pulled up on the huge open lot beyond the grandstand. Shedding his T-shirt, Dan began to bawl orders; within minutes the canvas was rising and the wonderland was being put together out of poles and canvas and lights, for a week's engagement.

Dan worked the men hard; the pitches were in place by seven. He got his supper in the cook wagon, but he ate alone. Most of the kids had gone off to see the big city, investigating the liquor situation. Crystal City ran wide open, Dan knew. They'd find the bars doing business on Sunday night. He made a mental note to check for hangovers the next morning.

Once again, his cigarettes were tasteless, as was the food. He pushed the plate away and stalked out along the midway. The sun sat on the horizon like a pale red ball. A fitful breeze lifted eddies of sawdust. Canvas flapped. The tent poles stood out like gaunt fingers against the paling sky.

Manny was playing solitaire in the trailer. He looked up as Dan came in. "Hi. Place is like a tomb, ain't it?"

215

Dan sat down, glum. "It sure is. I don't think there's a soul left on the lot."

Manny chuckled. "Even Dorman and his wife made a night of it. We still got the cats on our hands. Drives me nuts." Dan listened and heard the wild vicious tiger-scream floating along the midway. "That baby's gonna kill somebody someday," Manny commented. "Want to play some euchre, or should we go hit the bars, too?"

Dan wanted to say no, we might run into Angie and Chick. Instead he said, "Let's play cards."

About eight-thirty, a knock sounded on the trailer door. A short warty-skinned man with muddy dark eyes sauntered in. He wore cheap clothes, a silk shirt, a loud purple tie. His blue suede shoes squeaked faintly. Dan didn't like the insolent look on his face. He put down his cards and stood up. "Something?"

The man fished out a grimy white card. "I want to see the boss. Or the guy who runs your concessions. That is, if it's one and the same. Otherwise, the guy handling the concessions."

"I run the show," Dan said. "Chick Morrison handles the concessions."

"Where can I find him?"

"Depends on why you want him. Let's see that card." Dan stuck out his hand. The man's eyes met his for an instant, hard and insolent. He handed over the square of cardboard. *Mumford Mightier Midways.* And in smaller type, *Crystal City.* Dan returned the card.

"My name's de Packh. Lester de Packh. I represent Mumford," the man said.

"I've heard about you. We haven't got any business for you. We run a clean midway."

216

De Packh guffawed. "Jesus, don't tell me you're one of those. Listen, Mumford can make a profit for you while you're here. For a forty percent cut, we'll guarantee to double your volume of concession business. Maybe triple it." Manny watched, frowning.

"No thanks," Dan said. "I don't need that kind of profit. Rigged wheels and floating crap games and armed hoods to take care of any suckers who might object to being fleeced. I'm not buying."

"Listen here . . ." de Packh said sharply. Dan glared at him, but de Packh didn't scare. Dan searched for a bulge under the man's jacket and found it.

"Leave," Dan said. "Right now."

"I can give you plenty of trouble," de Packh said. "I just tried to make a little money for you. I don't like it when somebody refuses a friendly offer."

Dan took a step forward. "Are you going out, or do I have to break your neck for you?"

De Packh hesitated. Dan noticed that the man's right hand flexed almost automatically. But, de Packh finally shrugged and headed for the door. Before he went out, he turned.

"So long, sport. I'm not going to forget about you." He slammed the door hard, making the glass vibrate.

Dan went back to the table. Manny shook his head. "Boys like that I don't like. If you get on the wrong side of them, they can put the kibosh on things overnight. A few boys with axes and clubs and bang . . ." He snapped his fingers. "No more carnival."

"What the hell was I supposed to do? Write him a ticket to bring all his crooks in here? No dice."

Manny looked apologetic. "It's what they call the horns of a dilemma."

Dan scarcely heard. He thought again of the warty face of Lester de Packh, and remembered that he had mentioned Chick Morrison's name. That bothered him. He had no specific reason, and yet he was uneasy about it.

He tumbled into bed in a black, angry mood. He heard some of the kids come onto the lot about midnight, laughing and singing. He turned over restlessly and slammed his fist into the pillow. It didn't do any good. He kept thinking of Angie and Chick Morrison and Dorman and his kill-crazy cat and Lester de Packh and Mumford Mightier Midways. The more he thought, the worse it became. At last, around three, he managed to go to sleep. But then he dreamed of riding the rods, as he'd done when he was a kid, wandering, without a job, and he woke up in a cold sweat.

At nine a.m. Monday morning, the gates of the fair grounds opened and the first customer poured in. Monday was usually an off day, but by noon Dan could see that they were drawing crowds comparable to Saturday nights in smaller towns. The shows, the rides ran full tilt. The sun blazed down, the smell of sweat and tobacco and popcorn rose toward the sky.

Hogs trumpeted in the stock barns. Women gabbed about their quilts and preserves. Cows made mournful foghorn noises. The barkers screamed; Manny was hoarse by two in the afternoon, but the crowds kept coming. Dan lounged in the shade of the root beer stand, a cold mug in his hand, realizing that it would be a capacity week. Which meant more opportunities for things to go wrong. Nerves grew frazzled. Arguments sprouted into full-scale brawls. This could be a week to remember.

He saw Angie on the platform at Hawaiian Nights. She didn't notice him, they were through. He turned away, determined to put his mind on other things. He saw Chick Morrison approaching. Chick threw a flip, "Hi, boss," at Dan and hurried on. Dan turned to see him standing in the crowd, watching Angie. She had her eyes on him, a grin a mile wide on her lips. He had already moved in, and he was guarding the new treasure.

Dan caught Dorman between shows and dressed him down for fooling with the cats. The stocky foreigner was half drunk. Zelda, his fortune-telling wife, chipped away both of them in her purple English. Dorman cursed, too, yelling at her one minute, pleading with Dan the next. Dorman promised to reform. Dan determined to keep an eye on him.

Rajah, the Bengal, prowled his cage restlessly. The two mangy lions slept, but Rajah prowled. The cat had a killer look in his great yellow eyes. His flanks were lean, and he needed a good meal. Dan stopped by the cook wagon and told Freddie to get some extra rations over to Dorman's tent right away.

Despite Crazy Chad Chapman and his stunt drivers, who were crashing their Fords head on and ramming them through flaming wooden walls in front of the grandstand, the midway was packed to overflowing that night. Before nine o'clock rolled around, Dan had picked up three pickpockets, one shifty-eyed old man selling lewd pictures, and a drunken woman who insisted on taking off her clothes in public, laughing like a hyena all the while. Dan booted all of them off the lot. He hoped fervently that nothing worse would develop during the week. Things like this he could handle.

Ten o'clock came and went. Dan loitered in the trailer, drinking coffee. At ten-thirty the Hawaiian Nights girls came out again. Dan knew the time by heart. He swore at himself even as he left the trailer and headed down the midway. The

crowd was still big. Here he was, skulking around like a senti-
mental kid, waiting for a look at her.

Manny went into his spiel, obviously worn out. The girls
were listless in their dance, but that didn't seem to bother the
customers. Chick was in the crowd, down front. He gazed
raptly at Angie and she smiled back. Dan wondered if the
smile was sincere.

The trouble started with a fat man in the front row of the
crowd. His beefy face was flushed, his words clogged by too
much liquor. He began talking loudly, pointing at Angie and
making dirty cracks. Chick's face was rigid, angry.

The fat man kept on talking. Manny leaned over and said,
"All right, friend, if you make a disturbance you'll have to
. . ." With a roar of laughter, the drunk seized the ticket
booth, pulled himself up on the platform with a loud *oof*, and
lunged for Angie. Harriet screamed. The crowd stirred like
an awakened rattlesnake. The drunk lurched back and forth,
crooking his finger and saying, "C'mere, sugar, c'mere."

Before Dan knew it, Chick had vaulted up beside the fat
man. The flash of a fist, and the drunk dropped over the side
of the platform. Someone cursed at Chick; he leaped off the
platform, swinging.

Dan shouldered his way through the crowd hastily. Damn
him, he thought. He had his hooks in Angie and he thought
he owned her. That temper of his . . .

But it didn't help matters to think of Chick. The brawl was
on.

Chick swung at the fat man's friends. Others charged in;
the crowd became a heaving mass of angry men, slugging at
each other, yelling at guys they'd never seen before. The girls
had fled the platform, all except Angie. She stood watching
the spectacle; watching Chick.

Dan dodged a punch and jabbed a man in the stomach with his elbow. He kicked his way through the mob, aware that boys had left the concession stands and were already quieting the rowdies on the fringe of the crowd. By the platform, Chick and his adversaries, unknown and unnamed, brutally continued to slug it out. Dan shoved one out of the way, placing himself in front of Chick's rocketing fist. He rolled his head with the punch, standing his ground. Chick lowered his fists, glaring. He was breathing heavily.

Almost at once, the fighting stopped. Dan faced Chick angrily. "Chick," he said, "I can't have you wrecking the show because of personal feelings. Manny could have handled that guy."

"Lay off me, Dan," Chick shouted hoarsely.

"Dammit, you're not going to mouth off around here."

"I said lay off!" Chick's voice rose to a yell as he belted Dan in the stomach.

Dan doubled over, side-stepping to miss a sizzling uppercut. Talking wouldn't do any good now. He waded in.

Chick was strong, and fast. But neither he nor Dan moved around. They stood firmly, feet planted wide apart, pounding blows home, ripping piledriver punches into each other's face and stomach. They hammered each other, shaking like great trees under the bite of the axe. But neither fell. Dan's face was a mass of pain. He kept slugging. He put all his strength into it. Chick faltered. Dan pressed his advantage, smashing home one thundering blow after another. Chick's nose dissolved into a red smear. Dan could see him clench his teeth. Stubborn—He wouldn't give. Dan kept pounding. At last, Chick dropped to one knee, shaking his head dazedly. It was all over.

Dan stepped back, wiped his raw knuckles on his trousers.

John Jakes

Most of the crowd had been herded away by Manny and some of the concession boys. A few passing marks gawked. Dan paid no attention. He looked up at Angie. Her face showed a mixture of shock and contempt. Chick looked at her, too, his cut lower lip stuck out petulantly. He seemed to be demanding something.

Angie came down off the platform and helped Chick to his feet. Chick mumbled, "Thanks," rubbing blood out of his eyes.

"Morrison," Dan said, "you're through. You can stay till we finish our run here. By then I'll have someone to replace you."

Chick's chest was heaving. "You fire me, you'll really have trouble. I can be pushed around just so long. This isn't the last time we'll tangle." Dan could see that he meant every word of it, meant it.

Angie stepped in front of Dan, the hurt look still in her eyes. "Why, Dan? You didn't have to beat him like that."

Dan pushed his hair back off of his forehead. "We can't have disturbances like that on the midway."

"You caused a worse one," she said hotly. "And you did it because of me." Discouraged, Dan realized that she was right. She was hurt and angry. Angrier than he had ever seen her.

"Well, honey," Chick said, "you heard the big boss. I'm through. How about you?"

She glanced at Dan, and quickly away. "Yes, I'm coming with you. Saturday will be my last day with the show. Come on. You've got to get cleaned up." She took Chick's arm and led him away. But not before he faced Dan once more.

"Today's Monday. I'm here till Saturday. So watch yourself."

They disappeared around the Hawaiian Nights tent. Dan hunted for a cigarette and got it going. *Damned little broad,* he

222

thought. *Great times she'll have with Chick. On the rebound all the way.*

But are you any better?

No, he had to admit, he wasn't. The fight with Chick had been more personal jealousy than anything else.

He bumped into Lester de Packh before he recognized him. De Packh munched on popcorn from the bag in his hand. His smile looked pasted on his unpleasant face. "Get the hell out of my way," Dan said.

De Packh didn't move. "Why, I'm just wandering around having some fun. That was some brawl. You having trouble here, Wilde?"

Unthinking, Dan brought his fist up. De Packh let go of the popcorn bag. His hand slapped down hard on Dan's fist; the other dropped to his jacket pocket. De Packh's eyes glittered in the glare of the colored lights. "Easy, tough guy. This isn't a candy bar in my pocket."

Dan shoved him out of the way and walked on. De Packh's laugh floated in the air, contemptuous. Dan looked around, but the man was gone.

He sat a long time in the trailer, brooding over the untasted cup of coffee. The calliope music dinned. Finally Manny arrived, whistling. He stopped after he saw Dan. He pulled down the shades and poured himself a cup of coffee. "Dan, I've got something to say."

"What is it?"

"The kids are talking. They're saying big tough Dan Wilde is going to pieces. Letting a broad twist him around her finger. Letting his feelings run him. Things'll loosen up around here if you let that happen, Dan. They'll be a lot tougher than they already are."

Dan stared at him, hollow-eyed, dried blood still smearing his cheek. He didn't speak.

Manny sighed. "End of sermon. Want me to help you go over the receipts?"

"Sure, I'd appreciate it."

Later, he lay in bed staring at the ceiling. Dan Wilde, the smooth-running machine, was breaking apart. That's what they were saying. And why not? Trouble piled on trouble, creating a maze he couldn't get out of. Angie leaving on Saturday, hurt and angry. Chick hotheaded and potentially dangerous. Wart-faced de Packh hanging around. The finely precise machinery that kept Clay Bros. in the black was disintegrating, while he stood by and watched. He'd have to take hold. Really take hold, no more kidding around. *Clamp down,* he thought. *You've got to last the season. You've got to do that, or you'll be back riding the rods, so clamp down.* In his dreams, he was caught in a giant vise, with Angie and Chick twisting the lever tighter and tighter. He got smaller and smaller, but at the end of the dream, he exploded, just like a balloon.

Tuesday came and Wednesday and Thursday—the crowds grew larger. By Friday night, you could hardly move on the packed midway. The shows turned people away, the vendors ran out of food, men and women with bills in their fists stood three deep at the wheels and the games. For Dan, the week had passed with agonizing slowness. There had been no big troubles, just the usual stuff—drunks, and an attempted stick-up on Wednesday afternoon.

Dan saw Chick Morrison occasionally. Chick kept to his job, playing the shill for his own stands. On two occasions, he looked drunk, and thoroughly angry when he saw Dan. Lester de Packh had disappeared, but Dan couldn't escape the uneasy feeling that the warty man was somewhere close by. Dan went about his job in a controlled way, not giving in to the emotions battering him.

Friday was hot and humid. By mid-afternoon the sky was a mass of angry gray clouds. But still the crowds came. Night darkened the world and the lights came on. In the grandstand, a vaudeville show featuring a washed up singer from Hollywood was scheduled, but still the midway was jammed beyond capacity. Biggest crowd they'd ever pulled, Dan thought.

The air remained hot, heavy, but the storm didn't show up. There was only an ominous rumbling in the distance, and flashes of lightning over Crystal City. The crowd pushed, laughed, shouted, howling, surging up and down the sawdust avenue in pursuit of pleasure. Dan had trouble getting around. To him, the air smelled of trouble. One spark, and that mob of people could erupt into a frantic stampede. It brought clammy sweat just to think about it.

He moved past the Hawaiian Nights pitch, startled to see that Angie was missing from her spot. Another girl filled in between Harriet and Bubbles. Dan caught Manny's eye. Manny jerked his head toward the rear of the tent.

Dan moved down the shadowy aisle between the walls of canvas. In the girlie tent, he heard a feminine voice exclaim, "Aw, knock it off, sweetie," followed by a chorus of piping giggles. Dan rounded the corner of the tent. A cigarette glowed orange; Angie rose to meet him. He could see lines of tension around her mouth.

"Dan . . ." She put her hand out, then quickly drew it back.

"Manny sent me back here. I didn't know he was sending me to see you."

She nodded her blonde head. He noticed that she hadn't even changed into her costume. "I couldn't do this show," she said. "I had to talk to you. I told Manny to keep an eye on the midway, in case you . . ."

He cut her off. "I haven't got a lot of time to waste. If it's anything personal, let's not talk about it. We settled things last week."

He saw the hurt look flare in her eyes. "Oh, Dan . . ." She shook her head, as if confused. "It's Chick. I . . ."

"If you've gotten me back here to give me a sob story about your troubles, forget it, Angie. I'm busy."

She seized his arm. "Dan, I can't kid myself. I don't love Chick. He's too . . . I don't know . . . too conceited, maybe. But that isn't it." He stared at her accusingly. "Dan, believe me, it isn't. There's going to be trouble. Chick's been drunk almost all week, he's said he was going to get you for beating him like you did. Tonight . . ."

Dan could see that she wasn't faking. "What about tonight?"

"Well, after the eight-thirty show, he came around and we sat out here, having a cigarette. He had a bottle with him. He was sweating a lot and . . . and this man came from somewhere and Chick laughed when he saw him. Dan, it was terrible, that laugh. Cruel. He knew the man. He said he had business with him. He and the man walked off and stood talking. I heard the man say everything was set. The man had a gun. He gave it to Chick."

Dan frowned. He shot a quick description of Lester de Packh at Angie. She nodded.

"Yes, that's the one."

Dan gripped her arms. "Angie . . . I appreciate your telling me this. I'm sorry if I was rough with you. You know how I feel about you."

She smiled, but he saw a tear gleam in the corner of her eye. She shook her head. "I tried to forget about it, Dan. I couldn't."

He patted her shoulder and started to say something else.

226

Then he heard the commotion on the midway—voices pitched high, frenzied. A woman screamed. Someone came running around the tent. Dan whirled.

"Manny . . ."

"Holy Christ, Dan. This is it, Dan. *Rajah's loose.*"

The woman's scream sounded again, hellishly shrill. Dan's stomach hurt. Manny kept babbling until Dan slapped him across the cheek. "Listen to me. Have you got your thirty-eight?"

"In the tent," Manny gasped.

"Get it." Manny disappeared. He returned in a few moments, pressing the gun into Dan's hand. Without another word, Dan bolted down the line of tents. He could hear the panic out on the midway. Wild confused voices . . .

He came to Dorman's tent. A huge gap had been torn out of the canvas. On the sawdust, Dan saw prints of animal pads, impressed in reddish-brown blood. Dan rushed into the tent.

Joe Knox, one of the roustabouts, stood at the front of the tent. "Christ, Dan, am I glad to see you." Dan looked down. He choked. He recognized Dorman's red uniform, but the man's head was a featureless mass of blood and gray gore. Zelda stood over him, head buried in her hands, sobbing.

Dan grabbed her hands and pulled them down. "What happened, Zel?" She gazed at him dumbly and went on crying. He shook her hard. "What happened?"

"The bastard, said he'd kill me. We . . . we had another argument. He hit me. Threatened me. I didn't know what I was doing. I opened the cage and let Rajah out right before the nine-thirty show. He tried to fight the tiger with his blank cartridge pistol. Oh, God . . ."

Dan motioned to Knox. "Get a dozen men and try to catch

227

the cat. I've got two rifles in the trailer. Take them, kill the cat if you have to. Find Manny Fedderson and get some of the other boys onto the midway, to calm the crowd. Tell people somebody had an appendicitis attack, any damn thing." He whirled on Zelda. "Anybody see the cat get loose?"

She shook her head blindly. "But they must have heard Boris scream."

Joe Knox disappeared. Dan made sure that the cage door was locked. The two lions were still inside, prowling restlessly. They smelled blood. Well, they'd smell a lot more if things got much worse. Dan ran outside, hurling himself into the crowd on the midway. "Nothing's wrong," he yelled, "somebody just got sick, that's all."

Somebody shouted, "You're a damned liar, I heard screams."

"Somebody got sick and fainted and his wife screamed," Dan shouted, hurrying on.

There was new commotion up by Hawaiian Nights. Manny was outside with a dozen men around him. He was gesturing wildly when Dan came up. Dan grabbed Manny's shoulder. "What's wrong now? Did they corner the cat?"

Manny shook his head. Frantically, he pointed to the far end of the midway. His mouth moved spasmodically for a second before words came out. "He's . . . he's up there . . . with . . . with a whole army of goons . . . they're wrecking the midway . . . clubs . . . axes . . ."

"Who?" Dan shouted. "Who's up there?"

"De Packh."

"Come on!" Dan gathered the carney hands around him and they went plunging down the midway, a flying wedge that battered the crowd apart. Most had clubs of some sort. Manny had found a butcher knife.

From up ahead, Dan could hear the chunk of axes in

wood, the sound of ripping canvas. Savagely, he pushed people out of his way.

The crowd had scattered near the end of the midway. The hoods, tough-looking bruisers in Levis and work shirts, swung their axes and clubs on Hell's Motordrome. The tents and stands around the motorcycle show were a shambles. Dan's men waded in, swinging. One of the thugs caught a club behind the ear and went down.

Dan shoved through the melee, hunting for two men. A hairy arm seized his neck, jerked him back. Dan sent a series of triphammer blows into the man's belly, doubling him over, then rabbit-punched him to the ground. Dan saw one of the men he wanted. Chick Morrison, swinging an axe into the plank sides of the Motordrome, a flushed drunken look on his face.

Dan swung Chick around. Chick's face knotted up savagely as he swung the axe. Dan ducked and felt the blade swish past his head, heard the ugly sound as it buried in the wooden wall. Chick had his arm back, ready to throw a punch, when a voice said sharply, "Hold it." A gun barrel jammed into Dan's spine.

Dan lowered his fists.

"All right," Lester de Packh said, "let's go. Around the back."

Dan started walking. Chick grinned and walked a few steps behind. They rounded the tent into relative darkness. Lightning flickered on the horizon. Searchlights blazed in the grandstand and Dan heard a ripple of applause as the singer finished a number. It all seemed very far away.

"Turn around," de Packh said.

Dan turned. Chick stood beside the warty crook, hands on his hips. "Well, Danny," he said thickly, "I guess you got

229

yourself into something you couldn't handle. All you'll have left when de Packh's boys finish is a mess of wood and canvas that even a junk dealer won't buy."

"So you were in on this," Dan said.

"Yeah, I was in on this. De Packh here thought I might like to join up with him. He was only going to tear up one or two pitches, but I persuaded him to knock the hell out of the whole midway." Chick laughed. "And right now, I'm going to have the pleasure of knocking the hell out of *you*."

De Packh waved his pistol. "You shut up. We're going to handle him my way."

"What do you mean?" Chick asked.

"I mean I don't like guys like this. I told you I'd fix you, Wilde. If something happens to you, old man Underwood and all the other carneys will sign with Mumford. And that'll make me happy. I'm going to be a lot happier killing you, though."

"Killing . . ." Chick said.

"Yeah, killing, we aren't in kindergarten, buster. Mr. Wilde is going to get a nice neat bullet through his skull. Then we'll take a club and beat his brains out so they'll never know he got shot. Just a casualty of the brawl." He laughed, a sound like wind rattling dry leaves.

"I didn't deal myself in for any shooting," Chick said uncertainly.

"Well, you're in now. Stand back."

Dan watched Chick, aware that he was debating with himself. All at once, he was stone sober. Suddenly Dan heard a low rough purring in the darkness. The pit of his stomach went cold. The other two men didn't notice.

Finally Chick shook his head. "No. I'm not going to kill him."

De Packh threw Chick's restraining arm off. "Get out of

my way, you dumb . . ." Chick's hand dove into his pocket and came up with the gun Angie had spoken of. De Packh pushed him, firing at the same time. A lance of red cut the darkness and Chick shouted, clutching his left side just above the belt. He reeled back and collapsed on the ground.

Before de Packh could swing his gun around, Dan twisted it out of his hands and tossed it away. De Packh raised his fists to fend off a blow. Dan belted him in the stomach and then on the jaw. Lester de Packh sagged, his eyes closing. Dan rubbed his knuckles, starting toward Chick. Then, he froze.

Baleful yellow eyes gleamed out of the darkness, two feet behind Chick. "What's wrong?" Chick groaned. He heard the growl. "My God. That sounds like . . ."

"Keep quiet," Dan whispered. The cat was crouching to a spring. Rajah would be on Chick in one leap. Dan calculated that if he moved hastily, Rajah would come for him instead.

He felt the thirty-eight Manny had given him weighing heavily in his pocket. He moved his hand slowly, pulled it out, watching the cat. The hissing rose to a hoarse growl. Dan bolted abruptly and ran to the left.

Rajah hesitated, and then sprang for Dan. Dan brought the thirty-eight up, frantically remembered to check the safety. The cat's body was a black shape off the ground, coming for him. Dan got the safety off and tried to run. The huge animal struck him and bore him to the ground. Claws tore into his arm. The yellow eyes shone like giant moons; the fangs dripped; the breath roared like a blast from a stinking oven. Desperately Dan raised the gun and pulled the trigger.

He kept on firing, hearing the cat's scream as the bullets blasted up through the roof of his mouth into his brain. Dan rolled over wildly, escaping a last furious snap of the jaws as Rajah rolled in his death agonies. Cat screams cut the night air.

Dan heard a siren somewhere. He staggered to his feet and only then did he feel intense pain. He looked down at the ripped flesh of his bloody arm. Chick said something he couldn't hear. Rajah whimpered, his huge body quivering.

Dan tried to hold himself up, but it was impossible. He slammed into the dirt and lay still, his mind floating down into a deep dark well that swallowed him completely after a moment.

He awoke in his bunk in the trailer. Morning sunlight poured in through the windows. He groaned and rolled over. Manny and Angie were bending over him. His arm was in a sling.

"I feel like I went through a meat grinder."

Manny laughed weakly. "You practically did. One more minute and Rajah would have made hamburger out of you."

Questions flooded his mind. He poured out words until Angie said, "Hold on, Dan. One at a time and we'll answer them."

"How badly did they wreck us?"

Manny said, "I'll take that question, doctor. Nothing much beyond the Motordrome. The crew stopped them. Then the Sheriff arrived with a party of deputies and finished off the rowdies. Chick charged de Packh with attempted murder before they took him to the hospital. The Mumford outfit's through. With Chick's evidence, they've got enough on them to close 'em down for good."

"How's Chick?"

Angie spoke. "The bullet went in and came right out again. He'll be up in a week or so."

"Good." He listened a minute. "Hey, that sounds like the calliope. Are we still in business?"

Manny grinned. "Why not? You're not the only guy that

can run a midway. They dragged Zelda Dorman off to the local jail by the way. So that cuts out the cat show. But we've still got enough to run, and today's Saturday. Carneys can't pass up a day like Saturday."

Dan smiled tiredly. "No, I guess they can't." He yawned.

Angie leaned over and patted his hand. "You'd better sleep some more." He started to protest. She bent down and pressed her lips to his. "No more talk," she whispered. "Sleep."

"Aye aye sir," he said, dropping off.

He got up Sunday morning, ate a giant breakfast in town with Angie, and the two of them went over to the Crystal City Hospital to see Chick. He was sitting up when they came in. He grinned, but sheepishly.

"How you feeling?" Dan asked.

"Swell," Chick replied. "The nurses here are classy."

"You'd better hurry up and get well. The concessions will go to pieces without you."

Chick stared at him. "You mean I'm still working for you?"

"If you want to."

"Hell," Chick said, "wild horses won't stop me. Dan . . ." His eyes grew serious. "After what I did . . . de Packh and all . . . you could have left me there for Rajah. No one would have blamed you."

Dan shook his head. "No, Chick. We lost our heads over a woman. This one right here. Men don't think straight when that happens. We'll forget about it."

"I sure was off my head," Chick agreed. "Angie, you'll have to persuade this lug that you and I just weren't made for each other, and I'll have to wait until some lady comes along who can stand my being jealous of her. Maybe one of the nurses . . ."

"You'll find her, Chick," Angie said softly.

"Well, in the meantime . . ." He looked at Dan. "Thanks," he said.

The afternoon was cool, a relief after the heat of the preceding week. Angie put her arm through Dan's as they left the hospital. When they reached the edge of the fairgrounds, he stopped, stood looking out over the deserted midway, bare of tents, strewn with pop bottles and paper sacks and cigarette butts. Angie tugged his sleeve gently. "Hey. You're not saying much."

"Thinking," he answered. "No matter how well I tell it, old man Underwood isn't going to hand me that desk job at least not for a couple of years. So there's only one thing for me to do."

"What's that?"

"Marry you. That is, if you think you can wait for the house and the new car that'll go along with the desk."

She squeezed his arm. "You're crazy, Dan Wilde. But I love you for it. Maybe I'll resign my title as a Hawaiian princess."

They walked on across the fairgrounds, watching the wind lift sawdust, seeing the trucks loading. Dan felt good. In an hour, two, they would be rolling again. The highway waited for them, the towns waited for the laughter and the lights of their wonderland.

And beyond, the future waited. A very fine future indeed, Dan thought.